D0408426

THE
UNFORTUNATE
SON

CONSTANCE LEEDS

VIKING
An Imprint of Penguin Group (USA) Inc.

VIKING
Published by the Penguin Group
Penguin Young Readers Group, 345 Hudson Street, New York, New York 10014, U.S.A.
Penguin Group (Canada), 90 Eglinton Avenue East, Suite 700, Toronto, Ontario, Canada M4P 2Y3
(a division of Pearson Penguin Canada Inc.)
Penguin Books Ltd, 80 Strand, London WC2R 0RL, England
Penguin Ireland, 25 St Stephen's Green, Dublin 2, Ireland (a division of Penguin Books Ltd)
Penguin Group (Australia), 250 Camberwell Road, Camberwell, Victoria 3124, Australia
(a division of Pearson Australia Group Pty Ltd)
Penguin Books India Pvt Ltd, 11 Community Centre, Panchsheel Park, New Delhi – 110 017, India
Penguin Group (NZ), 67 Apollo Drive, Rosedale, Auckland 0632, New Zealand
(a division of Pearson New Zealand Ltd.)
Penguin Books (South Africa) (Pty) Ltd, 24 Sturdee Avenue, Rosebank, Johannesburg 2196,
South Africa

Penguin Books Ltd, Registered Offices: 80 Strand, London WC2R 0RL, England

First published in the United States of America by Viking, a division of Penguin Young Readers
Group, 2012

10   9   8   7   6   5   4   3   2   1

LIBRARY OF CONGRESS CATALOGING-IN-PUBLICATION DATA
Leeds, Constance.
The unfortunate son / by Constance Leeds.
p. cm.
Summary: Luc, a youth born with one ear and raised by a drunken father in fifteenth-century
France, finds a better home with fisherman Pons, his sister Mattie, and their ward Beatrice, the
daughter of a disgraced knight, and even after being kidnapped and sold into slavery in Africa, he
remains remarkably fortunate.
ISBN 978-0-670-01398-2 (hardcover)
[1. Identity—Fiction. 2. Luck—Fiction. 3. Abnormalities, Human—Fiction. 4. Fishing—Fiction.
5. Slavery—Fiction. 6. Kidnapping—Fiction. 7. France—History—15th century—Fiction.
8. Africa—History—To 1498—Fiction.] I. Title.
PZ7.L51523For 2012
[Fic]—dc23
2011027530

Printed in the USA   Set in Goudy Old Style   Book design by Jim Hoover

For my Brother

WHAT WOULD DOUG DO

THE
UNFORTUNATE
SON

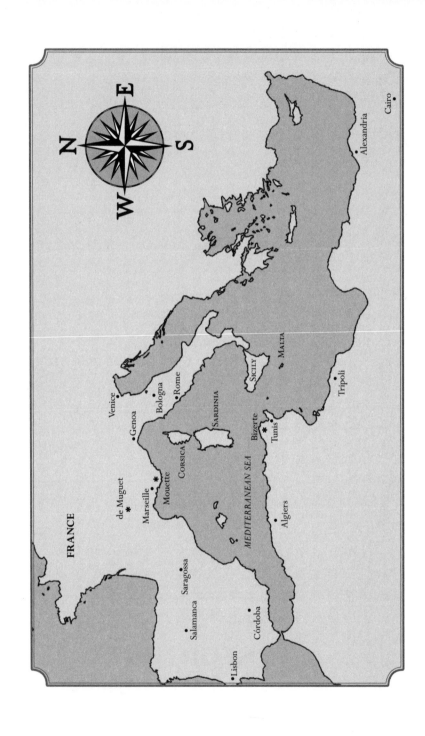

❦ CONTENTS ❧

1486

A Son

THE MIDWIFE BRAGGED that the beautiful countess dropped her first three babies as easily as a peasant. When the fourth was delivered even more quickly, the old woman cackled. She tipped the last drops of wine into the mouth of the exhausted mother, snipped the cord, and handed the slippery infant to the young wet nurse, who wrapped him in a warm blanket.

"Perfect. A second son for Count de Muguet," announced the midwife.

She hoped the count would be generous. His lordship's bad temper was certain, but his generosity was unpredictable. Leaving the other servants to attend the mother and child, the midwife rushed from the chamber with the good news.

The baby cried, a cry strong enough to be heard through the thick oak door. Muguet nodded and flipped the midwife a gold coin. Delighted, she scuttled away.

Inside the dim, candlelit room, the wet nurse cradled the blanketed baby in one arm and wiped his nose and mouth with a damp cloth. The infant was plump and alert, with a lovely little face. She carried him to a windowed alcove.

Perfect, the young woman thought, with a bittersweet smile.

As the sun's first light brightened the room, the wet nurse ached for her own little boy. Her son would be waking; he would cry for her, hunger for her milk, but he was a year old, old enough to be weaned. From today, her milk belonged to this baby; the count would pay handsomely. But this was the first morning apart from her son, and she fought her tears as she rocked the newborn in her arms.

This child will never know hunger, she thought, and she kissed his forehead.

Laying the baby on a table, the wet nurse unwrapped the blanket and began to rub olive oil into his skin. She studied the rosy infant: five toes on each foot, five fingers on each hand, bright eyes, pale downy hair. But something was missing. She gasped and covered her mouth. On the right side of the baby's head was a tiny seashell of an ear. But on the left side, there was nothing at all. Just smooth skin where an ear ought to have been.

The young woman crossed herself and set a drop of

honey on the baby's tongue with her finger. Taking a deep breath, she now wondered if this unfortunate child would ever have a happy day. The wet nurse knew what everyone in the castle knew: the count despised imperfection. And here was his son, with an obvious and strange flaw. She swaddled the baby from head to toe in fine white linen just as the count stormed into the birth room.

"Where is my son?"

The startled nurse held up the linen-swathed child for his father.

The count was not a tall man, but he was square, with short legs and broad shoulders; his arms were thick, his fists were enormous, and his voice was loud. His presence was big. He nodded with a rare smile.

"Good. Another hearty boy. Wrap him in this, and bring him to the chapel," he said, and he tossed the wet nurse a priceless golden cloth, embroidered with pearls and silken threads of all colors. "I shall welcome this fine son into my family before God."

1500

CHAPTER ONE

The Fisherman's Cottage

SITTING IN THE shade of a large linden tree, the old woman worked a knife along the edge of silvered driftwood, flicking the blade until the shape of a fish was unmistakable. A small, perfect fish. She laughed and shook her head, plying the knife with her knobbly hands, carving a scaly surface and tiny fins.

"Another fish for my lady Beatrice's sea," she said, and then she laughed again.

Glancing sideways at the old woman next to her, Beatrice smiled and picked at the rows of a fishing net; she gathered loose cording with a hooked needle made of sheep bone.

The old woman, Mattie, had a round face framed by willful white curls; her brown eyes were deep-set under heavy dark brows, and her wide smile dimpled both cheeks. As she dropped the carved fish to the ground and reached for another piece of wood, Mattie looked up at the clouds. Overhead a black kite wheeled in the sky; the edges of its wings looked like fingers as the bird dipped and rose, moving from left to right across the sky. She pointed to it and smiled.

"That bird brings us luck. A good change is ahead," said Mattie.

"We are lucky enough already," said Beatrice, tying knots in the net's loose ends.

Mattie put down her knife and squinted at the girl. "There's never enough luck, dear one."

"Never *too much* luck, you mean?" said Beatrice.

"You're too smart for me, Beatrice," Mattie chuckled, putting her arm around Beatrice and drawing her close. She kissed the girl's forehead.

Shaded from the September sun by the yellowing leaves of the linden, Beatrice and Mattie sat on a long wooden bench in front of the home they shared with the old woman's brother, Pons. The limestone cottage had two sturdy doors and four shuttered windows that lit its one room. Inside, each beam was hung with more wooden fish than anyone could count, strung on threads of different lengths, so that when the shutters were open, any breeze brought the room to life with fish and their swimming shadows. Every wooden surface in the cottage was carved with shells and sea creatures. The heavy table was wave-edged, and a starfish trimmed each corner. The place was magical, and children from the village would scamper up to the old woman and beg to come inside. The children believed that the beautiful Beatrice, with her long dark chestnut curls and her milk-white skin, was a mermaid who had come to live among them and that she could calm the mistral, the sudden and biting wind that blew from the northwest.

Beatrice was not from the sea. But like the mistral, she came from the northwest, from a corner of Provence a four-day horse ride from the Mediterranean fishing village of Mouette. Beatrice was the daughter of a disgraced, and now dead, knight; Mattie had been her nurse from the time she was weaned.

There had been children born before Beatrice, but none had survived. Her father, Sir Étienne, had been a handsome, pleasant man but an inattentive master to his tenant farmers and an indifferent husband. He had loved his little daughter as much as he loved anyone, but he was absent from their stone manor house most of the year, serving Count de Muguet, so Beatrice rarely saw him. Her mother was timid and anxious, quick to worry and slow to laugh, but Beatrice was a beautiful, sunny child, with glossy brown hair, clear blue eyes, and rosy cheeks. She was liked by all and loved by Mattie.

Seven years ago, when Beatrice was eight years old, Sir Étienne was accused of stealing from his liege, Count de

Muguet, to cover gambling debts. His debts were undeniable; whether he had stolen was unproven, but the accusation was enough. The count was the law, with the power of life and death and everything in between, so Sir Étienne was brought before him.

That terrible morning the sky was blue, and the spring sun was warm; warblers and larks sang from the trees. Green nubs poked through the earth that edged the castle's pebbled courtyard, where a rowdy crowd had gathered. Mattie had been taking Beatrice to her mother on the other side of the castle gate when the child slipped free from her grasp and wove through to the front of the thick throng. Mattie desperately pushed forward to regain the little girl's hand, but the mob was too tightly packed. Beatrice watched as her father rode in alone through the castle gate on his bay courser.

The count waited on the threshold of his château. Sir Étienne rode across the courtyard and pulled his horse to a stop; he removed his helmet and faced his accuser. In a deep and growling voice, the stout Count de Muguet spoke: "Sir Étienne, you have failed me, your lord, and yourself. You have shown yourself to be no more than a scoundrel and a thief. You have brought disgrace upon my name, upon yourself, and upon your family. That knighthood by which you received honor is brought to nothing, and you and yours are undone. Let all who are witnesses here today take example and beware."

Sir Étienne dismounted, and a soldier led away his horse.

A herald stood on each side, and another took his shield, spoiling it with dog feces. Then the shield, once proudly displaying Sir Étienne's coat of arms, was hung upside down from a post near the castle entrance. The crowd jeered and whistled as, one by one, each piece of his armor was removed and broken into pieces. His spurs were hacked off. Stripped of all that was knightly, Étienne turned his face to where his young daughter stood motionless. He placed his right hand over his heart and hung his head. Then he dropped to his knees and knelt in the dirt. The count stepped forward and took Étienne's sword. He raised it high and, with all his strength, smashed the flat of the sword down on the crest of the kneeling man's head. The crowd fell silent except for a little girl's scream. Étienne slumped forward into the dirt.

The count leaned over the dying man and said, "Now you are nothing."

A coffin was dragged forward, and the heralds threw Étienne's body into the wooden box. Four soldiers hauled the coffin from the courtyard, leaving it beyond the castle walls. Beatrice screamed again and ran after her father. As she knelt sobbing over the coffin, her mother, who had remained outside the gate waiting to say farewell to her daughter, tapped her shoulder.

"Poor little Beatrice. Don't cry for him. Look what his carelessness has done to us. The count has confiscated everything. We have no home. We have nothing," she said, trembling and wiping her eyes. "Say good-bye to me now, Beatrice.

Mattie has promised to look after you. She is a good woman. Good-bye, Beatrice."

Beatrice's mother kissed the top of her child's head, and turned to mount a small palfrey; the little girl watched her mother and a servant ride off. Earlier in the week, their priest, Father Thierry, had visited Beatrice to explain that the count was angry with her father and intended to punish him. Because her mother was going to a convent, Beatrice was told that she would travel far away with Mattie. Beatrice hadn't understood that she would be saying good-bye to her parents and to her home forever.

Beatrice knelt and put her hand to her father's cheek. He wheezed, and blood pooled under his cracked skull. His eyes never opened. His breathing roughened, and he was still. She pushed his shoulder, first gently, then again, with more force.

"Papa! Please!" she cried, tears running down her face, pushing his lifeless shoulder harder and harder. "Please don't go. Don't leave me."

Beatrice felt a hand on her head, and looking up, she saw Mattie, who had struggled through the mob and finally caught up to the little girl.

Mattie pulled Beatrice to her feet and drew her close; in the warmth of Mattie's arms, the girl wept. Mattie wiped her own eyes and kissed Beatrice's forehead.

"There, there, my dearest. No worries. You're with me now, my child."

Beatrice sobbed, "You won't leave me?"

"Never."

"Why couldn't Mother take us?" sputtered the little girl, sniffing and gulping air.

"Father Thierry told you, dear child. Your mother is going away. She'll become a nun at the Abbey of Saint Clotilde. They only accept noblewomen. They would never have someone like me, and since your father, God rest his soul, is no longer a knight, they won't take you."

Beatrice wiped her eyes with her sleeve.

"Why won't they take me?"

"Hush, my Beatrice. It doesn't matter. You are still my lady."

"Always?" asked the little girl.

"Yes," replied Mattie. "Always."

CHAPTER TWO

The Helper

AS THE AFTERNOON shadows lengthened, Beatrice rolled the fishing net and left it by the cottage door. She followed Mattie inside and opened the shutters, which had been closed throughout the day to keep the cottage cool. Mattie snapped apart a head of garlic, slipped off the purpled husks, and chopped the smooth white cloves. The chickens clucked, and the goose hissed, scratching and pecking under the kitchen table. Beatrice shooed them to the back annex, a space in the rear of the cottage where Pons kept the animals: three or four hens, sometimes a goose, and the annual pig. Adding sticks to the hearth, she knelt to fan the flame with a flat piece of wood. A pot hung from a hook, and Beatrice used her skirt to protect her hand as she removed the hot cover. Onion slices simmered in fish stock. Beatrice tipped in a basketful of mussels that she had gathered and cleaned that morning, added Mattie's garlic, and replaced the cover.

On a shelf by the window, there were three blue-glazed bowls, three wooden mugs, and three wooden spoons. Beatrice set them on the table as Pons came through the door. He was a wiry man, with bandy legs and bare feet, a thick head of white hair, and a short gray beard. His face was dark and creased by the sun and sea, and he carried a basket of beets, onions, and two waxy aubergines.

When she saw the eggplants, Mattie clapped her hands and said, "I knew this was a lucky day!"

"I traded the carpenter's wife a couple of mullets for these," said Pons, holding up the basket of vegetables. "Who made my net good as new?"

"The mermaid, of course, Brother," answered Mattie.

Pons handed the basket to Beatrice, kissed her forehead, and collapsed on the bench.

"Lord, I am weary. And hungry," he said. "I'd wager that heaven doesn't smell as good as this cottage."

He rubbed his eyes and began to knead his hands.

"Your hands are bad, aren't they?" asked Beatrice.

"I can barely make a fist," answered Pons, opening and closing his fingers.

"It's time you had a boy to help you," said Mattie.

Pons shook his head. "Would you have me spend my days worrying about a boy instead of the fish?"

"Mattie spends her days worrying about me," said Beatrice.

"Worrying about you *and* about Pons," corrected Mattie. "And I'd worry less about my brother if he had an extra pair of hands, young hands. Besides, I could use help too. It isn't right having Beatrice digging in the dirt, under the sun," she added, gesturing to the left where a garden hugged the side of the cottage. There Mattie grew the cabbages and cauliflower and the beans, peas, and carrots that filled their soup pot throughout the year.

"Mattie, will you ever understand that I *want* to work in the garden?" asked Beatrice, heaping a ladleful of mussels into each bowl.

Mattie raised her eyebrow. "You may like to garden, but I never saw anyone so terrified of a little ant or, heaven forbid, a wasp."

Pons laughed.

"I hate bugs," said Beatrice.

"That's because you're a delicate lady, who shouldn't be out in the sun, working like a peasant," said Mattie, wagging her finger at the girl.

Beatrice wrinkled her nose and handed Mattie a loaf of bread.

"The carpenter's wife told me that our swineherd took a bad fall and won't be able to work for a month, maybe two. Starting tomorrow, the son of that olive grower from over the hill will be taking the village pigs," said Pons.

"Which olive grower from over the hill?" asked Mattie, cutting the bread. "I don't know who you mean."

"Yes, you do, Sister. Pascal. The one everyone says is a lazy drunk. I hear he never prunes the trees. Never does anything. Pascal's mean-spirited and without a friend."

"That's the family from the north, right?" asked Mattie, pointing over her shoulder with the knife.

"Yes," Pons said, leaning over his bowl and inhaling. "Pascal served Count de Muguet. Got the place as reward for something. Can't imagine what. A farmhouse and a grove of trees?"

"Well, the count ordered deeds you might not reward a good man for," said Mattie.

Beyond memory, Pons and Mattie's family had fished the Mediterranean Sea and lived in the little village of Mouette, a day's ride east of the ancient city of Marseille. Although his castle was inland, on the north side of the mountains, Count de Muguet had acquired Mouette as part of his wife's dowry. Every fall the count's men delivered salt and olive oil so the fishermen of Mouette could preserve mullet and bream, anchovies and sardines. Each spring the count's men would return to collect the cured fish as rent for the village homes. As a young woman, Mattie had married a foot soldier in the count's service. But her husband had died in an accident in the second year of their childless marriage, and she had stayed in the north. After serving as a maid in the Muguet household, she became the nurse to Beatrice in Sir

Étienne's nearby manor. When the count executed Beatrice's father and the child's mother abandoned her, Mattie took the girl and returned to Mouette. Though far away, Count de Muguet remained an inescapable presence in their lives.

"Perhaps Pascal's son will be looking for work when the swineherd's healed," said Mattie.

"Maybe he could help you, Pons," added Beatrice.

Pons shrugged. "I hear it's a big grove," he said, scratching his stubbled chin. "Dozens of fine old olive trees."

"Really? Then why would a boy whose father owns a large grove of olive trees be helping a swineherd?" asked Beatrice. Using a shell half, she dug out a mussel and sucked it into her mouth.

"That's a good question," said Mattie as she stood up and poured wine into their mugs. "I suppose, we'll find out more tomorrow when the boy comes for our pig."

By the flickering glow of the hearth-fire, Beatrice, Pons, and Mattie settled into a cozy supper. They finished the mussels and sopped up the broth with bread that Mattie had baked in the shared village oven early that morning. The sun was setting, and the cottage went from gray to dark. Beatrice sloshed water to rinse the bowls, kissed the foreheads of Mattie and Pons, and climbed the ladder to the loft. For the past seven years, she had slept under the cottage rafters, beneath the little round window from which she could see the moon and the sea. It was snug in the winter, and in the summer, the unglazed window let in a cooling breeze. She was comfortable and content, but Mattie had begun to worry. What would the girl's future be? It was time they considered a husband for Beatrice, but Mattie could think of no one good enough for the girl. Not in their little village.

In the morning, laughter woke Beatrice. She crossed herself, stretched, and peered out her little window. The brightening peach sky was noisy with birds, so she pulled her faded slate wool dress over the linen smock that she wore night and day, and climbed down from the loft. Pons was scratching his head and laughing with his sister.

Mattie wiped her eyes. "Did you notice it right away?"

"No," said Pons.

Mattie sat with her elbows on the table, beaming across at her brother.

"Of course not," she said. "If he had three, you would have noticed. But just one?" Mattie shook her head.

Pons nodded, "Never in my life."

"Who are you to talking about?" asked Beatrice, slipping in next to Pons.

"Good morning, my lady," said Pons, brushing the girl's hair back from her face.

Beatrice's unbraided hair tumbled to her waist. She rubbed her eyes and combed her fingers through the curls.

"You're not fishing today?" she asked Pons. Usually he went out in his boat before the first light of day and didn't return home until midafternoon.

He shook his head. "No, I stayed to meet the boy, the swineherd's helper."

"What's he like?" asked Beatrice.

"You'll never guess," said Mattie, and she pushed a hunk of buttered bread across to the girl.

"Our new pig boy has only one ear," announced Pons.

"He lost an ear?" asked Beatrice.

"Don't think he ever had more than one. Just one, on the right," said Pons, pulling his own right ear.

"And on the left? Nothing!" said Mattie, snapping her fingers. "No scar, no sign that an ear should be there."

"How strange!" said Beatrice, tucking her hair behind her own ears. "Can he hear?"

"Better than most," said Pons.

"You think he didn't notice when you started speaking so softly to him?" asked Mattie, laughing. "You should have heard my brother," she said to Beatrice, "speaking soft as a mouse."

"Well, I was curious," answered Pons. "Anyway, there's nothing wrong with his hearing. Can't tell how old he is. Seems older than he looks. Slight and smooth-faced. Almost pretty, don't you think, Mattie?"

Mattie nodded. "Such light eyes. And his hair? I'd like to have had that hair as a girl. Yes, he's a pretty one."

"You're saying the pig boy, this boy with one ear, is *pretty*?" asked Beatrice. "I can't wait to see him."

"He was very polite, seemed like a quiet boy. He might do for you, Pons," said Mattie.

"Let's see how he does with our pig for now. I really don't want anyone in the boat with me."

"Not a question of what you want, Pons. It's what you need," said Mattie.

"Train a boy who knows nothing of the sea? What if he can't swim? How many hooks is he going to lose? I'm used to being alone in my boat."

Pons shook his head.

Beatrice looked thoughtful for a moment. "Didn't you feel the same about Mattie and me coming to live here with you?" she asked.

Pons smiled. "You two are the best thing that ever happened to me."

"How come you never married?" asked Beatrice. The question had not occurred to her before, but with Mattie talking lately about finding Beatrice a husband, marriage was on her mind.

"My brother never spent enough time on dry land to find a wife," said Mattie.

"Where would I have found a wife who would turn my cottage into a sea full of fish?" asked Pons. "Or a beautiful mermaid who could fix my nets?"

CHAPTER THREE

Rain

OVERHEAD THE SKY was bright, but the horizon was streaked with green and lavender, and a cool salty wind was blowing. By noon, the autumn rain fell loud and heavy. Pons sharpened Mattie's knives and wrapped strips of leather around fraying basket handles. Beatrice and Mattie raked the floor and pushed the pile of old rushes outside; Pons shoved aside the table so they could tamp the dirt floor until it was smooth and hard. Pons and Mattie spread fresh rushes while Beatrice sliced a roasted beet into their soup.

"Wonder how our new swineherd is faring in the downpour? Not an easy first day," said Pons, blowing to cool his soup.

"Nasty to be out in this weather," said Beatrice.

The rain drummed loudly on the cottage's stone roof, and rainwater seeped in along the edges of the shutters, streaking the walls and puddling on the floor.

"The pigs won't mind," said Mattie. "Not so long as the beechnuts are plentiful."

"I wouldn't stay out there. He'll be soaked," said Beatrice. "Maybe the pig boy will come back early."

But the boy with one ear did not return with their pig until dusk. When Pons saw the boy, he insisted he dry off by the fire.

"You're drenched, and your hands are white with cold."

The boy led the pig to the annex in back of the cottage and fastened the door that separated the animals from where the people lived. When he saw Beatrice, he stopped.

Mattie laughed. "She's a mermaid, but you needn't be afraid. She is very kind. Warm up by the fire. Have you eaten today?"

The boy nodded, rubbing his hands over the hearth; he kept craning his head to look up at the carvings.

Mattie winked at Beatrice, who ladled steaming soup into a bowl and offered it to the boy.

"I'm not really a mermaid," she said. "My name is Beatrice." She waited for him to introduce himself, but he didn't say a word. Or even take the bowl. He just stared. At Beatrice and at the cottage. At the fish suspended from the ceiling. At the smiling old woman and the kindly fisherman. But mostly he stared at the beautiful girl. Beatrice stared back. She was unsure which was more startling, the missing ear or his coloring. His complexion and hair were golden, and his light, wide-set eyes were bluer than any she had ever seen.

Mattie prodded the boy onto the bench and set the bowl in front of him. Beatrice cut two chunks of bread and watched as the boy slipped one onto his lap before bringing the bowl to his mouth greedily. He mopped every last drop from the bowl with the other piece of bread and jammed it into his mouth. She sliced more bread, and again he slipped one piece into his lap.

"What's your name?"

The boy wiped his mouth on the shoulder of his shirt and looked at her. He swallowed.

"Luc," he said.

"Why are you taking the bread?" asked Beatrice.

Luc blushed, and he answered softly, "For my dog. He's had nothing to eat today."

"Where is he?" asked Beatrice.

"Outside with my father's two pigs."

Pons was standing at the doorway, peering out.

"The rain's starting to let up, Luc. You ought to head home before your family worries you washed away," said Pons.

"Thank you for the soup and the bread." Luc rose and pointed to the wooden fish overhead. "Did you carve all these, sir?"

"None of them," answered Pons. "It's my sister's work. That and all the other carving."

Luc shook his head. "Would it be all right if I brought my brothers sometime?"

"Of course. All the village children come knocking to see the fish. Mattie loves to make them smile," said Pons.

"The soup was the best I ever tasted."

"Well, for that you must thank Beatrice," said Mattie.

"Thank you, miss," said Luc, turning to Beatrice.

She studied him and wondered what his age was. He was at least her height, but slight, with a child's smooth skin. She guessed he was a couple of years younger than she, maybe thirteen years old.

"Your father has olive trees?" asked Mattie with her hands on her hips, staring at the boy and smiling.

"Yes, he has more than forty trees."

"Why are you working as a swineherd?" asked Beatrice.

"I'm just helping the swineherd until his leg heals, but my father thinks I'm better suited to this work."

Mattie scowled. "Does he now?"

Pons stepped out onto the threshold and pointed to the dog, "That's a fine-looking dog. What's his name?"

"Cadeau. He's mine," said Luc proudly.

His father's two pigs were backed against the front of the cottage while Cadeau ranged back and forth, growling and pinning them in.

"He's doing a good job with those pigs," said Pons.

"Lucky they aren't hungry," said Beatrice, coming out from behind him.

"Right," said Luc. "If they weren't so full of nuts, Cadeau would have a hard time. But he's good at everything—herding, hunting, guarding."

He rubbed the dog's head, and Cadeau wagged his tail and shook his wet fur, spraying the boy. Luc wiped his face with the back of his hand. And grinned.

"Can he fish?" asked Beatrice, taking a step back.

"Probably. And sail a boat too," said Luc with a laugh, picking up a long staff that he used to prod the pigs. "I'd better go now. You have been kind to me *and* to my dog." He pulled the two chunks of bread from his sleeve. "Thank you."

CHAPTER FOUR

Pascal's Farmhouse

DESPITE THE DOWNPOUR, Luc's first day as a swineherd's helper had not turned out badly after all. His clothes were half dry, and his belly was full. Cadeau gobbled the bread and trotted along, splashing through puddles and nipping and dodging the two pigs. He was a big, beautiful dog with a shiny brown coat, a freckled cream muzzle, and a long feathered tail. As Luc trudged home in the moonlight, he thought about the remarkable fish-filled cottage and the beautiful Beatrice. He'd never seen anyplace like the fisherman's home, nor anyone half as pretty as the girl with long dark hair and deep-blue eyes. She was probably his age, but, of course, no one guessed that he was almost fifteen; he looked younger than his brother Hervé, who was two years his junior.

Hervé was as tall as Luc and already stronger. His upper lip was shadowed, and his voice was deep. Luc's father often reminded Luc that Hervé could lift the heavy harvest baskets more easily; that Luc was the better climber and picked more olives went unremarked.

"Maybe you're missing more than an ear," said his father all too often.

Luc was no stranger to his father's insults, but he was learning to shrug them off. He was a wise, able boy who loved his mother and his little brothers. Until his work as a swineherd in Mouette, he had spent little time with anyone outside his immediate family. They lived a very quiet life; they avoided the fishing village along the shore below and rarely visited the farming village up the road except to attend the tiny hill chapel on Sundays and holy days. For as long as Luc could remember, their only visitors were the same two soldiers, who arrived twice yearly, in the spring and fall. The soldiers brought white flour, cheeses, honey, and woolen cloth for Luc's mother, Blanche. They brought a barrel of wine for his father, Pascal, and sometimes shoes for the boys. They talked to Pascal privately, but before they left, they always spoke with Luc and his brothers, asking how they spent their days and what they needed, or even what they wanted. Four years ago, the older soldier, a knight named Sir Guy, had given Luc a puppy. Sir Guy said the dog was for Luc alone, a gift because Luc was turning into a fine young man. For once, Pascal said nothing.

The soldiers had not come this past spring, and Luc had asked his mother why.

"Hush," Blanche had said. "Don't say another word about it, Luc. Especially to your father."

Luc rarely said anything to his father, but he remembered earlier years when his father had been kinder, and Luc had been happier. His brother Hervé was born when Luc was two, and baby Pierre followed six years later. The three boys were healthy, and the harvests were good, but Pascal began to drink after Hervé was born, and over time, he went from a hardworking family man to a sullen drunk and, increasingly, a mean one. As his father became more difficult, Luc noticed that his mother had stopped singing. His mother used to sing all the time. Before Pierre was born, Blanche would put baby Hervé on her hip, and taking Luc by the hand, she would sing softly to him as they climbed the hills beyond the grove. They would look down at their house, and she would ask Luc if he could see his father in the olive grove. Could he spot their chimney? Could he see the pigs in their pen? Could he see the chickens? Luc loved her games. He squinted and concentrated until he not only could point out the chickens but could tell which was the rooster and which was the spotted old hen. His mother hid tiny pieces of broken crockery in the dirt, and Luc raced to spot them. Blanche was surprised by all that he could do. When Luc was no more than four, Pascal was taking him to hunt because the remarkable little boy could hear a rabbit breathe and see the movement of a whisker. But that changed as Hervé grew. Hervé had never been good at his mother's games; he did not have Luc's quickness or his gifts. Now, when he went hunting, Pascal took neither boy, and his mother's games had ceased. Now, nothing Luc did was good enough for his father.

Cadeau barked and ran ahead to the house. Luc urged the pigs along with the staff. Pierre scampered to his older brother and threw his muddy arms around him.

"Luc! Luc! Papa said you drowned in a puddle."

Leaning the staff against the farmhouse, Luc lifted his mud-splattered little brother and swung him around and around by his arms. When Luc put him down, Pierre giggled and stumbled in a dizzy circle.

"Are you hungry, Luc?" called his mother from the doorway.

"You gave the boy cheese as he left. And he must have had nuts and berries with the pigs. Or he should have," said Luc's father, who stepped in front of his wife and stood on the threshold with his arms folded across his chest.

Luc said nothing. Their farmhouse was stone, a long rectangular building, much larger than the fisherman's cottage. The separate kitchen opened into a courtyard with a well and a generous shade tree. On the far side was a small stable, to which Luc led the pigs. He filled a pail with well water and rinsed his face and his muddy feet. Luc's legs ached, and his shirt was damp; he was tired and very glad for Beatrice's soup. He dried his face on his shoulder and smiled. It had been a fine day. He looked forward to tomorrow, when he would again see Pons and Mattie. And the girl.

Every day, throughout October and most of November, Luc shepherded about two dozen pigs from Mouette to the woodlands above. Most of the men in that village were fishermen, but each household kept at least one young pig, raising it in the spring and summer on table scraps and market waste, until the fall, when the pig was fattened on the acorns, beechnuts, and chestnuts that covered the forest floor. At the end of November, the pigs would be slaughtered and turned into meat for the winter. Luc's last stop at the end of every afternoon, after he had returned all the other pigs, was the cottage of Pons and Mattie and Beatrice, where they always saved supper for him.

"Have you ever been out on the sea?" asked Mattie one day as Luc was finishing his soup.

"Never," replied the boy.

"Would you like to go out in my boat one day?" asked Pons.

The boy nodded. "If my father will allow it."

"Tell him you'll bring home some fresh mullet."

Though he longed to go out in Pons's boat, Luc never asked his father. Their silver-leafed olive trees were filling with purple fruit, and the swineherd recovered in mid-November, just as Luc was needed for the harvest.

On his last night with the pigs, Luc was very quiet at the table in Pons's house.

"I hope you'll visit us after the harvest," said Mattie.

"Yes," said Beatrice. "We'll miss you. And Cadeau."

"I'll return. I promise," said Luc. "But tomorrow I'll be picking olives."

"Come back after the harvest. Maybe take a ride in Pons's boat, too," added Beatrice.

Luc nodded and waved good-bye.

CHAPTER FIVE

The Olive Harvest

EACH DAY, AFTER the sun was high and the dew dried, Luc and his brothers scoured the ground for the wind-fallen olives. Afterward, Blanche spread a rough woven cloth under an olive tree. With wooden rakes, Luc and Hervé combed its branches while Pierre crawled on the cloth beneath and sorted though the growing piles of olives, discarding twigs and leaves. They dumped the cloth-load of picked olives into a basket and moved to the next tree. After the trees were raked, Luc and Hervé strapped sacks to their waists. Climbing narrow ladders, they stretched to snap off any remaining olives. The family could harvest four or five trees each day. At the end of the second week, when all the olives on his forty trees were picked, Pascal would borrow a donkey from the

miller and haul the full baskets up the road to the mill. In return for a portion of the oil, their olives would be pressed, and
the oil would be poured into clay jugs for sale in the markets.

It was hard work; the olives had to be picked as soon as
they ripened, before they began to spot, or the oil would be
ruined. Pascal was a strong man, but by the middle of each
afternoon he was useless and asleep, and the work was left to
Luc and his brothers and their mother. On the last day of the
harvest, Pascal tripped over a rake that was propped against a
tree and smashed a couple of toes on a rock. He grabbed Luc
by the back of his shirt and yelled at him.

"You careless idiot. See what you did? You're not fit for
this work."

Luc glared at his father. Maybe it had been his rake, but
there had been nothing careless about where it was placed.
He was the best picker in the family, and he knew it. And he
suspected his father knew it as well, and that only seemed to
make matters worse. But Luc said nothing; he was almost too
tired to care.

That night, he fell asleep in no time. The harvest was
exhausting, and his arms and shoulders ached. The rake blis-
tered his hands, and his legs were scratched and scabbed from
the branches. He awoke at dawn the next day and slipped
away from the straw bed he shared with his brothers. Luc
sat outside with Cadeau and watched the sunrise; the gray
sky turned pink, illuminating the reds and yellows of autumn
trees. Maybe his father was right. Even though he was a good

picker, maybe the olive grove wasn't where he belonged. He buried his face in his dog's furry shoulder, and whispered.

"Think I could be a fisherman, Cadeau?"

Later that morning, to celebrate the end of the olive harvest, Luc's family gathered around the scrubbed kitchen table. The door was propped open, filling the room with sunlight. Blanche heaped a steaming platter with rabbit and onions. The rabbit had been a gift from one of the villagers to Luc on his last day of work with the pigs; Blanche had killed and dressed it that morning. The boys wolfed down the meat, too busy eating to speak a word. Pascal was slumped at the far end of the table, tearing off bits of bread, eating no rabbit. Blanche spooned out roasted red pears that had been given to Luc by another pig owner.

"How come you got pears and rabbits, Luc?" asked Pierre, between bites.

"What's it like in the village?" asked Hervé.

As the boys ate, Luc recounted tales of the fishing village. During the harvest he had been too busy to tell his brothers about Mouette, and now he entertained them with stories of the carpenter who had no teeth, and the baker who had eleven children.

"More, Luc. Tell more," begged Pierre with a greasy smile; the little boy's curl-framed face was slick with rabbit grease and pear juice.

When Luc began to describe the fisherman's cottage, Hervé leaned forward, and Pierre's eyes grew huge. Blanche asked questions about Pons and Mattie, but his father said nothing.

"Please can we see the fish?" said Pierre, clapping his hands.

"Yes, please, Father?" asked Hervé. "I would love to see the fish cottage."

"No," said Pascal. "It's a wonder no one complained that this lazy boy spent more time in the village than in the forest."

Luc shoved away the rest of his food.

"Hervé, would you have wasted time like Luc?" asked Pascal, pushing himself back from the table.

"Luc always came home tired, Papa. He worked hard," answered Hervé.

"You're too generous, Son. You always defend him."

Then, cursing under his breath about the toes he had stubbed, Pascal limped to a shelf and took down his old knife. It had a smooth horn handle and a sharp blade.

"I won this knife in a fight when I was a little older than you, Hervé. I was the strongest boy around. Like you, Hervé. Now it's yours."

Pascal handed it to the boy, and Hervé stared at the knife in his hand.

"Thank you, Papa," he mumbled, looking anywhere but at Luc.

Luc stood. He took a deep breath and charged from the house, slamming the door. He whistled, and Cadeau bounded from the garden. Luc was sitting under a tree scratching his dog's ears when Hervé and Pierre tumbled outside.

"Papa is really mad," said Pierre.

"Hush!" said Hervé. "Sorry, Luc. The knife—"

"As if I wanted that old thing," said Luc.

"Don't lie. You wanted the knife."

Luc stood up. "I never expected the knife. Or anything else from him."

"But—"

"Leave me alone, Hervé. Shut your mouth, and leave me alone."

"It's not my fault," said Hervé, squatting to pat the dog.

Luc swatted Hervé's arm away from Cadeau. "I said shut your mouth."

"I *am* stronger than you, Luc. Besides, you have a dog," said Hervé, still squatting.

"Not thanks to Father," said Luc, and he shoved Hervé.

Hervé rocked backward and bumped Pierre, who tripped and fell face down. Luc helped the little boy to his feet. He was crying, and blood dribbled down his chin. When Pierre wiped his face and saw the blood on his hand, he began to scream. Pascal rushed, hobbling, from the house. Luc was kneeling, dabbing his brother's cut lip with his shirt when his father slapped him hard across his face.

"Get away from Pierre. You have done enough damage. You broke my toes, and now this," he snarled, pointing at the little boy.

"It was an accident."

"Get out of my sight. Cursed freak."

Luc glimpsed his mother watching him from the doorway. She said nothing. He rubbed his cheek and turned away. Pierre was sobbing as Pascal lifted him and carried him back into the house. He slammed the door, leaving Hervé and Luc in the garden.

"Papa is angry, but it won't last," said Hervé.

"He hates me. Why wouldn't he? I *am* a freak. And a weakling."

"You're neither, Luc."

"There's no place for me here," said Luc, touching his face where a red handprint marked his cheek.

"Take the knife, Luc," said Hervé, holding it out.

"No. He gave it to you. But go inside and get my shoes for me, Hervé."

"Your shoes? Why? Where are you going?"

"I'll be back tonight. But I won't stay here much longer," said Luc.

Hervé came out with Luc's shoes under his shirt. He handed them to Luc, who sat on the ground and pulled the soft leather over his feet. He stood up and wiggled his toes.

"Thanks, Hervé," said Luc, patting his brother's shoulder.

As Luc headed down the hill, away from the olive grove, he turned to wave at Hervé, who stood watching him leave. Then he looked down at his shoes. Except for Sunday church,

Luc was always barefoot. These shoes had been too big for the past season, but now they fit well, and he liked the way he couldn't feel the stones underfoot as he began to hurry down the path. Cadeau loped along, sometimes nosing the boy in the back of his knees, sometimes whining, his tail always wagging. Towards the bottom of the hill, Luc stopped and looked at his dog.

"What is it, boy? Do you know where we're heading?"

Cadeau woofed, and they both began to run toward the fishing village.

CHAPTER SIX

A Gift

THE HOUSES OF Mouette were strung below Luc along a narrow road. Cadeau barked, and Luc stopped running to greet the baker, who was strolling uphill with three of his sons.

"Good afternoon, Luc," said the baker. "We've missed you."

"It's good to see you," said Luc once he caught his breath.

The run had reddened his face, and he breathed deeply. He bent over and put his hands on his knees for a moment.

"Are you all right, boy?" asked the baker, pointing to Luc's bloody shirt.

Luc nodded, cleared his throat, and stood up. "I fell. It's nothing."

"Well, it looks like you and your dog are in a hurry, so I won't keep you. But be careful."

"Thank you, sir," said Luc, and he jogged down the road, breaking into a run.

Luc and Cadeau raced to the last cottage in the village, where Luc fell to the ground and lay breathing deeply. The goose honked, and the chickens scattered. Cadeau licked the boy's face, and Luc pushed him away. When he sat up, he saw Pons rushing toward him.

"What's the matter, Luc?" asked the old man.

Luc huffed. "Nothing. I ran here."

"Well, catch your breath. It's good to see you again, Luc."

Mattie and Beatrice hurried from the cottage.

"Look who's here," said Pons.

"Welcome back," said Mattie.

"Hello, Luc," said Beatrice. She noticed the welt on the boy's cheek and the bloodstains on his shirt. "Did you get into a fight?" she asked, patting Cadeau.

Luc stood and brushed himself off. "Brother stuff. It's nothing," he said, rubbing his face.

She pointed to his shoes. He smiled and rocked back on his heels.

"How was the harvest?" she asked.

"Good," said Luc.

"Now you'll take the oil to market?" asked Beatrice.

"No," said the boy. "I won't."

"Why?" asked Pons, putting a hand on the boy's shoulder.

"I'm leaving home."

"Come, Luc. Help me fold my net."

The heavy net was draped over a large rock to dry in the afternoon sun. Taking two corners each, Pons and Luc folded the net into a neat rectangle. Beatrice watched from the doorway, until they finished. She called to Luc.

"We're just about to eat. Join us."

"Thanks, I've eaten," said Luc, patting his stomach.

"Has Cadeau?" asked Beatrice.

Luc laughed.

"Keep us company then," said Beatrice, shooing the chickens and the goose to the annex.

"I was hoping to see you, boy. I have a surprise," said Mattie.

Luc pulled the benches to the table, and Beatrice ladled brown soup studded with bits of orange carrot, gray beans, and flakes of white fish into three bowls. She cut four slices of bread. Then she smiled and cut one more.

"Here, Luc, have some bread at least. And some for Cadeau. I've missed that dog," said Beatrice, handing him two pieces of bread.

"And the boy?" said Pons, shaking his head. "Haven't you missed Luc too?"

Beatrice looked up at the rafters and bit her lower lip. "Well, maybe a little."

"But not as much as you missed Cadeau?" asked Luc.

"Not half as much," said Beatrice.

They talked and ate and laughed. Luc began to feel better.

After the meal, Mattie wiped her mouth with her fingers. "Wonderful as always, my Beatrice. Now," she said, rubbing her hands together. "Aren't you curious, Luc? I said I had a gift for you."

"A gift? You said a surprise."

Mattie walked to the shelf that hung beneath the window. "Close your eyes, and put out your hand."

Luc did as he was told. When he opened his eyes, he found, resting in the middle of his palm, a carved wooden ear, the mirror image of his one ear. A perfect left ear. He was speechless.

"You don't know what to say?" Mattie chuckled.

Pons laughed. Beatrice shook her head, but she, too, was smiling.

"What do I do with it?" puzzled Luc.

"You're no longer the boy with one ear," said Beatrice.

"I can't stick it on my head, can I?" asked Luc, arching his brows and scratching his neck.

"Of course not. How would you do that? Drive a wooden peg into your skull?" asked Mattie.

Pons tousled the boy's golden hair, and added, "And I thought you were a smart boy."

"I don't understand," said Luc, flipping the carving and looking at each side.

"It's a joke. When anyone says something or when they don't, but you can tell they're bursting to say something—" said Mattie.

"—you pull the ear out of your sleeve, and drop it on the table," finished Beatrice.

Luc began to laugh. "It looks just like my real ear. I wish I *could* stick it on my head." He tucked the ear into the pouch on his belt. "Thank you," he said, standing up.

"Where are you going?" asked Beatrice.

Luc blinked and turned to Mattie. "Thank you. For everything."

"But where will you go?"

"Home," he answered softly.

"I thought you said you were leaving home," said Beatrice.

Luc nodded.

"Why?" she asked.

He did not answer, and Mattie scowled at Beatrice.

"Hush," she said to the girl. "If Luc wants to tell us, he can." Then Mattie smiled at Luc and leaned toward the boy. "Pons needs a helper. He meant to ask you before your last day with the pigs."

The old man nodded.

"Wouldn't you like that?" asked Beatrice.

"You would live here with us and learn to fish," said Mattie.

"We could use a watchdog, too," said Beatrice, looking at Cadeau asleep near the hearth.

"What do you think?" asked Mattie.

"I–I," Luc stammered, and his voice thickened. "Yes," he said hoarsely.

"On Sunday, in three days' time, I'll go and speak to your father," said Pons.

"Well, now," said Mattie, "this has turned into an extra-fine day."

"I agree," said Beatrice, nudging Luc. When Beatrice pushed the boy, Cadeau barked.

Luc cleared his throat and smiled. "A fine day for all of us."

He helped Beatrice rinse the bowls. When he went to fetch more water from the well down the road, Beatrice walked with him. Cadeau trotted behind.

"I hope your father says yes," said Beatrice. "Wouldn't you like to live here with us?"

Luc nodded because his throat was tight again. Now and then he glanced sideways at Beatrice.

"Have you ever been out in a boat?" she asked.

Luc shook his head.

"Do you know how to swim?"

Luc nodded.

Beatrice stopped walking and put her hands on her hips. She scowled at him.

Luc halted, baffled. "What?" he croaked, his voice cracking.

"I hope you'll talk more when you live with us."

Luc laughed, "I will, I promise."

"Shoes?" asked Beatrice, pointing to the boy's feet again. "*You* always wear them."

"Only because Mattie insists. But Pons never does. Except to church."

Luc nodded. Beatrice frowned at him. He smiled and put a finger to his lips. Beatrice rolled her eyes.

The sun set before Luc waved good-bye. As he headed back to the olive grove, he stopped now and then to rub Cadeau's head. It had taken Luc less than an hour to run down to the village, but the walk home was uphill, and he didn't run, so it took more than twice as long. The sky was dark, and the moon was high when he reached the farmhouse. Hervé was sitting on the ground outside the door with a blanket wrapped around his shoulders, scratching in the dirt with his knife. He jumped to his feet when he saw his brother.

"Where've you been, Luc?"

Luc didn't answer. Instead he asked, "How is Pierre?"

"He broke a tooth, but it's just a milk tooth. Where were you? The fishing village?"

Luc nodded.

"Father is passed out in the courtyard. Help me drag him inside," said Hervé.

"No," said Luc. "Why should I? Let him sleep in the dirt all night. Besides, I'm too much of a weakling to move such a big man. Even with your help, Hervé."

CHAPTER SEVEN

Fishing

AFTER CHURCH ON Sunday, Pons climbed to the olive grove. The door to the house was open, but no one was inside, and there was no sign of Luc or his brothers. Pons found Blanche in the courtyard, drawing water from the well. When he asked to see Pascal, she led him wordlessly through the back of the house to the garden, where Luc's father was sprawled against the trunk of a tree, drinking from a wineskin. A breeze rattled the leaves, and they floated to the ground around the man. As Pons spoke about taking Luc as an apprentice and teaching him to fish, Pascal glowered. When the old man finished, the sullen man rose, mopped his red face with his sleeve, and, without a word, staggered back inside the farmhouse, banging the door behind. Pons waited a good while for Pascal's answer, but the door remained shut, so he returned home.

At dusk, there was a knock at the fisherman's cottage; Beatrice opened the door and clapped her hands. Luc was on the doorstep with a wagging, whimpering Cadeau at his side.

"My father said he won't pay Pons anything."

"I never asked for anything," said Pons, coming to the door.

The banked orange embers whispered and popped under the stew pot. Mattie led Luc to the table. Beatrice dished up a bowl of warm turnips and broth. She sat across from Luc and smiled as he gulped down the soup. Beatrice filled the bowl again, and Luc finished every drop. Pons cleared a corner of the cottage, where he unrolled an old straw-filled pallet; Mattie handed the boy a blanket. With a full belly and Cadeau curled against his side, Luc fell asleep easily.

When Luc opened his eyes, it was dark; the hearth lit only one corner of the dim cottage, but he could pick out the silhouettes of fish overhead. He rubbed his eyes, stretched, crossed himself, and smiled. Luc went outside with Cadeau, and when he returned he saw Mattie by the fire, filling a loaf of bread with hard yellow cheese. She tied it in a cloth bundle with four apples. Nearby, Pons baited the last of his hooks with salted fish. Each time a hook was baited, Pons spit on it. Only Beatrice was missing as Mattie handed Luc and Pons bread and mugs of linden-blossom tea.

"Why do you spit on the bait?" asked Luc.

"My father always did," said Pons, shrugging and looking at the boy. "Well, Luc, it's your first day as a fisherman. Are you ready?"

"But it's still dark," said the boy.

"Sun will be up in a few hours. After midnight the wind stops blowing, and the fish start feeding. Early morning is the best time to fish," said Pons as he sipped his mug of tea.

"Where is Beatrice?" asked the boy.

The old man pointed to the loft. "Ah, now, she sleeps well into daylight, like a regular lady, on a bed Mattie made for her, with a feather-stuffed mattress. It's the only part of the girl's day that hasn't changed since she left the house of her father."

"Her father?"

Pons nodded. "He served Count de Muguet."

"Who?" asked Luc, blowing to cool his tea.

Pons dunked his bread in his mug, and Luc copied him. Mattie added sticks to the fire, and the flame brightened.

"You don't know who Count de Muguet is? He's a powerful nobleman from over the mountains," said Pons, shaking his head. "Owns land everywhere. The count owns this village, and his holdings in the northwest would take you more than two days to cross. Your father used to serve him. You and your parents are from up north."

"*Me?* From the north?" asked Luc. "No, I've always lived in the farmhouse on the hill," he said, pointing in the direction of the olive grove.

Pons cocked his head. "No, boy. You're from the same place as Beatrice. Count de Muguet gave the grove to your father."

Luc frowned. "I've never heard any of this. Why would a count give my father an olive grove?"

"I've told you all I know," answered Pons. "Your father must have earned it. The count is anything but generous. He's a cruel and dangerous man."

Luc shook his head and dunked some more bread in his tea; then he frowned and asked Pons, "You said Beatrice is from there too? She's not your family?"

"No. Mattie was her nurse. Beatrice's father was one of the count's knights. She's noble born."

"Her father is a knight?" Luc asked, tea dribbling down his chin as he chewed.

"Like I said, her father *was* a knight, but now he's dead, and her mother might as well be. Poor girl still has nightmares about her father's death."

"Shhh, Pons!" said Mattie. "The less said, the better."

"Right, Mattie. Let's be off, Luc. First thing we need to do is teach you to row. Don't suppose you can swim?" asked Pons.

"Enough to keep from drowning. For a while, anyway. Sometimes I swim in the river with my brothers."

"Then you might just live long enough to grow a beard," said Mattie, thumping the boy on his back.

"I don't think I'll ever grow a beard," said Luc, grinning

and rubbing his chin. "I'm about as hairy as an eggshell. But you should see my brother. He—"

"The fish don't care. Let's be off," said Pons.

Luc patted Cadeau, and held his palm over the dog's head. "Stay, boy. Stay."

The dog whined once and lay down on the threshold, watching as his master shouldered the net and labored behind Pons.

Countless stars pricked the early morning sky as they walked to the beach, where Pons's boat was drawn up on the damp, pebbled shore. It was a small sailboat with a rounded hull that came to a point in the bow and in the stern. The narrow mast had a single triangular sail. The old man struggled to drag its bow into the water until Luc leaned his shoulder against the stern and pushed. Then the little boat slipped easily from the beach into the sea. When they were knee deep, Pons managed to roll himself in without swamping the craft. He was pleased by the ease and lightness with which Luc pulled himself up and over the gunwale.

"See these?" asked Pons. He picked up a pair of carved oars and began to row. "See the blade, how it cups to a ridge in the middle? Works better in the water than a flat oar. Mattie carved them, but Beatrice came up with the shape. She figures everything out. Fearless too, except about bugs. Even so, she's a wonder in the garden, gets anything to grow. Beatrice just has to watch how to do something, and then she knows it. Anything at all, except sewing. Can't sew worth a lick. And what about my sister and her carvings? Those fish look real enough to salt. And your ear? What do you think?"

"The ear? I never saw anything so lifelike. Tell me more about Beatrice."

"Not until I teach you to row and to fish. And that's going to take some time."

Throughout the remains of the dark and well after dawn, until the sun was high in the sky, Pons and Luc took turns rowing. Pons showed Luc how to pull, feather, and push the oars—circling and stopping and making headway. Luc caught on quickly.

Pons began to notice more than the boy's grace. Luc had an uncommon sharpness of vision, easily noting the sea's faint color change that marked a school of fish. He spotted distant gatherings of birds, another telltale sign of fish. Pons handed him a line, and as soon as it sank, Luc caught a fish. It wasn't just beginner's luck, either. It seemed to Pons that every time Luc dropped a line, he caught another fish. Pons played out the long line, strung at intervals with baited hooks, and before long, that line, too, began to tug with bites.

"Pull in the lines, now," said Pons as he hoisted the sail to catch the sea breeze. "It's time to head home."

"What kind of fish are those?" asked Luc, pointing to three silver creatures that appeared just beyond the stern, diving and leaping out of the water, riding the draft of the little boat under sail.

"Those are dolphins, boy," said Pons, with a broad smile

that creased his eyes. "That's the best luck a fisherman can have, seeing dolphins like that. You caught the first fish today, and now this?" Pons patted the boy's head. "Lucky signs, Luc."

That day Pons's nets filled with more fish than on the best of days, and Pons suspected that the boy's value might go beyond his young hands and his good nature.

CHAPTER EIGHT

Luc's Visit

LIFE IN THE fisherman's cottage was good and getting better. Throughout the day, Cadeau followed Beatrice until each afternoon when the dog caught sight of Luc and tore down the road. December was often a rainy month, but this year the weather stayed fine, and Pons declared that the fishing had never been better.

Pons and Luc napped most afternoons after they returned from fishing. The winter sun set earlier, but whenever Luc awoke before day's end, he would help Beatrice and Mattie until nightfall, when they would all share supper. Pons had slaughtered the pig at the end of November, and Mattie was curing its hide in a shallow ditch behind the cottage. She had soaked the hide in quicklime and then in the residue of her cider pressing. Next, the pigskin steeped under a layer of dung. Mattie never let Beatrice help with the unpleasant task of leather tanning, but she welcomed Luc's assistance. He was good-natured even during the worst of jobs.

"Luc," said Beatrice one afternoon, pinching her nose. "You stink worse than the privy."

"That he does, poor boy," said Mattie, stepping back from Luc. "Give me your shirt."

Luc peeled away his shirt, and Mattie took it to rinse in a bucket. Luc washed himself with a basin, a cloth, and soap that Beatrice readied in the yard for him. When he came inside, he was shivering, and Beatrice handed him a blanket to wear until his shirt was dry.

"That's better," she said, sniffing.

"Better for you," said Luc. "I'll probably catch my death from the cold."

As Mattie was hanging Luc's wet shirt on a hook by the hearth, they heard children's laughter. Cadeau barked, and Mattie went to the door to find three smiling barefoot village boys standing on the cottage threshold, caps doffed.

"Please, ma'am, can we see the fish?" asked the biggest child. He was slender, snugly dressed in a heavy shirt of mustard-colored wool.

"And the mermaid?" added the littlest, who wore a shirt of the same cozy yellow wool. The middle boy was heavier than the other two, and Mattie recognized him as one of the baker's sons.

Luc ducked out the back door as Mattie chuckled and ushered the children into the room. They were hushed and slack-jawed, looking up at the fish. Beatrice smiled and handed each child a small apple. The littlest was afraid to take the apple, and Beatrice was crouching to reassure him when Luc burst through the front door with the blanket draped over his head, running at the children, hooting and braying.

The children screamed and headed for the back door as he whipped off the blanket, laughing. The boys turned, and the two older ones started to laugh, but the little one was terrified. Beatrice took him in her arms and wiped away his tears.

"Bad Luc," she said, and she began to sing softly to the little boy.

Luc was smiling at the older boys, who were giggling and making fun of the crying child, when the biggest boy stopped and stared at Luc. He pointed.

"It's the pig boy," he said, elbowing his friend. "He has only one ear."

"Nope," said Luc. "Look here."

Luc opened his palm and showed the boys the wooden ear that Mattie had carved. All three boys were silent. The oldest thanked Mattie and Beatrice, and the three children backed out of the cottage, keeping their eyes on Luc until they were outside. With a roar of laughter they were off, running from the yard.

"I'll see you scamps in church," yelled Luc.

When the three boys spotted Luc that Sunday at Mouette's little church, Saint Olive's, they rushed to him with big smiles on their faces. He had already been known to the villagers as the swineherd's helper. Now, after several weeks of fishing, he was becoming known as Pons's lucky boy, because Pons had bragged about Luc's good fortune to his fellow fishermen. Everyone began to notice the increase in the old man's haul.

Saint Olive's was a small stone church with a wide nave and a barrel-shaped chancel that held the village's only glazed window. It lit the simple wooden altar that today was decorated with Christmas greens and two beeswax tapers. The inhabitants of Mouette stood together in a space that would have been crowded if only half the village showed up. But every Sunday and holiday, everyone jammed together, stood, and listened to the old priest's Latin singsong mass.

When they returned to the cottage after church, Pons held out a basket with three plump sea bream. "Take these to your mother, Luc. It's been almost a month since you left home."

"She'll be happy to have fresh fish before Christmas," added Mattie.

"I'm sure she's missed you," said Beatrice.

"Stay for a meal with your family," said Pons.

Luc missed his brothers and his mother, and he was proud of the fish in the basket, so he and Cadeau marched happily up over the hills to see his family. When he saw Luc,

Pierre jumped into his brother's arms, whooping and laughing.

"Never leave again."

Luc laughed, rubbed the little boy's head, and kissed each cheek. "Smile for me, Pierre."

"My bad tooth's gone. It fell out as soon as you left. Papa said that meant you would never come back."

Hervé stepped from the cottage and nodded at Luc.

"Are you home for good?" he asked.

"Just a visit," said Luc, clapping his brother on the back.

Hervé smiled. "I miss you, Luc."

"Good," said Luc with another thump. "I've missed you and Pierre. Maybe you'll bring him to see the carved fish. Where is Mother?" asked Luc.

"Inside. Father is asleep in the garden."

Luc shook his head, and went into the house.

When Blanche saw Luc, her eyes filled; she pulled him close and held him. Then she pushed him away and looked at him.

"You look older and stronger."

"In one month?"

"You still have stork legs," she said, gently pinching Luc's cheek. "But you're filling out."

"Look what I brought."

"Did you catch those?" asked his mother.

Luc nodded, handing her the basket of fish.

"We'll have a good dinner today, after all," she said.

"And Father?"

"He's asleep."

Blanche chewed her lip. "You should leave before he wakes. His temper is worse and worse. There isn't even time to fix you something to eat."

"That's all right; I'm not hungry."

But Luc's stomach rumbled as he sat at the table and studied his mother. Her thin hair was pulled back under a small cap, and her cheeks were pale and hollow. Her apron was spotless, but her sleeves were frayed, and her cap was torn. She sat down across from him and pulled the basket of fish to her. Looking at the fish, she shook her head and smacked her dry lips.

"I can't remember the last time we had fresh fish," she said.

"No," said Hervé, slipping in next to Luc. "It's always herring. Salty old herring. Like eating old shoes."

Blanche reached across, cupped Luc's chin, and smiled.

"Pons said we come from the north. Is that true, Mother?" Luc asked.

She pulled her hand away from his face and looked down.

"What?" asked Hervé. "I thought I was born right here in this house."

"You were," she said, glancing at Hervé.

"But I wasn't, was I?" asked Luc.

Blanche squeezed her eyes shut. "Someday I'll tell you, Luc."

"Tell me now."

"There isn't time," said Blanche.

Luc stood, and waited for his mother to look at him.

"Why does Father hate me? Is it because I am a freak, or something else?"

"Hush, Luc. You're not a freak. Pascal is a good man. But go, before he wakes."

"He's a mean, drunken fool, Mother."

"You had better go now. Thank you for the fish," said Blanche, without a glance at Luc.

Luc nodded and left the house with a throat too tight to speak. Hervé followed Luc outside, where they found Pierre throwing a stick for Cadeau.

"What's all that about being from the north?" asked Hervé.

"I don't know," said Luc.

Hervé shrugged. "Who cares?"

"I do."

Luc whistled for Cadeau, and Pierre ran with the dog to him.

"Be good, Pierre," said Luc, rubbing his little brother's shoulder.

"Don't go, Luc," pleaded the little boy, dropping the stick and hugging Luc's legs. "You have to be here for Christmas."

Luc shook his head and kissed the top of Pierre's head; his dog fell in behind as he left for the fishing cottage.

1501

CHAPTER NINE

Winter in the Village

A FEW DAYS later, Luc helped Mattie and Beatrice hang greens and holly over the cottage windows. Early in December, on Saint Barbara's day, Beatrice had planted three saucers of lentils and wheat, which now were green with new growth. She and Pons set up a nativity scene on a wooden chest by the hearth. Luc had never seen anything like it.

"Mattie started these carvings on my first Christmas here in Mouette," said Beatrice, lifting the figure of Joseph and showing it to Luc. "First it was just the holy family."

Luc picked up a lamb and rubbed his thumb along its wooden curly coat.

"Every year Mattie carves something secretly," Beatrice

said, pointing to the stable animals and the shepherds. "This year it's the three kings."

"Now she has nothing left to add," said Luc.

Beatrice scowled. "I hope you're wrong. It's a wonderful surprise every year when she adds the new figures."

On Christmas Eve, Pons killed the goose, and Luc awoke on Christmas morning to the delicious aroma of the bird roasting, its fat popping and sizzling, as Mattie turned the spit. Luc took deep breaths and let the wonderful smells fill him to his spine. This promised to be his best Christmas. He went out to the pile of wood at the back of the cottage and split several logs for the hearth.

When it was time to eat, Beatrice helped Mattie dish out the food, and Pons motioned to Luc to sit next to him at the table. Then the four of them bowed their heads, and Beatrice said a prayer.

"Thank you, Lord, for all that we have and for what we are about to receive." Then she raised her eyes for a moment and caught Luc watching her. With a half smile she added, "And thank you for bringing Luc into our home. Amen."

"Amen and Merry Christmas," said Pons. "Let's eat."

After the Christmas feast, Mattie shooed everyone outside.

"Look how beautiful that sky is," she said, pointing to the low December sun. "You three go for a walk while I clean up."

"That's not fair," said Beatrice. "We'll help."

"No," said Pons. "You young ones go out, and enjoy the afternoon. I'll help Mattie."

So Beatrice took her shawl, and Luc wore an old cloak of Pons's, and they headed toward the village with Cadeau. Pons watched from the doorway as the two walked along, and he turned to Mattie.

"I like that boy. You were right, Mattie."

"Aren't I always right?"

Pons laughed. "Yes, you are."

Mattie collected the dishes, saving any scraps of meat and vegetable for a soup that was already simmering.

"Not much left over, is there?" he said.

"No, the boy eats a lot," answered Mattie.

"But he brings in more than he eats. He's special," said Pons, rubbing his chin. "And Beatrice seems to like him. Nice for her to have someone her age around."

"I just hope she doesn't fall in love with the boy."

"Why not, Mattie?"

"Beatrice, a fisherman's wife?" she asked with her hands on her hips.

"It was good enough for our mother," said Pons.

Mattie rolled her eyes. "Maybe."

The rest of that winter was mild, and Luc and Pons fished almost every morning; now and then a storm kept them home. When the mistral blew down from the hills and across the water, the winds howled without pause for three or four days. The wind pressed the bare branches, and the trees whined; the blue sea turned white and dangerous. Then Pons and Luc sharpened Mattie's knives, or made rope, or they worked on the nets. Pons showed Luc how to waterproof the boat using a narrow mallet to drive hemp caulking and pine tar into the seams.

One bright but gusty morning in February, instead of fishing, Pons and Luc were repairing loose and cracked stones on the shallow-pitched cottage roof. Most of the village roofs were thatched, but Pons and his father had long ago replaced their roof with flat stones, which would last beyond the lifetimes of those who dwelled within. After a long morning, Pons and Luc climbed down from the roof at midday, when Mattie and Beatrice brought out bread and sardines. They all sat against the cottage in the afternoon sunshine, sheltered from the dying wind. Roofing was hard work, and Luc was sweaty and chilled.

Beatrice went inside and returned with a blanket that she handed to Luc. He wrapped himself in it and smiled at her.

"This wind is just about played out," said Mattie, tucking a curl into her cap. "You'll fish before dawn tomorrow."

"Fishing is the life for me. One day I'll buy a new sail for your boat, Pons, and I'll get Mattie a cloak made of the softest lamb's wool and dyed crimson," said Luc between bites.

"Crimson, eh? What would the neighbors say if I showed up at Saint Olive's in crimson? Ah, but I would love it," said Mattie.

"What would you bring for Beatrice?" asked Pons.

"A silk dress. The color of the sea," said Luc, shading his eyes with his hand as he looked toward the beach.

"Buttercup yellow," corrected Beatrice. She had a rough brown shawl wrapped around her shoulders, and she drew it tightly against the breeze.

"Buttercup yellow it will be," said Luc, turning to Beatrice and smiling again. He pulled his blanket tight around himself.

"A crimson cape for me and a yellow silk dress for Beatrice?" asked Mattie, raising an eyebrow. "Do you really think you'll get rich enough fishing?"

"I think he might. Never had so many fish in my nets," said Pons. "Luc's already a skilled fisherman, and what's more, he's good luck." Pons crunched down on a sardine, and oil dribbled down his chin. He wiped his face with the back of his hand and leaned against the cottage wall.

"Father said I was cursed," said Luc, leaning back next to Pons.

"No, Luc." The old man closed his eyes and turned his face to the sun. "Mmm. Feel that warmth? Spring will be here soon. Lent is coming. The price of fish always goes up. Good times, my lucky boy."

Mattie squinted against the sun as she scanned the skies. She bit her lip and sighed.

"What is it?" asked Beatrice.

Pons sat up, and Mattie pointed with her chin but

said nothing as the other three looked up at the sky.

"The devil take it," said Pons, spitting on the ground. "Not what I want to see."

"What?" asked Luc. "That's a stork, isn't it? I thought they were good luck."

"No, Luc. You're looking too far out. See right over there?" said Beatrice, pointing to a bird that had just landed nearby. "The heron. It's too close to the house. You don't want a heron near."

"It's a sign of something bad to come," said Mattie.

"Pshaw!" said Pons. "I'm not going to worry now that I have my good-luck boy," he said, rubbing Luc's head. "He sees a lucky stork over there. Come on, Luc, finish up eating so we can sleep. Tomorrow we'll spot your dolphins, and then we won't worry at all."

Luc and Pons napped; when Luc woke in the late afternoon, he joined Mattie and Beatrice, who were planting peas.

"What did you do all day, Lady Beatrice?" asked Luc, bowing at the waist as he took a sack of seed peas from her.

"Are you asking what I did while you slept half the afternoon?" asked Beatrice.

"I worked on the roof all morning with Pons, and I'll be out fishing before dawn while you're snug in your feather bed," said Luc.

"I just sleep the day away," said Beatrice, yawning and stretching her arms.

Luc laughed and dropped to his knees. Crawling down

the rows, he released one pea into each hole that Beatrice punched with a stick. Mattie followed, closing the holes with her foot. Now and then Beatrice poked Luc with the stick, and Mattie shook her head and muttered, until Luc popped up to his feet suddenly. He opened his hand under Beatrice's nose; in his palm was a large, striped, hairy centipede. Beatrice screamed and ran into the house.

"That was not nice, young man," said Mattie. "You *are* lucky, though. Those darn things sting something nasty. But it didn't get you, did it?" she added as she hurried after Beatrice.

Luc chuckled and finished planting peas alone. He brushed the dirt from his knees and hands and went inside as the sun set. Beatrice was stirring a pot suspended over the fire. Luc sat next to Pons at the table. She slapped a bowl of soup in front of him. Broth splashed over the rim and puddled around his dish.

"What do *you* do all day except float around in a little boat?" she asked Luc, still furious.

Luc bit his lip and grinned. Pons shrugged his shoulders and picked up his spoon.

Mattie was at the hearth tending oatcakes that sizzled on a flat stone. Using the heel of a wide knife, she slid a hot cake in front of Pons. When she got to Luc, she said, "Not a word from you, Luc. Just eat up, and hush up."

Beatrice sat down without speaking; she finished her meal, rinsed her bowl, and climbed into the loft.

Luc helped Mattie, fetching water and sweeping the floor. It was dark when he and Pons rolled the net to ready it for the next day.

Luc said good night, curled up on his pallet with Cadeau, and fell asleep.

Hours later, but well before dawn, Luc was sitting with Mattie and Pons in front of the fire in the dark early morning.

"Time to fish," said Pons, standing up. "Ready, Luc?"

As Luc stood, he saw Beatrice backing down the ladder.

"What are *you* doing awake?" asked Mattie.

"What can I do to help?" asked Beatrice, yawning.

Mattie rolled her eyes and laughed, "Sit down, Luc; the fish can wait a little. I'll pour more linden tea for you, Pons."

Pons nodded and held up his mug. He sat down next to Beatrice. Luc sat across from the girl, facing the hearth.

"I'm sorry about the bug," he said.

Beatrice stuck her tongue out at Luc, but then she smiled.

"This is nice," he said. "Having you here in the morning, Beatrice."

Mattie leaned down and kissed the girl's head. "Yes, but don't you make a habit of it."

Beatrice yawned, "I don't think I will. Aren't you tired, Luc?"

"I'm used to it," he answered.

Mattie handed Beatrice a steaming mug. She took it in both hands and held it under her nose.

"Mmm, I love this tea. Don't you, Luc?"

He nodded.

Beatrice watched him over her mug. "Yesterday you said that you like this fishing life, right?"

Luc rubbed his brow with his palm; he looked at his lap and sighed.

Mattie patted his head. "Something troubling you, boy?"

He didn't say anything.

"Tell us," said Beatrice.

"It's two things," he finally said.

Pons cocked his head and rubbed his chin. "Two problems?"

Luc nodded.

"Out with it," said Mattie, sitting down.

"Pons is a wonderful man," said Luc.

"The best," said Beatrice, yawning again.

"But?" asked Mattie.

"He breaks wind something fierce. Even in the open air of the boat, I worry I'm going to die. I'll just fall over dead in the boat."

Mattie opened her eyes wide, then she noticed the growing smile on the boy's face. "You rascal."

"I am not joking," said Luc, sucking in his cheeks.

Beatrice began to laugh. "He's been like that as long as I've lived here."

Mattie began to laugh harder. "I could carve a plug for him."

Pons looked at all of them. "You are meaner than a nest of hornets."

Mattie nodded but had to stop laughing before she could reply. She wiped her eyes. "Well now, I hear a spoon of fennel seed and honey taken morning and night might help."

Pons smiled. "Honey, eh? Not going to argue with that cure."

The fire flared and spit, and a spark popped and sizzled in the dirt near Beatrice's foot. Luc smothered it, pushing earth over it with his heel.

"You said there were *two* things," said Beatrice to Luc, yawning again.

"Are we keeping you awake?" asked Luc.

"Yes."

"Poor Lady Beatrice," said Luc, standing and adding a log to the fire.

Beatrice frowned. "You said there were two problems."

"It's nothing," answered Luc, without turning. He stared into the hearth.

"Out with it, Luc," said Mattie.

Luc turned and plonked down next to Beatrice. She elbowed him, and he elbowed her right back.

"Ooof," said Beatrice, pinching Luc.

"Ow, that hurt," he whined.

Beatrice sucked in her cheeks, imitating Luc. "What's the *other* thing?" she asked.

"Well," said Luc, rubbing his arm where he'd been pinched, "it's about you, Beatrice."

"About Beatrice?" said Mattie. "The perfect Beatrice?"

"I thought *I* was near perfect," muttered Pons.

"You are," said Mattie. "*Nearly* perfect. Beatrice is just plain perfect."

"Tell us, Luc. What's wrong with Beatrice?" asked Pons.

"You mean you don't know?"

"No," said Pons. "Nothing I can think of."

"Me neither," said Mattie.

"Beatrice snores," said Luc.

"I do not," she insisted.

"Yes, you do. Louder than you could imagine. Like a big noisy storm," insisted Luc.

Mattie raised her eyebrows. "Well, now."

"Luc is lying, right, Mattie?" asked Beatrice.

Mattie shook her head. "Oh no. Some nights you're like thunder."

Pons added, "We never wanted to hurt your feelings."

"It's a wonder you don't loosen the roof," added Luc.

Beatrice shook her head. "I'm sorry. I had no idea. I snore?"

Luc asked, "Mattie, anything you could carve or brew up for snoring?"

Mattie drummed her lips with her fingers. "I could maybe carve some plugs for our ears."

"Lucky me," said Luc, "I'll only need one plug."

Beatrice frowned at Luc.

Luc elbowed her.

"Stop it," said Beatrice.

"We're just joking," he said.

"What?" asked Beatrice, her face reddening.

"You don't snore. You're perfect. Just like everyone says," said Luc.

"You're anything but," said Beatrice, but she was smiling.

"No one ever said I was perfect. Not even nearly," said Luc.

Mattie suddenly reached out and plucked more than a few hairs from Luc's head.

"Ouch! What did you do that for?"

Mattie took the hair and held it in the firelight. "Pretty hair."

Luc was rubbing his head. "Thanks."

She leaned over the hearth and dropped the strands onto the embers—the fire grew brighter for an instant as the hair coiled and disappeared in the flame.

"Good, good, good!" said Mattie, rubbing her hands together.

"What's going on?" asked Luc.

Beatrice answered, "Mattie says if your hair burns brightly, your life will be long."

"And lucky?" asked Luc.

"It already is," said Beatrice.

CHAPTER TEN

The Soldiers

THROUGHOUT FEBRUARY AND into March, every afternoon when Pons and Luc returned with their catch, Beatrice and Mattie spread the fish in big wooden tubs. Pons coated each fish layer with salt until the tub was filled. Mattie topped the tubs with wooden planks, and Luc weighted the planks with heavy rocks. After two weeks, the salted fish were washed in seawater and hung to dry in the front of the house with Cadeau standing guard. In this manner, they prepared the fish Pons owed to the count.

Winter ended with more fish in the nets each day, and as the days lengthened, the sun grew warmer. Luc would sit in the bow, cleaning the catch. First he sliced off the fins, and then, using the back of his knife, he flaked off the scales from the skin before slitting each fish lengthwise along its belly. He scooped out the guts, sliced off the tail, and pulled out the gills. After flipping these discards to the circling gulls, Luc rinsed each carcass in seawater. It was messy work, and Pons was impressed with the boy's skill.

One morning in early March, Pons presented Luc with a new knife. It had a fine steel blade, a yew-wood handle, and a leather sheath. Luc was speechless.

"It's time you had a good knife of your own, Luc. You've earned it."

Luc was quiet the rest of the day; Pons watched him take the knife from the sheath again and again, turning it over, weighing it in his palm. At one point the boy held it so that the sunlight hit the blade, and light danced in a patch on the floor of the boat.

When Luc and Pons returned from fishing that day, they found two soldiers in dark-blue tunics sitting at the table with Mattie. Luc recognized one of men as the soldier who had always accompanied Sir Guy on his biannual visits to Luc's family. He was a big-bellied man with unruly eyebrows and an easy laugh. With him was another soldier, a skinny, pigeon-toed youth whom Luc had never before seen.

"Hello, Pons," said the burly soldier, turning to snag a loaf of bread from the windowsill. He pointed to the young soldier. "This is Henri, my aide. See to our horses and the mule, Henri."

As Henri left, Pons nodded and sat down. "Hello, Alain. This is my helper, Luc."

Alain jammed a chunk of bread into his mouth and raised his bushy eyebrows.

"Luc? The boy from the olive orchard?" he asked between chews.

"The same," said Pons.

"I thought he looked familiar. Of course, the dog outside," Alain said, whacking his head with the heel of hand. Alain unbuckled the pouch on his belt and produced a wedge of leaf-wrapped cheese. "Help yourselves," he said, peeling the cheese and slicing himself a large piece. "How about some wine, Mattie?"

Alain turned to Luc. "What are you doing here?"

Luc answered, "Learning to fish. What are you doing here, and where is Sir Guy?"

"I'm here collecting the Muguet rents. We didn't visit your place last year, so you probably haven't heard about Sir Guy."

"What about him?" asked Luc.

"I am very sorry to tell you, he died last winter. One of many changes up north," said Alain breaking off more bread.

"And the count?" asked Pons. "Last spring you told us he was taken with a fit about the time Sir Guy died."

"Muguet is too mean to die," said Mattie, setting a mug of wine in front of Alain.

Alain took a big swallow and wiped his mouth on his

sleeve. "He lingered for a year, but the count finally passed this January. It was a bad death."

"Sir Guy worked for *that* count?" asked Luc.

"He did, and they're both dead now." Alain shook his head and offered Mattie a wedge of cheese. He cut another piece for himself

"What do you mean by a bad death?" she asked.

"Well, after that fit, Muguet couldn't speak a word or move his arms. Helpless and hated? You can wager his final days weren't filled with comfort. You ever hear about the count's hands?"

Pons shrugged, and Mattie nodded.

"Count de Muguet had huge hands, but tiny thumbs. Like a baby's thumbs. He hated anyone to see his hands. Always wore gloves or kept his hands balled into fists. Except after the fit, he couldn't make a fist. I heard the servants used to prop him up in bed with his hands spread out on a pillow right in front of him. He had to look at those ugly thumbs every day for the last year of his life."

"He deserved it," said Mattie.

Pons crossed himself.

"Now I'm in service to the new count. His only son," said Alain.

"And what's this one like?" Mattie asked.

"He's young. No more than twenty years. But he's been away most of his life, serving as a page, then as a squire. I don't know anything about the young lord."

"Well, the old Count de Muguet won't be missed," said Mattie.

Alain nodded; then he looked at Luc, who was standing, leaning against the wall, flipping his new knife from hand to hand. Alain pointed to Mattie's fish carvings.

"Ever seen anything like this cottage?" asked the soldier.

Luc looked up. "No, never."

"Me neither. Magic, like. Good food, too. But why are you learning to fish?" Alain asked, draining his mug and holding it up for more. "Fishing is hard, dangerous work. Your father has a fine olive grove."

Luc shrugged and looked away.

"How did the family come by that place?" asked Pons. "People around here always wondered. Didn't Muguet give it to Luc's father?"

"That's what I heard. I don't know the history. Sir Guy knew, but he never told me. Something secret in the past. Lots of secrets up in that olive grove."

"Secrets?" asked Mattie. "Like what?"

"Like, Pascal paid no rent to the count. Instead, we brought gifts each year. Then Sir Guy passed away. Poof!" Alain snapped his fingers with both hands, blowing on one, then on the other. "No more gifts. But I'll tell you, Sir Guy was very partial to this boy," said Alain, pointing to Luc.

Luc lowered himself to the end of the bench farthest from Alain and reached for a piece of bread.

Alain finished his mug of wine. Mattie poured another.

"Luc looks like he's thriving here. Dog, too. Now that was a real fine puppy. From the count's prized bitch. Probably worth more than a year of my wages. I don't know how Sir Guy got that dog for the boy. Of course, the count trusted that old knight, as much as he trusted anyone."

"That's not saying much," said Mattie.

"True. Old Muguet was a mean, unforgiving man. One mistake, you were dead. But then, everyone liked Sir Guy," said Alain, scratching his neck. "Still, there was something mysterious up at the olive grove."

"Mysterious?" asked Mattie.

Alain tossed the last of the cheese into his mouth and held his mug up for more wine.

"I thought it had to do with Luc. He looks different from Pascal's other two boys. Guess it doesn't matter anymore, but I figured Luc was Sir Guy's bastard. It's a mystery, that and the kid having just the one ear. Damned strange. The old knight made me swear never to mention it."

Luc stopped eating, and scowled at Alain. "What are you saying? That Sir Guy was my father?"

"I'm saying it *might* be so," said Alain.

Luc stood, but Mattie put her hand on his shoulder and gently pushed him down, shaking her head at him.

"Well, we won't learn anything more from Sir Guy now," said Mattie.

"It all seems like a tall tale to me," said Pons.

"Probably. I may have said too much, as it is," said Alain,

wiping his mouth on the back of his hand, dusting the crumbs from the front of his tunic, and swaying to a stand. "Until the next time, if there is one. Muguet's son may let his rent collectors take this over. Never made sense that we did it. Like I said, something about Sir Guy and the boy. But I wish you all the best, Luc, whoever you are. Sir Guy was as good a man as I ever expect to know. Good health to all of you," said Alain, lurching as he turned to rejoin Henri, the younger soldier, who waited in the yard with the horses and the mule.

Pons and Mattie watched as both soldiers packed two large sacks with Pons's salted fish. After Henri tied the sacks onto the back of a mule, Muguet's men trotted through the village; they had other rents to collect before heading north. When she was sure the soldiers had left, Mattie called Beatrice down from the loft.

"Alain talks too much," said Pons.

"And makes himself right at home, doesn't he?" said Mattie.

Luc was slumped at the table, resting his chin on his crossed arms. He looked up as Beatrice slipped onto the bench facing him.

"Were you hiding from the soldiers?" asked Luc.

Beatrice nodded. "Mattie thinks it's better if no one up north remembers me."

"Why?" asked Luc.

Mattie shrugged. "We're just being careful. Her father's death was a terrible thing. Enough said."

Beatrice pursed her lips and looked at Mattie. Luc looked from Mattie to Beatrice, who reached across and patted his arm.

"How are you? I heard everything he said. It's a strange tale. About you and Sir Guy. Could it be true?" asked the girl.

Now Luc was silent. He felt as though he had been listening to a fable, as though all the talk had nothing to do with him. He sat with his elbows on the table and covered his face with his hands.

"You've had a long day," said Mattie, sitting next to Luc, patting the boy's shoulder. "Who knows if there's any truth to that story? What I know to be true was what Alain said. Sir Guy was a good man. He collected fish from us for at least a dozen years. Kind and honest, nothing like the count."

Then Mattie shook her head a few times; she looked up at Pons and chuckled, "What do you think, Pons? Might we have two noble brats living in our hut?"

Pons sat down next to Beatrice.

"I'm no more noble than you are, Mattie," said Beatrice.

Luc looked up. "If Alain spoke the truth, I'm just a bastard. A bastard with one ear."

"It might explain things, Luc," said Mattie gently. "About your family."

"It would explain why my father, or the man I thought was my father, despises me. Not only am I a freak, I'm not even his son."

"Luc, you don't know if there is any truth to that soldier's tale," said Beatrice.

"Alain never heard a story, true or false, that he didn't pass on," said Pons.

"You can think long and hard, but in the end, what comes of this? It's a fairy tale. Nothing more. Sir Guy has been dead a year, so that's the end of it," said Mattie.

Luc clasped his hands across his chest and looked at Mattie. "My mother knows the truth."

"If there is truth to Alain's tale, go easy on your mother. There is pain past and present here for her," said Mattie.

"Pain caused by my birth."

"But not by *you*, Luc," said Mattie.

"My father said I was his curse. It makes sense."

Beatrice came around and sat next to Luc. "It makes more sense to look at how lucky you and I are. Who could have a better home than this? It makes no difference who your father is."

"Easy for you say," said Luc.

"Me? I watched my father's execution, and then my mother abandoned me. What counts is that we both are here now with Pons and Mattie."

Luc swallowed and looked around at the cottage. He looked up at the carved fish, and then he turned to Beatrice, who was watching him. She took his hand, and he closed his eyes and nodded.

CHAPTER ELEVEN

Lilies of the Valley

IN THE LAST week of March, a storm and high winds kept Pons and Luc ashore for several days. Twice Luc started uphill to visit the olive grove, but each time, he turned back. He'd thought about Alain's story every day, but Luc hadn't decided how to ask his mother. One blustery afternoon as he turned the soil in the garden and helped Mattie plant cauliflower and cabbages, Beatrice appeared with a large oval basket and an iron pot.

"Mattie, can you spare Luc?" called Beatrice.

Mattie straightened, stretched her back, and clapped the dirt from her hands.

"I don't like to see you about in this wind."

"I thought we might dig *tellines*. Aren't you tired of beans?" asked the girl.

Mattie nodded and licked her lips. "Tasty, but don't you go into the cold water."

"That's why I need Luc," said Beatrice.

"Of course," said Luc. "Send the pig boy out into the cold water. What are *tellines* anyway?"

"Little clams," said Beatrice.

"Nothing better," said Mattie with a smile.

"Do I have to swim out for them?" asked Luc, putting down the spade and folding his arms across his chest.

"Oh yes," said Beatrice, nodding. "You'll have to dive deep underwater and hold your breath while you dig. Pons says you're a pretty good swimmer."

"Don't you think we might wait for warmer weather?" asked Luc.

Beatrice shook her head. "No."

"How deep do I have to dive?" asked Luc, picking up the spade again.

"The girl's pulling your leg, Luc," said Mattie, nudging Luc. "You just wade in up to your ankles. You'll find a basketful in no time, and you won't even get your knees wet. Beatrice knows the best spots." Mattie smoothed her dress and tucked her hair into her cap. "You two never stop teasing. Like brother and sister," she added, taking the spade from Luc.

"A sister like Beatrice? Now *that* would be unlucky," said Luc.

"And you're hardly *my* idea of the perfect brother."

"Exactly what any sister and brother would say," said Mattie. "But it's very nice having another young person around, isn't it, girl?"

"Come on, Luc. Let's go," said Beatrice with her hands on her hips.

Luc wiped his hands on the front of his shirt and rubbed his face on a shoulder. He called Cadeau and took the pot and the basket from Beatrice. The basket had a long leather strap, and he slipped it over his head and under his arm. He hurried after her on a path along the shore, away from the fishing village and any cottages, to a tidal inlet where there was a shallow eddy and sandy banks that were littered with powdery reddish rocks and fuzzy brown clumps of dried sea grass. The sky was leaden, and the wind was raw.

"How do I find these clams?" asked Luc, stopping at the water's edge to push up his patched hose. Cadeau licked his legs, and he brushed him away.

"We'll wade in, and you'll feel them with your toes, just under the sand," said Beatrice. "But *tellines* are tiny. Smaller than olives."

"That small? We'd better fill the basket, because I am hungry."

"You eat an awful lot for such a skinny boy."

"Skinny?"

Beatrice nodded.

Luc looked down at his legs. They were thin, and so were his arms. He sighed then shrugged.

"What's the pot for?" he asked.

"Seawater. After we collect a basketful, we'll soak the clams in the seawater until they spit out all the sand."

The sea was icy, and the wind was loud.

"Oooow. It's going to be hard to feel anything in this cold," he complained.

"Come on," said Beatrice, kicking off her shoes and tucking up her skirt so that her legs were bare to her knees.

"Mattie didn't want you getting wet," he said.

"Mattie is always trying to keep me from dirt and cold and sun. She thinks I am still a lady. But she won't know if you don't tell her."

"Mother of God, it's freezing," said Luc as he waded ankle deep into the choppy water.

"Stop whining and get some clams."

Beatrice reached down and scooped two fistfuls of wet sand that she let drain through her fingers. A dozen or so tiny silver-and-violet clams sat in her cupped hands. Luc held out the basket, and she let the clams slide in. He tightened the strap so that the basket nestled against his chest and stayed upright as he dug.

The basket was only half full when Beatrice ran from the water. Cadeau barked and rushed to her.

"Hey, where are you going? We don't have enough of these clams for a meal," called Luc.

"I can't feel my toes," she said.

"Of course, milady," said Luc with a chuckle, and he kept digging.

As Beatrice sat on the beach rubbing her feet, Cadeau started licking her face.

"Stop it!" she said, laughing and pushing the dog away as she slipped on her shoes.

Luc whistled, and Cadeau bounded into the water, barking and paddling in circles around Luc as he scooped.

"Call Cadeau, Beatrice. I can't find anything with him splashing around."

Beatrice called, and the dog charged out of the water, running to her. He stood over her and shook his coat.

She screamed, and Luc started laughing. The basket was full, and he ran out of the water. He lay the basket at Beatrice's feet, beaming, and grabbed the iron pot and filled it with seawater.

"I'm soaking wet, thanks to that mongrel," whined Beatrice.

"Mongrel? That dog is better bred than you or I."

"Certainly than *you*," said Beatrice standing up and wringing out her skirt. Then she added, "Whoever you are."

Luc puffed out his cheeks, exhaled, and stared at Beatrice. She was brushing the sand from her damp skirt; he leaned forward and dumped the pot of water over her head.

She didn't scream this time. She just glared at Luc, wide-eyed and furious. Then she turned and began to run home.

Red-faced, fuming, and muttering to Cadeau about how mean Beatrice was, Luc carried the basket to the water and rinsed each clam before dropping it into the pot of seawater. Then he strapped on the empty basket, heaved up the full pot, and sloshed along the path to the cottage, where he found Mattie in front of a roaring fire. She was wrapping Beatrice in a blanket.

"What got into you, boy?" said Mattie, her dark eyebrows low and her voice thick.

"I'm sorry," said Luc. "Is Beatrice all right?"

"I should think you're sorry. Poor girl was blue and hasn't stopped shivering yet. And you're not much better. Leave those clams here, and get yourself dry."

Beatrice turned her back to Luc and said nothing.

"I'll be back in a little while," said Luc.

"Don't you go out, soaked like that," said Mattie, but Luc was off at a trot, followed by Cadeau, whose coat was already half dry.

When Luc returned, it was dark, and Mattie and Pons were sitting by the fire with Beatrice, who was scrubbed clean and wearing a gray dress Luc had never before seen; her hair was brushed and gleaming.

"Where have you been?" said Mattie. "You missed dinner."

Luc held his hands behind his back. He bowed deeply and presented Mattie and Beatrice each with a bouquet of lilies of the valley.

Mattie shook her head and took a deep breath.

"Scamp. Do you know how I love these?"

"The very first of the season," said Luc proudly. "I spotted them this morning in a sheltered spot just off the path."

"Some say these little flowers are the tears of the Holy Virgin," said Beatrice. She smiled as she held the white bouquet to her nose.

"I'm sorry, Beatrice," Luc said.

Beatrice peeked at him over the flowers.

"I'm sorry too, Luc. I shouldn't have said anything about who you are."

"Like a pair of toddlers," muttered Mattie. "Get out of that filthy old shirt, Luc."

Luc stripped off his shirt and stood by the fire rubbing his arms.

"We saved you a bowl of clams. I'll get them," said Mattie.

Beatrice rose and handed Luc a cloth bundle.

"What's this?" he asked.

But he knew as soon as he took the bundle: it was a new shirt, a dark green tunic that fastened at the neck with leather braids. The wool was soft and warm and smelled of lanolin.

"Beatrice made that shirt for you," said Mattie, heaping steaming *tellines* into a bowl.

Luc smiled; he could see that the stitching was crooked. He pulled it over his head, and Beatrice stepped in and tied the leather laces. One sleeve was too short, and the other was too long.

"That looks good on you," said Mattie.

"Does it make me look like a gentleman?" he asked, flattening his hair and throwing back his shoulders.

"It's a shirt," said Beatrice. "Not a miracle."

"Well, it's a very fine shirt," said Luc, smoothing the front of it.

Mattie noticed that the boy had grown taller in the two seasons he had been living with them; his cheeks were rosy, and the sun had burnished and brightened his golden hair;. She smiled and shook her head. "You look very handsome," she said, handing him the bowl. "That shirt was supposed to be for Easter, but you need it now."

"That's the truth," said Pons, pinching the hem. "Good weight for fishing. Your old shirt was stained and your elbows were sticking out through holes."

"That's a new dress, isn't it, Beatrice?" asked Luc.

She nodded. "Mattie made it for me for Easter, but my old dress was soaking wet."

"You look nice," said Luc to Beatrice as he sat down next to her. "But someday I'll get you that buttercup silk dress."

"What would I do with a silk dress?" asked Beatrice, touching his arm.

"Go dancing with Sir Luc," said Pons.

"C'mon, Sir Luc, eat your clams," said Mattie.

CHAPTER TWELVE

Bad Luck

THE MOON WAS full, and the pale sky was almost day-bright as Luc and Pons headed out to fish. The mistral had finally ceased blowing, and the first days of April were warm and fair. Luc wore his new green shirt, cuffing up the longer sleeve. He whistled as he carried the net along the path that led to the beach. Pons had coiled the baited long lines around his shoulders, and he carried the rolled sail in his arms. His face was spiked with gray stubble, and his hands were worn, scarred by fish hooks and eel bites, his fingers crooked with age.

Mattie was right about the boy, thought Pons. *Just what I needed.*

He patted Luc on the back, and they shoved the boat into the water and climbed aboard. Luc leaned with the roll of the sea, watching the pitch-dark water meet the silver of the moon-bright sky. As dawn approached, he heard the cry of a sole gull and watched as it soared and disappeared toward the shore. On this early morning, there was no wind, and the sea sparkled as the moon slipped toward the horizon; the April morning was chilly, and Luc was glad for his new shirt. Pons rowed until his hands ached, and Luc took the oars. Because the sea was calm, they took the little boat into deeper waters.

"Pull in the oars; we'll drift for a while," Pons said as he lowered the baited long lines. Earlier they had passed a few other fishing boats, but now they were alone, without even a gull in the sky. "It's just us and the fish," he added.

As they bobbed gently, the sea went from black-blue to deep blue, and the sky went from pink to red. When the yellow sun rose, it hung in a blue, cloudless sky. A soft breeze ruffled the water.

"Guess I was wrong about the fish," said Pons after a few hours of drifting. "It's just us. No fish today." He handed Luc bread, cheese, and a handful of raisins, and they each took swigs of watered wine from a goatskin bag. "No sign of your lucky dolphins this morning, either. I hoped we'd catch your first tunny. That would be a fine way to start the spring. Land a big tunny. Though I'd wager you'd rather be ashore helping Beatrice mend the nets or work the garden."

Luc tore away at the bread and chewed big mouthfuls. He squinted and raised an eyebrow, looking at Pons. "Now, why would you think that? I love the sea."

"Oh yes, I see that, but I think there is something you're even more fond of, no?" When Luc just smiled, Pons added, "Though I'd have to say there is nothing in the world that could beat hooking a tunny."

Luc laughed and shook his head. "I don't know how it feels to hook a tunny, and I don't think I'll learn that lesson today."

"Perhaps tomorrow. Time to head in if we want to be home by midday. Take the oars while I check the lines. Maybe we'll have better luck on the trip in."

Luc settled into the middle seat and began to row. His hands had callused in his months of fishing, and although he was still slender, his shoulders and arms had strengthened. He leaned into each pull. The boat rose in the water and pushed ahead with each stroke. As he rowed, Luc scanned the water for the color changes that might mean a school of fish. Way out on the horizon, he noticed a dark speck.

"Pons, there's something out to the south of us," he said, pointing.

Pons squinted. At first he saw nothing. Luc continued to row, studying the distant edge of his vision, where the sea and sky met.

As he watched the speck grow, Luc said to Pons, "It's a boat. She's moving fast."

Pons looked up and across the water, shielding his eyes with his hand. He took a deep breath.

"We shouldn't have come out so far. Put everything you

have into those oars, Luc. I'll take over as soon as I have the lines in. I'll hoist the sail, too. Pray for more wind. I wish we had a second set of oars."

"That vessel has two sails. Three-cornered like ours but red and bigger. She's heading for us."

Pons raised his sail, and it luffed; he pushed the tiller until the canvas puffed out. He slid forward, and controlling the tiller with his bare foot, Pons took over the oars.

"Let me row. When you're rested, we'll each take an oar. We need to get in before they catch up to us."

"Who is it, Pons?" asked Luc, rolling and massaging his sore shoulders.

"I'll not say what I fear. Not yet."

The speck on the horizon grew, and soon Pons could pick out the two masts and the varnished hull of a dhow cutting fast toward the little fishing boat. Luc took one oar, and he and Pons rowed, pulling with every bit of strength. Together they hunched forward, and together they snapped back, the oars rising and dipping, both pulling hard against the sea. The little fishing boat surged ahead with each stroke, but they could not outrun the larger two-masted dhow that was closing in.

Luc saw the crew: dark-skinned, bare-chested men with shaved heads, leaning over the sides of the dhow. On the prow stood a robed, turbaned figure with his arms folded against his chest. The fishing boat continued to lose ground against the larger vessel, and soon Pons and Luc could hear the voices of their predators.

Pons turned to the boy; his face was gray, and his lips were pale. "Put down your oar, Luc. We're lost. Pray to the Lord, for surely this is the worst, and maybe the last, day of our lives."

Pons crossed himself and dropped to his knees, but Luc took both oars and put everything into his strokes. The dhow was pulling alongside; one of its sailors heaved a sharp and heavy iron hook. The smaller boat shuddered and rocked steeply as the hook crashed into its bow, tangling the rigging and splintering the mast as it fell. Before Luc could take a breath, strange men were screeching and howling, throwing ropes, and clambering into his boat. Pons was felled with a single punch.

Luc scrambled to reach Pons, but he was plucked up and tossed over the thick shoulder of a man who shinnied up a rope ladder to the larger boat. In vain, Luc hit, kicked, and squirmed. The sailor tossed him onto the dhow's deck, and someone bagged him with a rough cloth. Luc struggled, but unseen hands tied a rope around the sack, binding him in a dark, airless roll. He could barely breathe, and he felt himself being lifted and dropped, falling a distance into what felt like a pile of cloth. Gasping for breath, he sucked in sacking and little air. Luc rocked madly to and fro. He coughed and almost choked before the fabric was pulled away from his face. Luc gulped hot air, and then he screamed. A tall man with a scarred face and a neckerchief crouched over him. The sailor kicked Luc in the side, before he turned and disappeared up the narrow stairs. The hatch slammed shut, and Luc was in darkness, trussed and desperate.

Luc fought against the ropes, but he was bound tightly; he couldn't free himself. The hold was dark and hot, and he heard only muffled footsteps and occasional shouts from above. His heart pounded, and he couldn't breathe fast enough. He rolled and struggled, until his chest burned. It was hopeless. Luc was exhausted, more than exhausted: he began to sweat and to shake until he grew cold and heavy. He wet himself, and he didn't care. He was falling, slipping out of the awfulness of this nightmare and into a dream.

Luc became half aware that the tall sailor with the kerchief was back beside him, untying the rope binding and unrolling the sacking. The sailor wrinkled his nose and stripped off Luc's green shirt and his hose. Luc had no idea where he was; his thoughts had ceased to form words. He sat up slowly and blinked in the half-light from the open hatch. When the sailor tried to hand him a cup of water, Luc just stared at it, and the sailor threw the water in the boy's face. Luc didn't move. Then the sailor seized Luc's legs and clamped a thick iron ring around each ankle; the rings were connected by heavy links. Luc watched. His mind was empty. The sailor fetched another cup of water. With one hand pinching Luc's chin, he forced open the boy's jaw and poured in water. Luc sputtered and coughed. The tall sailor laughed and turned to Luc's discarded clothing. He tucked the knife that Pons had given Luc into his waistband and emptied the pouch that had hung from the boy's belt. Squatting, the sailor sifted the contents: a scrap of woolen cloth, a strip of leather, a dried white flower. When the tall sailor picked up Mattie's wooden ear, he turned it over and over. Then he grabbed Luc by his hair and began to comb through it with his fingers. He backed away, scowled at the boy, and vaulted to the deck, taking the steps two at a time.

Luc was alone again, but not for long. Three men, including the tall sailor and the turbaned, robed man who had been on the prow, descended into the hold. The tall sailor grabbed Luc's chin and wrenched his head to the left. A short, toothless sailor with a lantern frowned and pointed his thumb downward. The robed man—who, Luc would later learn, was the captain of the boat—squinted at Luc and stroked his beard. The tall sailor handed the captain the wooden ear. The captain turned it over and over in the lantern light. He began to laugh.

"He's a scrawny, worthless freak," the toothless sailor said. "Why waste water and bread on him? One ear? We won't be able to give him away. Throw him overboard."

The captain juggled the wooden ear. "This is a marvelous piece of carving. If the boy made it, he's worth something. If not, well, look at his hair. Someone will buy him for that."

Luc understood nothing that was said, but if he had, he would have learned that the wooden ear had saved his life.

CHAPTER THIRTEEN

Pons Returns

THROUGHOUT THE AFTERNOON and the night, the little fishing boat drifted shoreward in a calm sea. Finally, slowly, as day broke, Pons sat up and rubbed his head. He closed his eyes and relived the horror of the afternoon. He was alone. Luc was gone, and the old man wept. He had a tender lump on his head, but he was sound. He noted the position of the rising sun and figured that, overnight, he had drifted north and a little east. When he scanned the horizon, Pons saw that he was near enough to shore to see the faint outline of a village. He looked about at his boat. The slavers' grappling hook had destroyed the rigging, and the sail was useless. The mast was splintered and ruined. Pons detached the torn sail and pulled the stub of the mast from its fitting.

Then he tipped the broken pole into the water and watched it roll away from the boat. Now the little boat was lighter, and Pons took the oars and slowly headed in. By afternoon, he had rowed back to Mouette. A returning fisherman and his son ran to help as Pons struggled to drag his boat onto the shore.

"Mattie's been worried sick, knocking on doors, asking if any of us saw you yesterday. She feared the worst, Pons, but I hoped you hooked a tunny and fought it through the night," said the father. He was a tall man with a wide-brimmed hat pulled down low on his forehead. "I was a lad when you brought in a tunny that was bigger than your boat."

"Father still talks about that fish," said the son, a lanky youth with dimpled chin and dark eyes.

"Luc is gone," murmured Pons.

"Drowned?" asked the son.

Pons shook his head and could barely spit out the word: "Saracens."

The other two fishermen crossed themselves.

"Saint Pierre have mercy. Saracens? Here?" asked the father.

Everyone who lived on the Mediterranean coast knew the old stories of Saracens, heathen invaders from the East who pillaged the coast and kidnapped Christians. Hundreds of years ago, some coastal towns had been abandoned and people moved to new villages, perched on the hillsides, high above the sea, with sturdy walls and watchtowers to warn of the Saracens. But the maritime invasions had stopped long,

long ago. The coast had been peaceful for generations beyond memory, and once again villages were built on the shore. But just lately there had been new rumors of fishermen who disappeared at sea and reports of people who were snatched from the land, taken by Saracen ships, and never seen again. These tales of pirate invaders had been like the tales of sorcerers and dragons; the fear was distant and unreal. Until now.

Pons sat down on the beach and covered his face with his hands. Shoulders hunched, he began to weep. The father removed his hat, looked down at Pons, and waited until the old man was quiet.

"Come. We'll take you home," he said gently.

His son draped Pons's arm over his shoulders and helped the old man walk, while the father grabbed what remained of the sail, the net, and the fishing lines. Before they reached the cottage, Cadeau bounded out, tail wagging, licking Pons's feet and barking. Then he circled and sat, his tail thumping, watching expectantly for his master.

Mattie charged out of the cottage and threw her arms around her brother. Beatrice followed, and the three of them hugged and cried.

"Luc?" asked Mattie fearfully.

Pons shook his head.

Beatrice crumpled to her knees crying, "No! No!"

CHAPTER FOURTEEN

The Voyage

THE DHOW SAILED wide but usually within sight of the coast. Luc had no sense of day or night in the black of the hold. Most of the time he slept. Now and then the tall sailor jabbed him awake and handed him water or a piece of wormy black bread, a dry bit of salted fish, or a handful of oily olives. At first Luc pushed aside the filthy bread and merely sipped the stale water. But after what he guessed to be no more than a couple of days, Luc began to feel sharp pains in his stomach, cramps that would come on suddenly, disappear, and return. Only food eased the pain. He was starving, and soon he was gobbling down the infested bread and guzzling the sour water. Afterward, he would curl up, still hungry, and sleep. In his dreams, he was fishing with Pons or working in the garden with Mattie and Beatrice. When he awoke he was numb, aware of nothing but the pangs of hunger in his stomach.

One day, Luc was jolted awake by yelling. Footsteps tramped on the deck above. He was too bewildered to comprehend anything, but when the hatch opened, Luc watched four shivering men, shackled and naked like himself, stumble down the steps, pushed along by two seamen. Blood streamed from one captive's nose. Two wept. The fourth was silent, trembling and dazed. Luc covered his head with his arms and squeezed himself into the dim back corner of the hold. The words spoken by the captives were no more understandable than those of his captors.

For weeks, Luc and the four other prisoners—naked, hungry, and chained—ate and drank what little bread and water they were given and shared the stinking hold of the dhow. The air reeked of sweat, vomit, and excrement. As the dhow rose and fell with the sea, its foul bilge water sloshed over the prisoners and sent its rats scurrying. Now and then the boat stopped; more cargo, sponges, barrels, and sacks would drop into the hold. At first, the other captives tried to speak to Luc, but he understood nothing, and they ceased trying. When he listened to the other captives talking among themselves, Luc felt even more lonely.

Most afternoons Luc and the other captives were led above to the deck. Sometimes the tall sailor doused them with buckets of seawater. When they were forced to walk about or even march, Luc often stumbled. The iron cuffs chafed his narrow ankles, he had sores on his shins, and his skin was flea-bitten.

For days the dhow sailed with no land in sight, but the sea remained mercifully calm. At times, when he was up on deck, gazing out at the sea, Luc noticed a patch of choppy water that signaled a school of fish. One afternoon he leaned against the railing that edged the boat and watched as the tall sailor with the neckerchief dropped a small fishing line into the water. In daylight Luc could see an old scar that marked the man's dusky face from the corner of one eye to the corner of his mouth; his thick, muscled arms were ribboned with more scars. When he grinned, he flashed a mouthful of brown-stained teeth.

Luc turned to the sea, and thought that if he managed to fall overboard, he would escape but only by dying. He did not want death. He wanted his old life back. He turned from the sea to the deck and found the tall sailor had stopped fishing and was watching him.

"Hassan," said the man, pointing to his chest.

Luc just stared.

The man frowned and spit out a red kola seed. He pointed again to his chest and, more loudly, he said, "Hassan."

Luc wanted to reply but he couldn't form the words. He looked at Hassan and managed a very small smile. Hassan returned it with his own wide smile, nodding.

The next day Hassan repeated his name, but Luc still

had no words, only the feeble smile. Then on the third day, when Hassan was standing next to Luc at the stern of the dhow looking at the sea, a dolphin leaped from the water, dived, and leaped again, weaving through the sea, its spray glittering in the sunlight. Hassan pointed to the creature and grinned. Again, he said his name. Luc pointed to himself and murmured, "Luc."

Hassan smiled broadly and nodded. "Luc. Luc. Luc." He sucked on the sound, rolling it in his mouth like a kola seed. "Luc!" he bellowed, and patted the boy's head.

The remaining days melted and melded; time passed without measure. Often Luc felt nothing but hunger. Beyond his name, Luc knew no words to communicate with his fellow captives or with Hassan, who showed moments of kindness to the solitary boy. He gazed out on the sea, but he saw no more dolphins. One afternoon when Luc was slumped at the rail, he noticed that the horizon was fringed by the ghostly mountains of a distant shoreline. By the next day, aqua and green stripes brightened the cobalt sea, and he saw droves of other dhows with sails of red or yellow or gray. Soon his dhow was threading between large square-rigged ships and small fishing boats. White gulls screamed and swooped, and black-billed terns plunged deep into the water from high in the sky.

The five captives received increased portions of wormy bread and olives. In the evening they were fed thin soup. Hassan slipped Luc a chunk of fresh fish.

"Thank you, Hassan," said Luc.

Hassan shook his head and said, "*Shukran*, Hassan."

"*Shukran*, Hassan," said Luc.

Hassan bowed slightly to the boy and smiled.

The next morning, Hassan scrubbed each of the prisoners. He returned their seawater-stiffened clothes. Then he took Luc's knife and shaved the heads of the others. Luc was left with his golden hair. The voyage was about to end, but the nightmare of capture was in full thunder.

CHAPTER FIFTEEN

Bizerte

THE DHOW SAILED through a crescent-shaped natural harbor and into a wide manmade canal. It was dawn, and the sky was white. Stone quays edged the canal, shadowed by the thick ocher walls of a crenellated fortress with high watchtowers at each turn. Beyond the fortress, low gray and tan buildings lined the channel. The dhow's sailors jumped from the deck, dragging ropes and pulling the craft into a berth. A plank was dropped, and Luc and his fellow captives hobbled ashore, where a crowd gathered. Robed and turbaned boys and gangs of young bearded men lunged, making faces and even pummeling the fettered captives as they stumbled on their weak and rocky sea legs. As Hassan steered Luc and the four other captives through the city and along the shadowed

streets, the crowd followed, whistling, jeering, and threaten-
ing the prisoners. At a city square, ringed by low windowless
buildings, the prisoners filed down rickety steps to an under-
ground warren of hot, hellish cells, a *matamore*. A grate in
the slimy ceiling opened to the street and yielded a dribble of
air and less light. Moldy, lice-infested straw mats covered the
mud floor. The door clanged shut. Luc listened to the sounds
of the city above and the weeping of his fellow captives. He
was beyond weeping, beyond thinking. Luc was empty.

Before the end of the first day ashore, the dhow captain and Hassan, now turbaned and robed in sky-blue cloth,
returned to the *matamore* and led the prisoners up to the
street. The afternoon sun blinded Luc and his fellow captives
as they were prodded to a pen on the edge of the square,
where a small group of men waited. All were mustached and
many had pointed beards. They wore long robes with wide
sleeves and had covered their heads with turbans or small
round caps. A few stepped forward to examine the captives,
forcing them to strip off their clothes and jump and bend and
skip. Fingers poked into mouths and pulled down eyelids. Two
customers admired Luc's hair but drew back when they saw
he had one ear. The captain displayed Mattie's carved ear.
For a moment Luc was flooded with memories of home, and
tears streamed from his eyes. The men laughed and moved
on to the next captive. At the edge of the group, a singular
man watched. He was old and taller by a head then any other
man, taller even than the blue-robed Hassan. The old man

was thin, with a lined, narrow face and a trim white beard. He wore a white cap and a long white robe, all spotless as milk, except for his butter-colored pointed shoes. With him was a very short man with a bare, bald head and a crooked smile. He was dressed in a striped gray robe with a pointed hood that hung behind him. Although he was the height of a young boy, he had the face and the broad shoulders of a man. The old man motioned at Luc with a nod of his head, and the little man scampered over to the captain.

"How much for the boy with one ear?" asked the little man. Luc understood nothing as they began to haggle about his worth.

The captain looked down at the little man and frowned. "Two gold pieces."

"You're mad," screeched the little man.

The captain drew a small, curved dagger from his belt.

The little man ducked his head and put up his hands. He simpered. "Forgive me, kind sir. I meant only the price is too high. The boy is not whole. Can he hear?"

"As well as you. Maybe better. You're but half a man."

The little man smiled and thumped his head. "Yes, yes. Less than half a man, *sayyid*, but no one says his own butter-milk is sour. Not when he wants to sell the buttermilk."

"What?" asked the captain.

"This boy is worth little. Maybe nothing. Maybe less than nothing," said the little man, flicking his teeth with his right thumbnail.

"His hair alone is worth the price," said the captain, cleaning his fingernails with the tip of his dagger.

"What use is a head of hair?" asked the little man, rubbing his bald head. "Just a luxury bed for vermin."

The captain shrugged. "Get on with it. One gold piece for the boy. That, or move on."

"A fair bargain," said the little man, bobbing his head up and down. "Do we agree, you will pay my master a gold piece to take the boy?"

The captain spit on the ground. "Infernal dwarf. Be gone." He tucked his dagger back into his belt and turned to walk away.

"The boy has one ear. He is bad luck. It is risky to bring such a thing into a household," the little man called loudly.

The captain's face reddened, and he turned around. "A piece of silver, and the boy is yours, but take him and get out of my sight before I use my knife on *your* ear."

The little man nodded and pulled a silver coin from a leather sack. The captain motioned to Hassan, who removed the shackles from Luc's scabbed and bleeding ankles. The tall sailor patted Luc's head gently before he tied a rope around the boy's neck. When he tried to hand over the rope, Hassan was ignored. Instead, the little man pulled at the captain's robe.

The captain narrowed his eyes. "Now what?"

The little man held out his hand and cocked his head.

"What?" asked the captain again.

"You have our boy's other ear."

"You did not *buy* the other ear. You bought the boy with one ear."

"My master bought the boy. Surely the wooden ear belongs to the boy. Now both belong to my illustrious master."

"Who is your master?"

The little man pointed to the tall man in white, who stood apart from the crowd. The old man nodded, and the captain touched the tips of the fingers of his right hand to his forehead and bowed slightly. He tossed the ear to the little man.

"Your master is a very respected man. But you are nothing. Stay out of my sight, or beware, insect."

The little man dropped the wooden ear into his hood and winked. As he led Luc away, he looked over his shoulder at the captain. With a wide smile and a second wink, he whispered loudly, "The right answer to a fool is silence."

"What? What did that troll say?" asked the captain.

But Hassan, who heard every word, spit out a red kola seed and shrugged. Then he called to the little man.

"His name is Luc."

The little man stopped and turned. He pointed a thumb to his own chest. "Bes," he said, and he bowed to Hassan. Bes turned to Luc, tapped his chest again, and repeated his name. When Luc said nothing, he frowned and jerked the rope. Luc stumbled after Bes, who trotted a few paces behind the tall man in white.

Bes pulled Luc through the narrow streets, yanking the leash and causing Luc to stumble and sometimes fall to his knees. Bes laughed each time until the old man turned, wagged his finger, and clicked his tongue. Bes shrugged and cocked his head to one side. "Yes, master," he said. But when the old man turned, Bes jerked Luc one last time and stuck out his tongue at the boy.

Along crowded streets, through narrow alleys and under covered archways, the three passed stalls selling leather slippers, copper cauldrons, and bolts of cloth. They passed mountains of almonds and dried dates and bushels of grains and green vegetables. There were tables stacked with brightly colored sweets, round loaves of bread, and noisy pens of hens and chicks. Blood-spattered butchers called from beneath fly-covered hooks of skinned lambs and goats. The trio stepped aside to let donkey carts pass, and everywhere they went, people bowed to the old man, calling out, "*Salaam alaikum.*"

Although the sun was hotter than home, Luc was shivering. He inhaled the scents of cumin and turmeric and burned sugar; he saw bolts of cloth in shades of saffron, orchid, and indigo. He heard people talking, arguing, and singing, in words he could not understand. Nothing was familiar to Luc. Nothing was identifiable. Then, as he hobbled along, he noticed a man carving wood with a pointed chisel, etching an intricate design of vines and flowers. Luc stopped to watch. Bes tugged at him. The rough rope scratched and burned Luc's neck, a harsh reminder of his status. He was naked and leashed.

Like a pig, Luc thought. *A pig to be slaughtered.*

He shuddered, and his hands were icy. Bes jerked the rope, and Luc fell to his knees. The old man had turned down an alley ahead. Bes grabbed a handful of Luc's hair and yanked the boy to his feet. He hurried Luc along, catching up with the old man at a long whitewashed wall; swallows nested in every hole in the wall, and twigs and grasses jutted from every fissure. Bes dragged Luc to a carved doorway and swung open an iron-studded cedar door. The huge hammered hinges squealed. The old man entered, and Bes jerked Luc over the threshold into his new home.

CHAPTER SIXTEEN

The Master

THE STREET WAS dusty and hot, noisy and smelly, but when Luc stumbled across the threshold, he passed into a different world. Behind Luc was the closed door and the window-less, thick white wall that muffled the city outside. The old man and the little man slipped out of their shoes and left them by the entry. A scalloped archway opened to a spacious blue-and-green tiled courtyard, planted with tall leafy trees and edged with a rose garden. Cages of songbirds hung from tree branches, jasmine tumbled from blue urns, and in the center of the tiled yard, sparkling ribbons of water splashed from a white marble fountain into a green stone pool. Twisted, fluted columns ringed the courtyard, and a covered walkway with colorful mosaic bands led off into the rooms of the house.

"Scrub him well," said the old man to Bes.

"Shall I shave his head?" chirped Bes, examining a lock of Luc's hair. Luc cringed at the little man's touch.

Luc had understood nothing of what was said, but the old man's voice was as deep as he was tall, and when he spoke it rumbled from down within his chest, forceful but not loud. "You shall not cut his hair, though the color is unfortunate."

"Unfortunate?" asked the little man.

"A red apple invites the thief. Be gentle, Bes. The boy has suffered."

Bes smirked and pushed a bewildered Luc to the ground near the fountain. He blinked at the songbirds; he had never before seen a caged bird. Bes pinched his nose, made a face at Luc, and scampered away though a doorway on the far side of the courtyard. He returned wearing a copper bowl on his head and carrying a dish of black greasy soap, a bristle brush, and a yellow sponge. Behind the little man, a sleek white cat with yellow eyes, ginger ears, and a ginger-tipped tail padded on fat round paws.

Bes poured several bowls of water over Luc's head. He slapped globs of soap on the boy and scrubbed Luc's skin with the brush. The soap burned, and the brush scratched. Bes rubbed soap through Luc's hair with his fingers. Now and then he pinched Luc or pulled his hair. Luc flinched, but he did not cry out. The runoff water changed gradually from gray to clear as each bowl rinsed away more filth. Bes dipped the sponge in olive oil and soothed the boy's reddened skin.

The old man returned and dropped a short beige tunic over the damp boy's head; he handed Luc a pair of wide trousers that tied at the waist. Luc pulled on the trousers. Then he smoothed his wet hair, straightened his shoulders, and stood tall, taller than the little man.

"Much better." The old man nodded. "Feed him bread and dates. Give him milk. Goat's milk. Almond milk. Whatever we have. Then bring him to my room. And keep Cat away from my songbirds. I don't want to see that infernal creature, Bes. Ever."

"Yes, master," said Bes, who waited until the old man was gone before he kicked Luc once, grabbed him by the sleeve, and dragged him to the kitchen. It was a high square room, separated from the house by another courtyard, where there was a garden of vegetables and herbs and a large cistern to collect the rare rainwater. A wide hearth with a large chimney took up one corner of the kitchen. The deep shelves that lined the walls were crowded with baskets, bright copper pans, heavy earthen pots, and red and yellow glazed jars. Bes pushed Luc down on the stone floor near the hearth. He tore off a large hunk of bread and tossed it to the boy. He poured milk into a small bowl that he set down in front of the white-and-ginger cat. Then he poured Luc a cup of water and handed him three olives. The bread was fresh and smelled yeasty and clean, and the water was sweet. Luc gobbled and gulped. For the first time in weeks, he was washed and fed. He closed his eyes for a moment and savored his relief. Bes squatted with his arms wrapped about his knees, and watched the boy. He threw Luc another big hunk of bread. Luc finished and waited for more, but Bes winked and gestured for him to follow. They passed through the central courtyard to a double-wide doorway.

Inside the large room, thick, colorful woven rugs covered the tile floor. The old man sat in a carved chair behind a long table strewn with jars and cloth packets tied in string, instruments and tools. On the floor behind his chair were high stacks of parchments and piles of leather-bound books. The old man beckoned Luc around the table; Bes shoved Luc from behind. The old man pursed his lips and shook his head at Bes.

"Leave us, Bes. Go find shoes for the boy. And a cap."

"A cap?" asked the little man.

The old man nodded. "And halvah for yourself. Maybe that will sweeten you, for a moment."

Bes bowed and smiled. "Am I not sweet enough for you, sir?"

"No, you are not, Bes."

Bes backed out of the room, quickly turned and, with a skip, was gone.

The old man motioned to Luc to come closer. He examined the boy from head to toe. Gently he prodded Luc's scalp where the ear should have been and checked the other ear. He examined the boy's eyes and his teeth, and he felt his neck and checked his spine. The old man dabbed ointment wherever Luc had welts and insect bites, and he bandaged the sores where the shackles had rubbed off his skin. Then the old man fastened thin steel bands around the boy's ankles.

"These show you are mine. They will protect you."

Luc blinked and stared at the man. He was confused by the gentleness and care. He looked down at the metal bands. Though he understood nothing of the man's language, he understood that the rings showed he was a slave, that they demonstrated that, despite the kindness, Luc was now the property of this stranger. The boy felt dizzy and swayed.

The old man pointed to a cushion on the floor and motioned to Luc to sit. He began to speak. His words continued to be meaningless until, suddenly, Luc understood. For the first time in five weeks, he heard words that he knew, and he put his hand to his mouth.

"Ah!" said the old man. "You understand?"

Luc nodded. And then he wept.

The old man twirled his beard and waited, tapping his fingers on the table. Luc sucked in a few breaths of air, wiped his nose on his sleeve, and was quiet.

"This is the language I learned in the city of Marseille. I thought I would find your tongue. I have spent many years in different foreign lands."

The old man pointed to the table and his chair.

"I have even learned to sit like a European, one of their few admirable habits. Now, I know you are not deaf, boy. You can speak. Yes?"

Luc nodded.

"You have survived the worst. Tell me one thing about yourself. Anything."

"My name is Luc."

"I am Salah. Now, Luc, tomorrow and for the nine days that follow," said Salah, holding up ten fingers, "I will address you in your language. I will tell you the words in my language as well. After ten days"—the old man folded down his fingers one by one—"I will speak only the language of this city, Bizerte. You are on the Maghreb coast of Africa now, and you must learn Arabic. I hope you are quick and careful. And I hope you are kind. Bes is quick and careful, and he is trustworthy, but he is not always kind. I want more kindness in my household. I am an old man. Every sun has to set. You are my property, Luc, but if you are a good servant, I shall be fair and generous. If you are not a good servant, I will sell you. I have sold boys who were lazy or dishonest or useless. Prove yourself worthy. Do your best. I am a good master. You could do worse."

Luc bent down and touched one of the bands on his ankle. He looked up at the old man.

With a voice that cracked, he asked, "Am I never to go home again?"

The old man paused.

"This is your home now, Luc. Do not speak again of the life you had. It is gone."

CHAPTER SEVENTEEN

Sunday

SIX WEEKS HAD passed since Luc's disappearance. Mattie and Pons had asked throughout the village. Whatever happened to those taken by the Saracens remained a mystery: no one had ever returned. One Sunday morning in early May, Pons tarried after church to speak with the owner of the saltworks, Oubert. Oubert was the richest man in the village, and traded with merchants from other towns and from faraway cities. Oubert was also a recent widower with grown children, and he had asked Pons for Beatrice's hand in marriage. He told Pons that Beatrice was the most beautiful young woman he had ever seen. Oubert was an honest man, but he was merciless in his bargains, and Pons thought he was neither young enough nor generous enough for Beatrice. But Pons had never given Oubert an answer and usually avoided the man.

"Do you know anything about these Saracens?" Pons asked him on this Sunday.

"Oh yes. These pirate raids are the fault of the Spanish king. He banished the Jews and the Muslim Moors from Spain. Now the sea is full of both. More than a few fishermen have disappeared. In Sardinia, a large island to the southwest, I heard that people were taken from their villages. Women and children, too. Stolen from their houses and fields in the middle of the day. The captives are sold into slavery and worked until death. Imagine the horror," said Oubert, shaking his head.

Pons closed his eyes and rubbed his forehead. "Where are they taken?"

"To Africa, the land on the opposite shore of our sea. Where there are man-eating beasts and man-eating heathens," said Oubert, crossing himself.

Oubert tipped his hat to a passing villager as he and Pons walked from the gray stone Church of Saint Olive.

"How do you know this?" asked Pons, stopping to remove his shoe and shake out a pebble. He shook his head; he hated wearing shoes.

"I know men who trade in Africa: gutsy merchants from Genoa who live in Alexandria, Tripoli, Tunis, and Algiers— all infidel cities along the African coast. It's very dangerous but very profitable." Oubert snorted and waited while Pons forced his foot back into the shoe.

"Is there any hope for the boy?" asked Pons.

Oubert pursed his thick lips. "Very little. But I'll inquire; I expect a ship from Genoa by week's end. I trade mainly in salt, but other goods as well." Oubert pulled a heavy purse from his sleeve and poured a handful of silver coins into his palm; he cupped his hand and tipped the coins back into the purse. "How is Beatrice?"

"Well . . . well enough," said Pons. "But she has sores on her feet that make walking difficult, and her soles itch something fierce. Mattie has been trying all sorts of salves, but the medicines smell terrible."

The salt merchant frowned and wrinkled his nose. "Bad feet, eh?"

Pons nodded. The merchant dabbed his nose with a linen handkerchief.

"Unfortunate business, losing that boy," said Oubert, and he blew his nose.

"Awful. I'd best get home. Nice to see you, Oubert. Mattie and I would be much obliged for whatever you learn. I'll bring a nice string of fresh anchovies to you next Friday."

Oubert nodded, and Pons headed home. Cadeau lay by the cottage door; his tail thumped once. Then he rested his head on his front paws, and watched the road.

"Good boy," sighed Pons, bending to pat Cadeau's head.

The dog waited for Luc every afternoon, but he had begun to follow Beatrice everywhere, and he slept at the foot of the ladder to her loft.

Beatrice had spit-roasted an old hen for their dinner, and Mattie boiled radishes and leeks from the garden. Pons's catches had slipped since Luc was taken, but the spring, which began rainy, had turned warm and sunny, and the garden was fruitful. The three ate their Sunday meal in their fish-carved cottage.

"I'm not sorry that this hen gave up laying. This is a meal a rich man like Oubert would envy," said Pons.

"What did you learn from him?" asked Beatrice.

"Oubert said others have been taken. From the shore, even. Just snatched by the Saracen boats." He shook his head. "They came at us so quickly. I never saw a ship move so fast nor turn so sharply."

Beatrice handed Pons a drumstick. He pulled the meat from the bone, chewed slowly, and wiped his fingers on a piece of bread before popping it into his mouth.

"Do the captives ever come back?" asked Beatrice, sitting down next to him.

He patted her hand gently before answering. "None that Oubert knew of. But maybe his foreign merchant friends will know something." He put his arm around the girl and kissed her forehead. "Oubert asked about you, Beatrice."

Beatrice rolled her eyes. She slipped a scrap of chicken to Cadeau under the table.

"He *is* very rich," said Mattie.

"He might as well be a poor man. He keeps his coins in his purse," said Pons.

Mattie nodded. "I never liked that man."

"I don't think he'll be bothering Beatrice for a while," said Pons with a smirk.

"Why is that, Brother?" said Mattie, wiping her fingers on her lips.

"I might have lied to Oubert. Just a little," said Pons, looking upward.

"Might you have?" said Mattie with a crooked smile, squinting at her brother with one eye closed.

"I told him Beatrice was suffering from sores on her feet. Nothing too terrible. Except—"

Beatrice was giggling, and Mattie, with a wider, dimpled smile, asked, "Except what, Brother dear?"

Pons scratched at his stubbled cheek and sniffed. He added softly, "I said you had mixed ointments for the sores, and then, maybe, I said the ointments smelled something terrible."

"And I suppose you said the ointment made all her hair fall out? Not such a bad thing in the spring, what with all the lice she's always picking and scratching at," said Mattie.

"And you told him I snore like thunder, right?" asked Beatrice.

"Ah, ladies, I wish you had been there," said Pons.

Beatrice reached out and clasped hands with Pons and Mattie.

"I love both of you," she said.

"I don't care how rich he is, Oubert's not good enough for you," said Pons, patting her hand again.

"Surely not, but I worry about Beatrice," said Mattie. "What's her future? Here with us, two old people? There is no one good enough for her here in this village."

"I'm nobody special, Mattie," Beatrice said, standing. She stacked the dirty bowls.

"You're a lady," said Mattie. "Never forget that."

Beatrice shook her head. "No, I'm no such thing, Mattie. But don't worry about me. Worry about Luc. There must be something we can do."

"Pray?" said Pons. "Hope?"

Cadeau barked, and then they heard three knocks.

Beatrice closed her eyes, and Mattie crossed herself.

Pons opened the door and found Hervé. Cadeau charged out, barking at the boy.

"I'm Luc's brother. Father sent me for the dog," he said.

Pons scowled at him. He was a thick, strong boy with wild brown hair and dark eyes.

"Cadeau is Luc's dog. And this is Luc's home," said Pons.

"Father says Luc is dead," insisted Hervé.

"I hope not. And until I know Luc isn't coming back, his dog stays here."

"Father said not to return without the dog."

"Let your father come see me."

Mattie came to the door and looked at Hervé.

"And never knock three times on a door. It means there's been a death. You gave us a fright," said Mattie. "Come, Cadeau."

Cadeau lumbered into the cottage, and Pons shut the door.

CHAPTER EIGHTEEN

Salah's Household

IN SALAH'S HOUSE Luc slept on a woven palm mat near the kitchen hearth until sunrise, when Bes kicked him awake. Salah's kitchen was a bright room with a garden doorway and east-facing windows that filled the room with morning light. The floor was made of stone, not dirt as it had been in the simple fishing cottage, and the walls were whitewashed stucco. Luc missed the sharp smell of Cadeau's fur when he woke, and he missed Mattie's laughter as he ate his morning bread. Ever since that terrible afternoon of his capture, Luc had worried whether Pons had made it back to the village alive. And each day, as he scrubbed Salah's floors and tended the gardens, as he weeded the roses and swept the courtyard tiles, Luc would daydream of Beatrice.

"Is that the fastest you can sweep?" Bes would ask, pantomiming a faster broom because, at first, the boy understood no words. Bes pointed to the birdcages; Luc cleaned them. Bes dragged him to the souks and markets. He tied bundles onto Luc's back as if the boy were a beast of burden. Whenever they went out together, Bes insisted that Luc wear a slouchy gray cap pulled down so that neither his hair nor his missing ear drew attention away from Bes as he jabbered and joked.

One afternoon, toward the end of Luc's first month in Bizerte, Bes beckoned to the boy to follow him. As they left Salah's house, the little man called, "Here, Cat," because Bes never went anywhere without the white-and-ginger cat. When they reached the market, Bes bought a stick of grilled meat and three honey cakes. He tossed scraps to Cat, but he shared nothing with Luc. At an alleyway, a gap-toothed man with a curly black beard whispered to Bes and flashed a handful of dice. Bes left Luc leaning against a wall just inside the entrance of the alley while he squatted to try his luck, but he never stopped watching the boy. Luc closed his eyes and waited. He imagined he was on the boat, fishing with Pons. He pictured three dolphins finning along until one suddenly arced and broke free of the water, flying for a moment before diving. Then Luc felt the tickle of Cat rubbing against his leg and the pinch of the little man waiting to hand him another bundle. When Luc opened his eyes, Bizerte replaced the fishing boat. Luc looked about at this strange city of bustling alleys and turbaned citizens. He heard the singsong calls of its merchants, the clop of the donkeys, and the whine of cart wheels. He smelled frying dough and spiced roasting meats. This was a foreign world, and as Luc shifted the bundles on his back, he leaned down and touched his ankle band. He was angry, and he was sad, but he was resigned. Escape was futile. He couldn't run across the sea.

At least Luc's work as Salah's slave, though tedious, was easy, and the kitchen was stocked with bread and fresh cheese, fruits, and vegetables, and there was often meat or fish. All were available to Luc whenever he was hungry. As the months passed, Luc regained more than the weight he'd lost during his captivity; his appetite returned, and he began to grow taller and broader.

Salah's family was originally from Arabia, but they had lived in Bizerte, the northernmost port in Africa, for almost eight hundred years; they had grown very rich as merchants and landowners. As a boy and as a young man, Salah had studied in Baghdad, in Córdoba, in Bologna, and even in Marseille. Salah was a scholar, a master of many fields: a physician, an astronomer, and a mathematician. Everywhere, he was revered for his remarkable intelligence and his matchless knowledge. Teachers, students, and patients seeking the old man's advice or opinion visited Luc's new home almost every day.

Salah was a kind but exacting master. When Luc cleaned his tools, the old man watched, and then he examined the boy's work. He'd make Luc clean every tool again if he found one fingerprint or a speck of dirt. He spoke slowly and patiently to Luc, rarely raising his deep voice in anger. Occasionally, he shifted to Luc's native language, but he never permitted Luc to speak anything but Arabic. If the boy uttered a word in his own tongue, Salah held a finger to his lips and shook his head. Once when Salah was showing Luc how to braid a leather thong, Luc struggled to tell him how Mattie had taught him. Though Salah was impressed with Luc's progress in Arabic, he cut the boy off with a wave of his hand.

"Never talk of your past, boy. I am pleased that you are speaking my language; you are not slow. But do not waste my time with talk of your infidel life."

Luc was glad that he recognized enough of Salah's words to understand their meaning, but that understanding was bittersweet because Salah's criticism was no longer just babble. Still, Luc listened carefully to everyone he heard. Luc asked Salah for the names of each object he saw. Salah was never too busy to supply the Arabic words. Bes would bark orders, and Luc would watch as the little man pointed and gestured; each day, he knew more, understood more.

The summer months passed slowly. Luc constantly yearned for his old life. When he left his father's house to fish, he had missed his mother and his brothers, but it had not been painful. The winter and spring he had lived in the fishing village of Mouette had been filled with more happiness and affection than he had ever known, and Luc had felt that he belonged on the sea, fishing in the early mornings with Pons. He knew he was good at it—good at spotting the signs of fish, and good with the little boat. He missed helping Mattie in the garden. And Beatrice; Luc would close his eyes and recall her face. He tried to hear her voice as he replayed snippets of their conversations. He remembered how she smiled when he gave her the lilies of the valley. His loneliness was physical, an ache and a heaviness that spread from his chest across his shoulders and sapped his energy. At times Luc was so sad, so desperately sad, that he did not want to continue, but as the days and weeks passed, he began to accept that this was now his life, and all it might ever be.

If Bes caught Luc daydreaming, he kicked the boy. He hissed insults that Luc was beginning to understand.

"Where there is too much sun, the people are overcooked, and their skin is black," said Bes one morning as he cooked. Luc was peeling onions and his eyes watered so that he had to stop to wipe his tears. Bes continued, "Where the land is cold, the people are undercooked. Here the land is perfect. The master and I," he said, pinching his own tan forearm, "we are toasted, just right. But you? You are an unbaked lump of dough. You cost next to nothing, but still the master overpaid. Worthless as a deaf-mute. With one ear and no talent," he said, wiggling his ears.

Bes stuck out his tongue and pulled Luc's hair, which now hung almost to his shoulders.

"I have talked to a wig man in the souk. I will sell him

your hair one day soon. Then I shall persuade the master to sell you. That won't be hard. The master always tires of his slaves, especially the stupid ones."

Luc said nothing, but later that day, when Bes was with Salah elsewhere, Luc sharpened a kitchen knife. He wanted to go home, but he knew that was impossible. Besides, Bes had told him of a slave who escaped the day before. Slave catchers sliced off his nose before returning him to his master.

Bes had said, "How would you look? Two eyes, one ear, and no nose?"

Tired of such taunts and tired of being powerless, Luc nicked his thumbnail with the blade to test the knife's edge. The knife was sharp. He grabbed a handful of hair and began to hack. When Bes returned to the kitchen and saw Luc with his cropped head and the pile of golden hair on the floor, he laughed so hard he had to sit down. When he stopped laughing, he stuffed the cuttings into a bag.

"Might be worth more than a slave with one ear," said Bes.

Luc tried to ignore Bes as he had his drunken father, and he never complained to Salah. Although Salah's eyesight was failing, he was wise and mindful; he waited for the boy to tattle. Luc's silence pleased him, as did the boy's diligence. Salah knew that Bes was often mean and rascally, but there was great affection between the wise man and the little man. Twenty years before, when Salah was consulting at the Mansuri Hospital, a renowned center of medicine in Cairo, Egypt, he encountered a tiny homeless orphan who had been beaten and robbed. Salah set the half-dead boy's broken bones and sewed up his wounds. The boy was Bes, and he was surviving by his wits: begging for bread, entertaining people with his banter and acrobatics. Salah was amused by the street boy's cleverness and stirred by his resilience. When the old man returned home to Bizerte, he invited the child. The little boy had never before known any kindness, and to Salah, Bes would always be faithful.

Salah was sitting at his desk. Moistening a finger, he turned the page of a heavy book and looked up to watch Luc dust the shelves with a damp rag. He said nothing about the boy's haircut.

"Your first summer is ending, Luc. You have grown taller. Do you get enough to eat?"

"Yes, master."

"Bes is treating you well?"

Luc nodded.

Salah stroked his beard and leaned back, studying the slave. "Bes can be difficult, but he has many talents. He has always insisted that I need no servants other than him. I have always disagreed, but every boy I buy is quickly sold. Except for you, Luc. You have been here for how long now?"

"Almost two seasons, master."

"Yes. Half a spring and now the summer."

"Yes, master," said Luc, wiping his damp brow on his sleeve.

Salah fanned himself with a woven disk. "I am quite pleased with you, Luc."

"Thank you, master."

Salah looked down at his book for a moment, but the boy stood in front of his desk looking at him. "Something else, Luc?"

Luc nodded. "May I ask a question, master?"

"Yes, Luc," said the old man, shutting his book.

"Why does Bes sleep on the roof?" asked Luc in stumbling but improving Arabic.

Salah smiled. "When Bes was a little boy, someone told him that if he slept inside, the sun would not rise in the morning."

"He believes that?"

"Bes is hardly a fool," said Salah. "But he cannot sleep inside. So every evening he takes a ladder and climbs to the roof. He goes to sleep under the stars with his cats."

"Cats?"

"There are seven or eight strays who sleep on the roof with Bes. Only Cat comes inside, and Cat is supposed to stay in the kitchen. I detest cats. Now, go help Bes. I expect a guest this evening, a physician from Fez," he said, dismissing Luc with a wave.

In the kitchen, Luc found Bes preparing lamb; he sent Luc to find spices from the pantry and herbs from the garden. Luc collected mustard greens and garlic, mint and cardamom, black cumin seeds and turmeric, marjoram and myrtle. Each time Bes asked, Luc produced the correct ingredient. Bes sent him to the souk for almonds and quince jam. Luc returned with both and with more than the expected change, for the boy had been observant, and he bargained well.

"Speechless dog," said Bes. "How did you bargain?"

Luc pinched his earlobe with thumb and forefinger. Bes scowled at him.

"Fetch seven carrots from the garden. Clean them. Slice them into coins."

Bes handed Luc a knife.

Luc pretended to test the blade, and he half grinned at Bes.

"I'd have your hand cut off before you came within a blade length," said Bes, flicking his front teeth with a thumbnail.

Luc threw the knife upward, turning his hand so the knife spun once in the air before he caught it by the handle. Bes reached for another knife, pitched it into the air, and caught it on the tip of his finger, where he balanced it on its point for several seconds. Then he tossed it up again and caught it behind his back. Luc shrugged and went to the garden. He pulled and scrubbed seven large carrots. He sliced the carrots into uniform circles and cut notches at even intervals around the edges of each slice. When he presented them to Bes, the little man chuckled. He motioned with his blade to the string of fish he had just brought from the fish market.

"Clean and fillet those. Leave a single bone, and I'll etch my name in your back with it."

Luc began to skin the fish. Bes was patting spices into the slab of lamb, but he stopped to watch the boy.

"So, you can wield a knife. You are a bit more skilled than a trained monkey. But only a bit. And twice as ugly." Then Bes began to hum. "Can you sing, baboon face?"

Luc said nothing.

"Can you play a lute or a flute?" he asked, pitching a scrap of lamb to Cat.

Luc said nothing.

Bes pretended to blow an imaginary pipe.

Luc shook his head.

"No, I didn't think so. Tonight you shall hear me play the *bendir*. You can *hear* music? With only one ear?" asked Bes, cupping his ear and holding up one finger.

Luc did not respond.

"A rock is better company."

Luc shrugged. Bes narrowed his eyes and hissed. He cut slits in the lamb, jamming the pockets with spices and herbs and slivers of garlic. Then he threaded the meat on a spit and set it over a low-burning fire.

"Turn the spit. If you burn the meat, I will beat the soles of your feet. Most masters flog their slaves every day. The old man is far too kind."

Bes dumped a basket of dates onto the table.

"Remove the stones and stuff each date with an almond. Can you handle that, wordless swine?"

The fragrance of roasting lamb drifted through Salah's

house. Bes pressed the filleted fish with crushed almonds and mustard greens and rolled the stuffed fillets. He layered slices of lemon on the fish and poured vinegar into the pan. He sprinkled the cut carrots over the top.

Bes wrapped a turban around his head, and Luc copied him. He was growing used to this Arab custom, which hid his missing ear and what remained of his golden hair. What would Beatrice think of him in this Moorish head wrap?

Later, as he served Salah and the elderly physician in a niche off the courtyard under the stars, Luc thought of the simple meals back home on a bench outside the cottage on a summer night. How he would love to show Beatrice the unimagined luxuries of this exotic place! The diners lounged on thick silken cushions. Oil lanterns hung from the trees, lighting the low dining table. Salah and his guest talked and ate with deft fingers, sharing beautiful, fragrant platters of fish and lamb. Bes whisked away the empty dishes, and Luc presented an alabaster bowl of sugared orange slices with shaved cinnamon and a silver tray of almond-stuffed dates and fresh figs.

Bes appeared leading a snake charmer to entertain.

The snake charmer glided in, holding a covered basket in his outstretched arms. He bowed to Salah and then to the other physician. Salah nodded, and the snake charmer slid to the ground, kneeling. He settled back on his heels, removed the basket top, and raised a wooden flute to his lips. Red and yellow tassels dangled from the instrument. Swaying and dipping his head and shoulders, the snake charmer played a high-pitched trill. He closed his eyes and threaded his tune with deeper notes; one snake slithered from the basket, then another, and another. Three snakes lined up in front of the man. The cadence shifted, and the notes accelerated; the serpents edged up vertically until they stood on their tails. They swayed to the music. Luc watched from a corner of the alcove. He hated snakes, but he couldn't look away. The snake charmer began to play a mellow, slow song, and two of the snakes slipped back to the ground and up into the basket. The remaining snake, the largest of the three, brown-speckled with a cream underbelly, slid into the flute player's lap and then rose, gliding up his chest, across his shoulders, and encircling his neck. The song was achingly sweet, and except for his fingers, the snake charmer was motionless. The snake's lidless eyes caught the lantern light, and a pink tongue flicked from its mouth.

The man opened his eyes and stopped playing, and the snake uncoiled from his neck and glided over his shoulders and down to the ground. The snake charmer nodded to Bes, who began to tap his fingers on his *bendir*, a small wood-framed drum strung with three strings under its goatskin drumhead. Bes's fingers moved quickly, and the *bendir* buzzed and thumped. Bes rolled his shoulders rhythmically and tapped one foot. The speckled snake moved toward Bes, who struck the drum more loudly and more quickly. Slowly, the snake slid over Bes's other foot and climbed up his leg, disappearing under the little man's robe. Bes danced more quickly, beating the drum more loudly. The *bendir* vibrated and hummed, and the snake charmer took up his flute and launched into a sharp, fast tune to the beat of the drum. The snake appeared, headfirst, slithering out from the left sleeve of Bes's robe.

Suddenly the music stopped, and the only sound was the splash of the fountain. Bes dropped the drum and snatched the snake in his fist. Then he put the head of the serpent in his mouth and bit down hard. He dropped the writhing carcass and spit out the creature's head. The severed snake head opened its mouth, hissed, and then its jaws clamped shut as it rolled across the floor to Cat, who pounced on it and carried it off to the kitchen. Bes bowed to the snake charmer. He bowed to Salah and his guest.

Then he turned to Luc, drew a finger across his neck, and winked at the boy.

CHAPTER NINETEEN

Blanche

PONS RARELY FISHED that summer. When the moon was bright, he sometimes left home just after midnight, but he returned by dawn because the sun was hot, his hands hurt, and he missed the boy. From Oubert, Pons learned of agents who would search in Africa for captives and arrange for ransoms, but the cost was beyond any sum that Pons could even dream of.

One midsummer afternoon, while Pons slept, Beatrice sat sewing under the linden tree. Mattie whittled a hollow stick of hazel wood.

"Ever smell anything better than linden blossom?" asked Mattie, looking up at the thick, dark leaves and remembering the yellow blossoms of early July.

"Lily of the valley," said Beatrice. She bit her lip as she pushed a needle through the rough linen cloth she was holding.

Mattie leaned over the girl's work. "Tsk, tsk, Beatrice. Make those stitches smaller. And don't pull the needle through unless the stitch comes up in line."

Beatrice puffed out her cheeks and put the sewing down in her lap. "It's no use."

Mattie put her arm around the girl. "Just takes time. And patience. Put it away for now. It's too hot for anything except sitting."

"And thinking," sighed Beatrice.

"Thinking about what?"

"About Luc," said Beatrice.

Mattie nodded and notched the wood. "It was good having a young person here for you. For all of us."

"I miss him," said Beatrice, rolling up her sewing. "Mattie, do you think we could talk to Luc's mother about what Alain said? If Luc *is* really Sir Guy's son, perhaps that family would pay his ransom."

"Sir Guy is dead." Mattie shook her head and added, "What's done is done. Besides, do you think the old knight's family would care that his bastard was kidnapped?"

Mattie put down her knife, and mopped her face with her apron.

"What other chance does Luc have?" asked Beatrice.

"I don't think there is any hope for the boy. But I

wouldn't mind hearing about those secrets Alain spoke of," said Mattie. "Perhaps we *could* pay a visit to Luc's mother. . . ."

"Today?"

Mattie shook her head. "In this heat?" Mattie looked at Beatrice's face, and patted her hand. "All right. Let's go while Pons sleeps. We'll just pay Luc's mother a call to say how much we miss the boy. Let's pray the woman's husband is napping. I don't want him lurking about."

"And we'd better not bring Cadeau."

Mattie held up the hazel-wood stick she'd been whittling. "I made this flute for the older of Luc's two brothers. Made a whistle for the little one last week. I thought we might be heading up there soon."

Beatrice smiled. "I'll pick Luc's mother a bunch of lavender."

"You watch for spiders."

"You didn't need to remind me, Mattie."

Beatrice stood and smoothed her gray dress. It was a plain kirtle of light wool, laced in the front with darker gray ribbon, over a linen smock with sleeves upon which Mattie had embroidered yellow flowers. Unlike Mattie, who wore wooden clogs, Beatrice wore good leather shoes that Mattie bought for her every fall from the cobbler who came to the village fair.

Mattie mopped her face again and said, "Wear that big straw hat I made you. Remember who you are."

"I know who I am, Mattie." The girl's hair was loose, and she pushed it back behind her ears.

"You are a lady, Beatrice. Never forget that."

Beatrice rolled her eyes, but she fetched the wide-brimmed hat and tied it under her chin.

"I should braid your hair, Beatrice."

"I'll tuck it up under my hat," she said.

Mattie and Beatrice looped their way under trees, wherever they found patches of shade. Neither had ever seen the olive grove or the stone house.

"This is a mighty nice place," said Mattie with a whistle. "Far grander than I imagined. And they let the boy work as a swineherd?"

Beatrice nodded. "Luc must have mattered very much to Sir Guy."

Mattie sucked in her top lip. "It might have nothing to do with Luc, Beatrice."

Beatrice put her arm around Mattie. "I pray it has everything to do with him."

Luc's mother answered their first knock. Two boys appeared behind her, and Mattie handed the whistle to Pierre and the flute to Hervé.

"Did you bring the dog?" asked Hervé.

"Shoo!" said Luc's mother to her sons, who disappeared happily to try their presents. Blanche buried her nose in the lavender Beatrice gave to her, and breathed deeply.

"Thank you. Come where we can sit in the shade," she said, leading them to the courtyard, where there were two benches under a large chestnut tree. "My husband is asleep. Just as well, if you have come to speak of Luc." She laid her palm flat against her chest. "I am Blanche. You must be Mattie and Beatrice."

At first the women talked of the hot summer weather, the lavender, and about Mattie's carving.

"Luc said your cottage is a marvel," said Blanche, tucking under the ragged cuffs of her sleeves.

"We miss the boy," said Mattie.

"Very much," added Beatrice.

Blanche blinked hard and put her hand to her mouth. "He was happy with you."

"A special boy," said Mattie. "Wise beyond his years."

"Most of the time," added Beatrice.

"Luc was clever. And handsome. People didn't really notice his ear, not right away," said Blanche, shaking her head. "I loved him," she added.

Mattie nodded. "We do too."

"He needs your help," said Beatrice.

"Help?" Blanche frowned. "Luc is dead. Pascal says he fell overboard. The old man couldn't save him, so he made up that tale about pirates."

Mattie shook her head. "Pons is more honest than sunshine. The boy was stolen, just as my brother said."

"Even if what Pons says is true, isn't it the same as if the boy drowned?" asked his mother. "Maybe worse."

"No," said Beatrice. "Luc could be ransomed. There are men in Africa who hunt for captives. But it's very costly."

"Costly? Who would pay for the boy? I've nothing of value," said Blanche.

"But," said Beatrice, "the olive grove—this house . . ." She motioned to the courtyard and the sturdy yellow stone farmhouse with its double roof of baked earthen tiles.

"My husband will never part with the grove or our home."

"Does it belong to him or to Luc?" asked Beatrice.

Blanche glared at Beatrice. "It belongs to my husband. It will belong to my sons one day. What stories have you heard?"

"Sir Guy—"

Blanche frowned. "Sir Guy is dead. This has nothing to do with him."

"We heard he was Luc's father," said Beatrice.

Luc's mother hissed, "Sir Guy was nothing to the boy."

Mattie rose. "That's enough, Beatrice."

"Won't you help your son?" begged Beatrice, ignoring Mattie.

"My son?" Blanche replied, covering her face, her voice breaking into sobs.

Mattie sat down next to the weeping woman and put an arm around her. Through Blanche's worn dress, Mattie felt the sharpness of the woman's shoulders and the knobbiness of her spine. "Hush, now," said Mattie. "We only came tell you how much we miss your son."

Blanche began to cry harder.

Her face was still covered by her hands when Blanche finally spoke.

"Luc is not my son."

CHAPTER TWENTY

One Ear

AS MATTIE AGAIN rose to leave, Blanche wiped her face with her apron and motioned for her to sit. "I shouldn't be telling you. If Pascal knew—"

"We'll go now, before he wakes," said Mattie, motioning to Beatrice to get up.

"Stay; Pascal's done for the day," said Blanche bitterly.

"Whose son *is* Luc?" asked Beatrice, as she stood up.

"Hush! Come, Beatrice," said Mattie, taking her by the arm.

Blanche shook her head. She gulped a few times and dabbed her eyes. "Stay. I *need* to tell someone. This terrible secret has dried up my heart, chewed at my soul. Now that

Luc's lost, I don't know what will happen. I fear we'll lose everything anyway."

"Will you tell us the whole story?" asked Beatrice.

Blanche looked at the girl and said, "I don't know if keeping this secret matters anymore. Now that Luc is gone. But it may, so you must promise to never tell a soul. Swear it."

"I swear," said Mattie.

"Me, too," said Beatrice.

Mattie and Beatrice sat down. Blanche blew her nose and continued.

"I'm not Luc's real mother. I was only his wet nurse." She began to rock back and forth as she talked. "He was such a beautiful baby.

"But when I saw that he was born with only one ear? I didn't know what to do. Who ever heard of such a thing?" Blanche crossed herself. "No one else had noticed. I had just bathed him and wrapped him when the count stormed into the birth room, demanding to see his son."

Beatrice gasped, "The count?"

"Count de Muguet?" asked Mattie. "Luc is the son of Count de Muguet?"

Blanche nodded.

Mattie pounded her hand with her fist. "Poor Luc. To have such a father."

Beatrice winced. "And the countess is his mother?"

Blanche nodded.

Mattie patted Blanche's knee, but Beatrice said, "Wait, if you were his wet nurse, you ought to have another child, a child near Luc's age."

Blanche nodded and took a deep breath. Again, she began rocking as she spoke. "When he first saw his son, the count was very pleased. But the child was swaddled, so he had no idea that anything was wrong. He ordered me to get the baby ready for the priest and tossed me a cloth to wrap him. I remember it was gold, stitched with pearls."

Blanche held the lavender to her nose and inhaled. She looked up at Beatrice.

"There was nothing I could do but pray no one would notice. I carried him to the family chapel. It's beautiful there. One window is filled with colored glass. A noblewoman held out her jewel-covered hands, and I gave her the baby."

Blanche rubbed her eyes. "I watched from the back. The baby was placed on a pillow, between two ladies—I don't know who they were—his godmothers? They began to unwrap him, but mostly they admired the gold cloth. They hardly looked at the child. *Maybe he won't be so unlucky after all*, I remember thinking.

"The old priest traced a cross on the baby's forehead. A younger priest was about to dip him in the water, but he stopped. He whispered to the old priest. The old priest shook his head. The young priest said something else. Muguet stepped forward. He was furious. The young priest held up the child. The count looked at his son for a moment, and then he slapped the young priest hard. I can still hear that hand on the priest's face. The monster. The young priest fell to the ground, holding the baby. The count was that strong."

Remembering her father's death, the awful sound of his skull cracking, Beatrice's eyes filled. She swallowed and wiped her tears. Blanche looked at the girl and continued.

"The count stormed out. The young priest left the infant on the floor, and everyone fled the chapel. All except me and the old priest. The baby was wailing, and the priest kept asking me for the child's name. What did I know? No one had told me what he was to be called. I remember the priest threw up his hands. 'This infant must have a name,' he said. Then he asked me for my father's name."

Blanche sighed. "My father's name was Luc."

Mattie put her arm around the woman. "There, there. You don't need to tell more of the story."

"No. You need to understand about Luc. He wasn't my son, but I loved him."

"Your husband doesn't," said Beatrice.

"Hush, girl," said Mattie sharply.

Blanche continued, "Poor Pascal. He was a good man. When the countess was heavy with child, and I was chosen out of all the young mothers in the count's great household, everyone was surprised. Such an honor! Me? Wet nurse to the count's baby? My husband and I were nothing. Pascal cleaned the count's horse stalls. We were so poor, but we had a baby boy who had grown faster and stronger than any baby in memory. And after I was picked?" Blanche smiled. "Oh, the almonds, hams, and honey—such wonders began to arrive from the count. Pascal was sure they'd make him a groom. All he ever wanted to do was work with horses. If only Luc had been born with two ears." Blanche shook her head.

"What happened to Luc's mother?" asked Beatrice.

Blanche shrugged. "There is an ugly history there. I didn't return to her chamber; after the baptism, I took Luc straight to the nursery. I never saw her again, but it was an easy birth."

Mattie said, "She was young and strong. I was surprised to hear that neither she nor the baby survived. Of course, by then, I was with my Beatrice in Sir Étienne's house. I wasn't hearing much of the castle."

Blanche untied her cap and then retied it. She smoothed her dress and looked at Mattie. "The baby and the countess survived the birth. What the countess didn't survive was her husband's temper. Count de Muguet was furious, crazed even. Pascal heard he killed his wife and the midwife."

"All this because the child was missing an ear?" said Mattie. "May Muguet rot in hell." She spit on the ground.

"What happened to *your* baby?" Beatrice asked softly, kneeling in front of Blanche.

Blanche covered her face with her apron. Then Beatrice reached up and wrapped her arms around Blanche's neck, and she and Blanche wept together. Blanche pulled Beatrice to the seat beside her and took her hand before speaking.

"The next day, two soldiers came to the nursery for me and Luc. One was Sir Guy. He led us outside the castle wall. My husband was there. His eyes were red, and he was alone. No one said anything. We got into a mule cart with Luc. Then the guards mounted, and Sir Guy rode in front and the other followed." Blanche dropped Beatrice's hand and smoothed her apron. She continued.

"The only thing Pascal said? 'He is gone.' Over and over. I knew he meant our son. Later I learned how. Sir Guy came to our home for Pascal and my baby and took them to the count. Pascal was so proud of our little son. He couldn't help bragging; he had no idea why he was there. He thought the count was going to reward him, but the count began to laugh and said, 'This peasant thinks he has a perfect child. Take the boy's ear.' He ordered the other soldier, not Sir Guy, to cut off my son's ear. So much blood." Blanche shook her head. "Our baby didn't live through the night."

Blanche pointed to the house and swept her arm all around. "This was the price he paid us for our son and for our silence. Land. As though I would trade my child for the moon, let alone a piece of land. But here it is, a fine stone house with a grove of olive trees, and it is ours, for always and for our children."

"And so you took Luc," said Mattie.

Blanche shrugged. "We were told to take him."

"Then that was the count's plan. He made Luc your son," said Beatrice. "With the theft of an ear."

CHAPTER TWENTY-ONE

Skills

IT WAS AFTERNOON, just after the the muezzin's mid-day cry. Luc had grown accustomed to hearing these calls to prayer, sung out from every mosque in the city, five times throughout each day. The heart of the summer's heat had finally broken, and the late September days started warm but cooled once the sun set. Salah sat at his desk, where he had been reading. Luc rubbed a lemon-soaked cloth on the silver pitcher Salah always used when he treated patients. Salah knew from practice and observation that there were fewer infections when silver, rather than a base metal, was used for medical tools and vessels. The precious pitcher's polished surface gleamed under Luc's cloth. When he saw the shine, Salah nodded.

"This is the third season you have lived here, Luc."

"Yes, master."

"You understand every word of our language now, don't you?"

"*Almost* every word, master."

Luc reached for Salah's tools. The blades of some of the scalpels were obsidian, a black, hard stone that could be honed to the sharpest point. The rest were silver: tweezers and tongs, picks and needles; Luc began to polish each one. Salah watched the boy.

"The unguent for skin disease?" asked the old man.

Luc looked up and said, "Olive oil and garlic. I made the paste this morning."

"What would I ask you to hand me for a patient who complained of flatulence?"

Luc looked up from polishing for a moment with a half smile. "Peppermint and dill seed. I shall try that on Pons when I return home."

"Home?" Salah frowned. He leaned back and twirled his beard with his long fingers. "You are more than I hoped for, Luc. You work hard, and in a short time, a remarkably short time, you have learned so much beyond the language," he said, pointing to the jars of dried herbs and powdered potions. "You have a fine mind and as strong a character as any lad I have ever known. You are made of iron, I think. But are you flexible?"

"I am a slave," answered the boy. "What does it matter?"

"Metal that will not bend is metal that cracks."

Luc shrugged. "I do know that I am fortunate to have you as my master."

"*But* you are my slave?"

Luc met Salah's eyes and said nothing. He put down the polishing rag and rolled the tools in a clean cloth before replacing them in the leather-covered box on Salah's desk.

Salah clasped his hands and rested them across his chest. "A tree is best measured when it is down, Luc," he said, raising one eyebrow. "Do you ever speak a word to Bes?"

Luc studied his master's face, searching for anger.

The old man continued. "Not a single word. I am right, am I not?"

The boy sucked in his cheeks and nodded.

"A traveler to distant places should make no enemies."

"I am not a traveler. I was taken."

Luc swallowed hard against the lump in his throat, fighting the bitterness that threatened to undermine the amity that he had recently felt from Salah.

"The remedy against bad times is to have patience. I have traveled to many places, Luc. I have spent much of my life, perhaps too much, as a stranger, living alone among foreigners, often among infidels. I even lived among your unwashed people. You are unlike them. You are unlike anyone I ever met. I am surprised by you."

"I was born different," said Luc, reaching his hand to his ear.

The old man smiled. "Yes, but that is just the obvious difference. You are different in many ways."

Luc put his shoulders back and stood up straight. "I don't understand what you mean, master."

"No?" asked Salah, raising his brows. "Your hearing is excellent."

The boy nodded. "Good enough."

"Yes, and you see things at a great distance, before others."

Luc nodded.

"Up close, you can discern the smallest of things?"

"Yes."

Salah held out his fist, palm up, and opened his hand for a single moment before snapping it shut.

"What is in my hand, Luc?"

"Coins."

"How many?"

"Four."

"Silver?" asked Salah.

"Three silver, one gold."

"Anything else?"

"A small stone carving," answered Luc.

"A carving of what?"

"A flower."

"What kind of flower?"

Luc shook his head. "I do not know."

"You saw the flower, but you do not know the name of the flower?"

"Yes, I do not know the name." Then Luc added, "But . . ."

"But?"

"The flower has three outer petals."

"And?" asked Salah, leaning forward toward the boy.

"And three inner petals."

Salah leaned back in his chair and smiled. "Your vision is remarkable."

"I have always seen things as I see them."

"I suspect that all your senses are exceptional. These are gifts, Luc. Gifts to be thankful for."

The boy bowed his head.

"You accept things, but do you appreciate them?"

Luc met the old man's eyes. He said nothing.

"You are like a distant shore, Luc. We both have much to discover about you. I do know that you have sure and steady hands. I have watched you in the kitchen with a knife. With your dexterity and your extraordinary eyes, you could be of use to me in surgery. Are you willing to learn?"

The boy hesitated. "How will Bes take this?"

"A curious response," said Salah. "Bes has an envious nature. He has envied you from the beginning."

"Me?"

"Of course—you are a tall, handsome lad."

CHAPTER TWENTY-ONE

"But I'm a freak."

"What is Bes?"

Luc did not reply.

"Never mind. It will not be easy. Not for any of us," answered the old man. "But understanding develops by degrees. I shall take care of Bes."

"As you wish," said Luc.

"An old man who has no children has nothing more than wishes."

"A slave does not even have wishes."

Salah frowned. "Listen to me, Luc. I am not offering you freedom. I am offering you knowledge. Unlike freedom, knowledge can never be taken away. If you work hard, you will have valuable skills. You will have a better future than fishing."

"I was happy fishing."

"Bloom where you are planted. Do not bore me with your past life. I offer you a wider world. Are you too stubborn to understand that? Perhaps you are too willful to be anything more than what you are."

Luc stood silently, head down, staring at the floor.

"One day your life will pass in front of your eyes. Make it worthy to look at," said Salah.

CHAPTER TWENTY-TWO

Autumn in Mouette

MOUETTE BUSTLED WITH harvest-fair preparations. Lemons, figs, and plums had been stewed in honey, candied, and preserved in sealed crocks for the lean winter season. Large wheels of cow's-milk cheese and small rounds of goat and sheep cheeses from upland herds were stacked alongside sacks of chestnuts and walnuts. Farmers carried baskets of cabbages, carrots, and cauliflowers. Tinkers arrived with packs of pins and pots and ribbons. The itinerant cobbler set up his stall. Everything would be sold for coins or bartered for salted fish. Mattie had worked for weeks carving more than a dozen pairs of wooden shoes that people would fight to buy from her. Soon she would set out for the fair with Beatrice, but first, she had other concerns.

"Come here, Beatrice. I won't have your hair looking like a sea monster."

"Turn me into a mermaid," said Beatrice, straddling the bench by the front door. Mattie sat behind her, and combed the girl's long hair. The chickens clucked about the yard, scratching in the dirt for insects. The swineherd had taken the pig for fattening on beechnuts and acorns in the hills above the village. Cadeau rested his head on the bench in front of Beatrice, and she patted him while Mattie worked the wooden comb.

"You are my mermaid," said the old woman, holding the comb between her teeth as she picked at a knot with her fingers.

"Can a mermaid make wishes come true?" asked Beatrice.

"I don't know." Mattie laughed, and took up the comb. "But if I *had* a wish, do you know what I'd wish for?"

Beatrice nodded. "I do."

"What would that be, my lady?"

"You'd wish for a husband for me. A lord, no doubt, who'd whisk me away on his fine steed to live in a hilltop castle." Beatrice held out her hand, trying to catch a twirling yellow leaf as it floated from the overhead branch.

"Sounds like a fine wish to me," said Mattie.

"But not to me," sighed Beatrice, dropping her hand to her lap. "What would I do all day? Sew? I prefer this life, here with you and Pons."

"So you don't have anything you would wish for?" asked Mattie.

"I have one wish," said the girl. "To bring Luc home."

Mattie stopped combing and patted the girl's shoulder.

"We all want him back. But you can't make wishes come true, and there's nothing we can do for him."

Beatrice shook her head. "What about the new count? Luc is his brother. What if he knew?"

"Do you think anyone will believe Blanche's story?"

"I believe her story, and it might save Luc."

"Your belief isn't enough, Beatrice. Now sit still so I can finish."

"There must be a way to prove who Luc really is," said Beatrice, flinching as Mattie caught a knot in her comb.

"Ouch!"

"Your hair is all tangled, Beatrice."

"You're not very gentle today, Mattie."

"You aren't very reasonable. The story of Luc's birth died with the old count and Sir Guy. You heard Blanche. She doesn't want to bring up the past. Can you blame her? She and her husband could lose everything. Remember, they paid a terrible price."

"But what about Luc?" asked Beatrice.

"Blanche is right. We don't even know that he's alive."

"But—"

"The count made sure no one would ever speak about this. Certainly not Blanche and Pascal. No one in the castle is going to listen to an old fisherman and his sister."

"Or the daughter of a disgraced knight," added Beatrice bitterly.

"If Luc is alive, all we can do is pray that he has figured out a way to survive. Maybe even thrive."

"If anyone might, it's that boy," added Pons, who had returned from fishing in time to hear the end of their conversation.

He carried a basket of late raspberries and a string of gray-feathered thrushes, which he handed to Mattie.

Mattie examined the string of little birds and said to her brother, "Odd fish, here."

"Cost me two fish," said Pons. "No problem making a trade today. The fair is already bigger than last year. Everyone's asking when you're coming with your shoes."

"What about the old priest?" asked Beatrice.

"You just won't let it be?" said Mattie. "The old priest had to be Father Thierry."

"Father Thierry?" said Beatrice. "I remember when he told me that I would have to leave home and go with you."

"Yes, Father Thierry was a good man but very old. I doubt he's still alive."

"Can we find out?" asked Beatrice.

"What good would it do? When the count killed Blanche's son, don't you think *her* child was buried as *his* son? Everyone who knows this history is dead or bought off." Mattie rose, handed Beatrice the comb, and took the string of birds and the berries. Beatrice stood up with a sigh.

"Poor Luc," said Mattie, walking with Pons and Beatrice into the cottage. "Pons always thought the boy was lucky. I guess he was wrong."

"Lucky? What does luck have to do with anything?" asked Beatrice, opening the wooden shutters to bring light into the room.

"Luck is often everything," said Mattie.

CHAPTER TWENTY-THREE

Education

LUC COULDN'T READ. Salah railed, not at the boy, but at his ignorance. It was a clear October morning, and they sat on cushions in the courtyard. Branches drooped under fat red pomegranates, and golden dates cascaded in strings beneath palm fronds. The old man made Luc try to read the same words again and again.

"Pay attention, Luc. You cannot remain illiterate."

"No one in my family can read."

"The ignorance of your race is breathtaking. We are supposed to be the three people of the book: Muslim, Jew, and Christian. My people read. The Jewish people as well." Salah shrugged. "Not the Christians. But where should I begin?"

"Teach me only what I need to know," said Luc. "Just the words I need to help you as a physician."

The old man shook his head and muttered. "Not to know is bad. Not to wish to know is worse. I have no time for you."

Salah snapped the book shut and closed his eyes, pinching the bridge of his nose.

"Can Bes read?" asked Luc softly.

"Bes worships his Egyptian gods. Or none at all. He has no use and no desire for reading. I had higher hopes for you."

Luc was frustrated. The surgery lessons had begun almost four weeks ago. Now, as he looked about the lush, flower-filled courtyard, heard the gurgling fountain and the songbirds, smelled the jasmine-scented air, and touched the smooth silken cushion where he sat, every sense told him that this beautiful place was his present and his future. The Arabic language was pushing into his thoughts and dreams. But as he sat struggling to read with this wise and generous man, Luc rubbed his thumb around one of his metal ankle bands. The cool steel proclaimed a larger truth: he was still a slave. Then he remembered something Salah had said: freedom could be taken away, but not knowledge. Luc looked at the old man, who sat with his fingers drumming on the closed book.

Bloom where you are planted, Luc thought.

"Teach me," he said. "I want to know."

Months passed, and Luc studied and learned. He was more than diligent. The old man drew pictures. The boy copied each drawing over and over until his were as good as his master's. Salah demonstrated the workings of the human body. During surgery on a chest wound, Salah captivated Luc by showing him a beating heart. Luc memorized the names of the organs and their functions. At first, the boy's medical tasks were simple. Luc handed surgical tools as the old man requested. Later Luc anticipated the need and handed Salah the appropriate instrument unasked.

"Listen to each patient. Ask questions. Examine carefully. The best way to treat the illness is to look for the cause."

Luc assisted in bandaging wounds. By the end of November, Salah did not need to tell Luc whether to put vinegar or honey on a wound. The boy learned to make poultices with herbs from the garden and spices from the souk; he bargained for stitching sinew from the butchers in the market. Wherever he went, Luc wore his gray cap or a turban pulled down low, so that he was simply known as a boy with sea-colored eyes, not the boy with one ear.

Luc began to do more. He removed splinters. He splinted broken bones. As predicted, Salah found his student was gifted, but the boy's love of the work and the science surprised both the teacher and the student. The teacher found his student soaked up education the way the dry Tunisian earth soaked up rain.

Usually Luc stood behind Salah to observe as the old man examined and treated his patients on a high wooden table in a corner of his room. One afternoon in early December, Salah handed Luc a scalpel and instructed him to lance a swollen boil on a patient's back. The patient, a prosperous carpenter with a large shop in Bizerte and many apprentices, protested when the boy took the instrument, but Salah put his hand on the man's well-muscled shoulder and spoke.

"The boy has sure hands. Mine are old."

Luc was afraid, but Salah waited until Luc pressed the silver point in, popping the angry flesh as he had seen Salah do.

Salah leaned over the boy. "Good, good. Just right," he said.

Luc looked up from the patient. For a moment he felt powerful. And proud. He remembered rowing Pons's boat: as he got stronger, he had felt a surge of pride as the little boat rose in the water and rushed forward with each of his strokes. Mastery. Except now it was less about physical competence. Luc could feel the gain in his intellect. He knew his questions were sharper, and his understanding was deeper. Salah recognized this change too. More and more, the old man looked forward to the lessons. So Salah began to teach the boy more than medicine; he introduced him to mathematics, geography, and history. Luc was quick, hardworking, and curious. And he was talented.

As the fall gave way to winter, Salah was increasingly impressed with all that the boy could do. Only Luc's reading lagged; Luc was easily exasperated with the written word and often lost his temper. The old man had no patience for impatience, and he would scold the boy.

"The key to all things is determination," said Salah one overcast December morning when Luc stumbled repeatedly over the same word.

"I am not good at this," fumed Luc.

"Only with patience do mulberry leaves become silk," said Salah.

"I will never get this," said Luc, pushing the papers away.

"Then leave. My head hurts today, and I've had enough of your mewling. Go to Bes."

Luc rose, bowed to the old man, and went to the kitchen.

Bes looked up when Luc appeared.

"What have you learned today?"

Luc said nothing.

Bes shook his head and continued, "It is no different from training a dog. You've learned some tricks. But you are still a dog."

Luc did not reply.

Bes pulled a sack of dried lentils from a shelf and dumped them on the floor, startling Cat, who squalled and fled to the garden.

"Look what you've done. Lentils are dear this season; waste none, slave," he said, tossing the boy the empty bag.

Luc was not surprised. Ever since he had begun studying with Salah, Bes often had punished him in a similar way. The little man would spill olive oil on a floor that Luc had just washed, or he would knock over a potted plant in the courtyard. Luc knew this was the price he had to pay for Bes's jealousy. He was down on his knees, muttering and scooping lentils from the floor as Bes watched, when they heard loud knocking at the front door.

Bes hurried to the door. Hearing voices and moans, Luc rushed to Salah's office. He found the old man asleep, with his head on his desk. Gently, Luc nudged him.

"Salah, wake up. Someone is here. An emergency."

The old man stirred, but he was confused; he did not seem to recognize Luc. He rubbed his eyes. Luc took a basin and ran for water. He washed the old man's face, and slowly Salah wakened, but his hands trembled, and he did not rise to meet his visitors.

Bes led four dusty men into the study; two of the men carried an injured man, who held a bloody cloth to his face. The fourth man followed, wailing and shaking his head. Luc rushed forward and helped lay the patient on the high table. Salah remained at his desk. He said nothing and made no attempt to stand.

Luc peeled the injured man's hand away from the cloth and looked underneath. Meanwhile, Bes tugged and pushed Salah and tried to get him to stand. The old man shook his head. He clutched the edge of the desk and closed his eyes. Luc looked at Salah before he turned to the visitors. From their sooty long robes, the dirt-covered feet, and the elaborate, long head wraps, Luc guessed that the men were camel drivers.

"What happened?" he asked.

The man who had been wailing spoke. "I've never had trouble with my camel. Not like this. Ibi was standing next to him, and the camel lunged. Ibi screamed."

"The animal had Ibi's cheek in its teeth," said one of the other men. "But Ibi's cry was so loud, the startled beast opened its mouth. And Ibi fell to the ground."

Luc examined the wound. Just below his eye, Ibi had two ragged gashes in his cheek. A triangular flap of his face hung open, exposing the cheek muscle. Luc took a deep breath and looked again to Salah for guidance. The old man was motionless. He was slumped over his desk with his chin resting in his palm, but he was watching Luc.

"Bes, get clean water, vinegar."

Bes scowled at Luc. The boy had never before spoken to him; now he was issuing orders.

"Hurry, Bes, please!" said Luc. "Bring me Salah's tools. Bandages. The silver needles and the gut thread. First clean water. Fill the silver pitcher. Make sure you use that pitcher."

Bes looked at Salah and back to the wounded man, and he said, "Ibi is my friend."

Luc looked at Bes. "I can do this," he said, pressing a cloth against the wound.

Bes frowned at the boy, but he fetched all that Luc requested, while the other men spoke among themselves.

"We don't want the boy," said the owner of the offending camel. "We need a doctor, not some infidel slave."

Bes shrugged. "My master is the best doctor in Bizerte,

perhaps the best doctor in Africa, but he is unwell today. He has trained the boy. Can one of *you* fix Ibi's wound?"

The visitors shook their heads.

"No? Nor can I. I have not been trained by Salah. But this boy works with Salah every day. The boy is all Ibi has."

Salah remained hunched at the desk with his head resting in his hands. He barely moved. Luc put a basin under the patient's head and flushed the wound with water from the silver pitcher. At first Ibi screamed, and two of his friends held him still. Luc placed a wad of cloth in his mouth.

"Bite down on this when it hurts. I apologize for the pain," said Luc, touching the patient on his shoulder.

Then the boy took an obsidian scalpel and gently trimmed the rough edges of the wound. Ibi trembled and squeezed his eyes shut. His friends looked away. Bes squatted near the door, rocking on his heels, watching. Luc worked quickly. He flushed the wound again, but this time, he added vinegar to the water. Ibi winced, but he did not cry out.

"Your wound is deep, but your eye is unhurt, and the cheek muscle was not torn. That is good," said Luc.

Luc pulled a silver needle in and out, pricking the flesh of Ibi's cheek, drawing the flaps of skin together, and closing the wound. His stitches were small and even, and he sewed carefully and quickly. As Luc finished, Bes rose and examined the work. He nodded and patted Ibi's hand. Luc wrapped Ibi's face and head in a clean cloth, tying the ends.

"Keep this bandage dry. Come back tomorrow. Perhaps

my master will be feeling better. Stay quiet. You will look like a warrior after this heals. You are a brave man, Ibi," said Luc.

"Should we pay the boy?" asked one of the men.

Bes frowned and asked, "Has Ibi's wound been attended to?"

But Luc shook his head. "No. Not this time." He looked over at Salah, who was watching. Bes led the men out.

Luc went to Salah. The old man was shaking his head.

"I couldn't move. My head felt as though it would burst," Salah whispered, and rubbed his face. "It's a struggle to pull the past hour into words."

"Are you feeling better?" asked Luc.

"A little."

"Can I help you to your bed?"

"Yes," said the old man. "I've never been more weary."

"Are you hungry or thirsty? Shall I bring you something?"

"Water."

Luc filled a cup, holding it while the old man sipped. With the boy's help, Salah climbed into bed, where he slept until almost midnight. When he awoke, Luc was still at his side.

"Was it my fault, master?"

"What?"

"Your head. Because I lost my temper?"

Salah smiled and spoke.

"No, Luc. I had a terrible headache when I woke this morning."

"Forgive me, master. I will be better."

Salah put his hand on Luc's head. "Every day of your life is a page of your history."

"My history?"

"Yes," said Salah. "Remember this day. You became more than you were yesterday. I became less. But you became more."

CHAPTER TWENTY-FOUR

Alain

IN LATE NOVEMBER, as the air cooled, and the days became short, Pons bound the fattened pig's feet and slit its throat. Mattie held a bowl to catch the blood pumping from the dying animal. When the pig was dead, they covered its carcass with straw and lit a fire. After the straw burned itself out, Mattie used a knife to scrape away the burned hair; this firing and scraping was repeated until the hide was clean. Then the pig was hung, draining, from a thick tree branch overnight. Cadeau stood guard beneath. In the morning, they set about skinning and butchering. The cut-up pork was soaked in seawater for three days and then smoked over a slow fire in a stone chimney behind the house. Mattie and Beatrice took turns feeding the fire.

Meanwhile, Mattie cleaned out the animal's intestine for sausage casing, soaking it in buckets of salted lemon water until the water was clear. Mattie was famous for the *boudin noir* that she made from the pig's blood and scraps of pork mixed with garlic, salt, and herbs, stuffed and tied into fat finger-length sections. After it was boiled, most of the sausage was smoked, but on the first night after it was made, Beatrice fried rounds of fresh sausage in butter with slices of apple and onion.

In the late afternoon of the following day, Pons, Mattie, and Beatrice were sitting at the table; the firelight flickered, and the shadows of the overhead fish swayed in the draft from the shuttered windows.

"Well," said Pons, "I expect we'll make it through the winter. Even if the fishing is only fair, we've a good amount of pork."

"Won't Alain arrive soon?" asked Beatrice.

"By week's end, I should think," said Pons.

"He'll be here any day," said Mattie. "That man can smell my *boudin* from over the mountain." Then she wagged a finger at Pons and Beatrice. "I don't want Alain to see Beatrice; I don't trust him."

Beatrice picked at a piece of bread. She did not look at Mattie.

"I know, Sister, but the boy?" asked Pons, pushing back from the table. "I could say something about Luc. *I* didn't promise Blanche anything. I could say I heard this rumor."

"Let sleeping dogs lie. Luc is in God's hands," said Mattie.

Beatrice nibbled at her food. She didn't want to argue with Mattie anymore—it was no use. Mattie's mind was made up. Now and then, the girl tried to catch Pons's eye, but he never looked at her. For the rest of the week, she kept the low fire burning under the smoking hams and sausages in the outdoor chimney. Pons tended the fire overnight and sometimes fished in the early mornings.

Alain and his young aide, Henri, showed up on Friday just as Pons was walking up the path from the beach. Cadeau barked at the soldiers.

"Shhhh!" said Pons, shifting his net and patting the dog's head. "Good dog." Then he added loudly, "Hello, Alain."

"Good day, Pons. So Luc is still with you?" asked Alain, pointing at Cadeau.

Pons put down his net and took a deep breath.

"Come inside, Alain. We have new cider," he said.

"And Mattie's black sausage, I hope?" asked Alain, handing the reins of his horse to Henri.

Pons nodded, and Alain followed him inside. Mattie was standing in the middle of the room, and Beatrice was nowhere to be seen.

"Hello, Mattie. I am hoping that you have made your *boudin*."

"You must have spies here, Alain. Just this week."

Grabbing a mug and sitting down, Alain asked, "Where's the boy?"

Pons stroked his chin and said, "I don't know what to say."

"Something happened to Luc?"

Pons nodded.

"Has he drowned?" asked Alain, holding up the mug.

Pons shook his head. "No."

Mattie put a trencher of bread in front of Alain, slid a thick slice of black sausage onto the bread, and poured him a mug of hard cider.

"This food rivals anything at the castle. I hope there's a lot more," said Alain, taking a big bite of sausage. "Now tell me about the boy."

So Pons told Alain about the dreadful day when Luc was lost.

"That child has had more than his share of misfortune," said Alain.

Pons shook his head. "That wasn't the way I saw it. I found that luck followed Luc. As soon as he stepped into my boat, my nets filled with fish like never before. All the time he was here, we had nothing but good fortune."

"Old man, look at the boy's life. He was born with one ear. And a bastard."

"We don't know that for a fact," said Mattie.

Alain raised his eyebrows and smirked. "No?"

"Anyway, luck or no luck, Luc was taken. I am a poor man," said Pons. "If I were rich, I would try to find the boy and ransom him. But it takes a lot of gold, and I have none."

"You see, Luc is unlucky. If Sir Guy were alive, then maybe. But Sir Guy died without acknowledging the boy," said Alain, washing down the last of the sausage with a big gulp of cider.

He leaned back, patted his stomach, and belched. Pons said nothing. Mattie was pouring more cider when she saw Beatrice descending the ladder. Alain looked at the girl.

"My God! Who is this?" He turned to Pons. "Who else is hiding in this cottage?"

"No one else," Beatrice said softly. "Just me."

"Is this another bastard?" asked Alain, still turned to Pons.

"I am no bastard. And neither was Luc."

Alain whipped around and looked at Beatrice.

"What's going on here? Who's this girl?" he asked.

Beatrice answered, "It doesn't matter who I am."

"No," added Mattie, glaring at Beatrice. "It's Luc we are talking about."

"First things first," said Alain, staring at the girl. "I insist you tell me who this maid is, Pons."

"You won't care who I am once I tell you about Luc," answered Beatrice.

"That's enough, child. Leave us. This is no concern of yours," said Mattie, pointing to the ladder.

Alain frowned at Mattie. "She's a brazen one. I will have my question answered."

He turned to Beatrice. Unblinking, she met his gaze.

"Luc is not Sir Guy's son," she said.

Alain shrugged. "I thought there was a chance he might be. But it matters little now."

"It matters more than ever," answered Beatrice. "Because Luc is the second son of the Count de Muguet."

"Hold your tongue, girl!" said Mattie as she stood up. "I'm sorry, Alain. I don't know what's gotten into her. This is nonsense."

Alain nodded and began to laugh. "Well, it's most certainly an outrageous claim. The old count's son, eh? If he were alive, you'd lose your pretty head for uttering that nonsense."

"I have no doubt that the count killed people for less. But he's dead. And as for the new count, Luc is his brother," said Beatrice.

Alain shook his head. "This is madness. Do you think your lie will get the boy's ransom?"

"It's no lie," answered Beatrice.

"What proof do you have, wench?"

Beatrice looked down at her feet and sighed, "I have no proof."

"And the olive growers? That drunk and his scrawny wife? What would they say?" asked Alain.

"They won't say anything. I had to vow not to say a word of this."

Alain frowned. "So you are not only impudent but also untrustworthy?"

CHAPTER TWENTY-FOUR

"I have to help Luc."

"And you would say anything, do anything?" asked Alain. "Am I supposed to believe you and not Pascal?"

"He and his wife have everything to lose. But there was a priest, Father Thierry," said Beatrice.

"He is dead. Maybe five years ago," said Alain, licking his thumb and smoothing his wild eyebrows.

"You see, Beatrice? You've said enough. This is just a tale. Leave us, child," said Mattie. "Forget this whole matter, Alain."

"Am I supposed to forget this beautiful maid as well?" he said, grabbing Beatrice's arm.

"Please," said Pons.

Alain shook his head.

"Who is she?"

"No one," said Mattie. "Just an orphan from the village. She helps with the chores. Leave us now, girl."

"You were hiding her, weren't you? Who is she?"

Mattie glared at Alain.

"You insult me," said Alain, still holding the girl's arm, looking at her from head to toe, at her dress and her leather shoes. "Do you think I don't remember you, Mattie, from the old days? You worked in that knight's household. The knight who stole from the count. I was there when the count killed the thief."

"My father did not steal," said Beatrice.

"Your father?" said Alain, pulling Beatrice closer.

The heavy soldier looked at the girl's face and began to nod his head.

"I recall now. There *was* a child. I remember her screaming at the execution."

Mattie sat down and covered her face.

Alain continued, "So you are Sir—? Ayiii! I cannot remember the unfortunate scoundrel's name." Beatrice was furious, pulling and struggling but unable to shake her arm free of Alain's grip. "Étienne!" said Alain, nodding. "I remember now. So you've lived here with Mattie ever since? And your mother?"

Mattie looked at Alain and answered, "Her mother left the child. There wasn't anyone to take her. Her grandparents died from the pestilence when she was small. She had no one else but me."

"So all these years you've hidden that disgraced knight's daughter in this peasant household? Oh and, of course"— Alain thumped his forehead with the heel of his free hand— "there was Luc, the count's secret son. And, of course! *He* was helping Pons fish? You're all mad." Alain shook his head. "What will become of the girl here in this village? Even if her father was a criminal, she is quite a beauty. I could make inquiries. Find her a position in a household back home. That would be more fitting. This is no place for someone of her class."

"My father lost his knighthood. That makes me as common as you."

Beatrice grimaced as Alain tightened his grip on her arm. "You don't know your place, girl. You should show me respect," he snarled.

"Please accept my apology," said Beatrice, glaring at Alain and finally freeing her arm. Her eyes filled; she was angry, but she was also scared.

"I beg you, Alain, forget you saw her," said Pons, stepping in between Alain and the girl.

"I promise only that I shall not repeat her outrageous claim about Luc. Thank you for the *boudin*; I must be going."

Alain rose to leave and stopped.

"What about the dog?" he asked.

"The boy's dog?" asked Pons.

"I'll pay you for that animal."

Beatrice wiped her eyes. "He is Luc's dog," she said. "And Luc will be back."

CHAPTER TWENTY-FIVE

Abraham

SALAH WAS SEATED on floor cushions in a corner of his room, reading by lantern flame and by the winter sunlight that filtered through the iron grillwork of a high window. A charcoal fire glowed in a brazier at his feet. Books were jumbled at his side. A paper scroll rested across his lap. He looked up when Luc entered carrying a bowl of dried apricots and almonds.

"It is a lovely December morning, Luc, is it not?" said the old man, pointing to the stripes of sunlight that patterned the floor.

Luc nodded and slid the bowl in front of Salah.

"Praise Allah," added Salah, nibbling an apricot. "I am as old as the mountains, but today I am as young as your eyes and your hands."

Luc tilted his head and smiled. The old man unfurled the scroll, and Luc knelt beside him.

But before Salah could begin, Bes ushered in an unexpected visitor from the nearby city of Tunis: a balding, bearded European with a small black cap and heavy-lidded eyes. When Salah saw the visitor, he smiled broadly and clapped his hands.

"Bring refreshment for my honored guest, Bes."

The little man bowed and turned.

"Abraham, my esteemed colleague, it has been too long," said Salah to his visitor.

"Good morning, learned friend," said Abraham. "Your face is a wonderful sight."

"My face? It is anything but."

"Ah, Salah, your smile is almost as famous as your wisdom."

"So much flattery, Abraham? You must want something."

"I want only your friendship, old man. And to see that you are in good health."

"I am alive, and that is enough at my age. Sit," said Salah, snapping his fingers at Luc, who pushed aside the brazier and scrambled to pile cushions across from Salah.

Abraham lowered himself onto the pillows just as Bes reappeared with a bowl of dates and two clear glasses of water, sweetened with sugar and infused with rose petals and mint.

"Thank you, Bes," said Salah.

When the little man bowed and took a step backward,

Luc turned to follow, but Abraham pulled Luc's sleeve.

Abraham asked Salah, "Your student?"

Salah nodded.

Luc made a slight bow to Abraham.

"You are most fortunate to have the great Salah as your teacher," said the visitor.

Luc nodded and began to back out of the room with Bes.

"Stay, Luc," said Salah.

Bes waited, but Salah said nothing. He bit his lip, glared at Luc, and left. Luc knelt next to Salah.

"Luc, this is the great Abraham Zacuto, a famous astronomer."

Abraham shook his head. "Not as famous as you, Salah."

Salah said, "Abraham, *your* fame will outlive a hundred generations."

"But not the smallness of man," said Abraham. "There are very few homes where a Jew is welcomed as a friend."

Salah clasped his hands in front of his chest and studied his visitor.

Abraham squinted at Luc. "Your student has the coloring of a Christian."

"Alas, it goes deeper than coloring," said Salah.

Abraham shrugged. "A poor choice for a student."

"To be sure," said Salah. "But you taught many."

"Look where it brought me."

Salah turned to Luc. "This man was an eminent professor of astronomy in Salamanca and Saragossa. He perfected the astrolabe and charted the skies. His work made it possible for Spanish sailors to explore distant seas."

Abraham smiled. "It did me no good. I was forced to leave Spain with the rest of my people."

Salah said, "A travesty. But then, the followers of Islam were defeated. Al-Andalus was lost."

Abraham nodded. "I fled to Portugal, where I found a place in the court of King Jaoa in Lisbon."

"Yes?" asked Salah. "And did you encounter the explorer Vasco da Gama there?"

Abraham nodded.

"What sort of man is he?" asked Salah.

"After a kiss from da Gama, you should count your teeth. I do not like that man. He will not end well. He sought my advice and my charts, but there was little reward for me. Jaoa's successor, King Manuel, was weak, and he bowed to the Spanish king. The Portuguese passed brutal, murderous laws against the Jews," said Abraham. "Almost everything I owned was confiscated."

"Being a king does not make a man wise."

"I had a terrible time leaving Portugal."

"Hate has no medicine," said Salah.

Abraham held his glass up. "Beautiful, Salah."

Salah held up his and said, "Yes. A gift from Venice; a visiting scholar brought this pair to me. They are indeed lovely. Glass is a thing of wonder; it's like holding water. And there is nothing more beautiful than water."

Abraham sipped his drink. "Except when one is forced to embark on a long sea voyage. My son Samuel and I thought we were fortunate to book passage to Tunis, but that journey was a horror. Twice we were set upon by pirates."

"This boy was captured from a fishing boat. It is how he came here," said Salah, pointing to Luc, who rubbed a thumb along one ankle band.

"So the boy and I are both unwilling travelers, longing for home?"

Luc nodded.

"This life is neither easy nor fair," said Abraham, turning to Salah. "A man ought to be measured for his merit. I never cared if you followed your god. Just let me have mine."

"My god?" Salah smiled. "My god is the same god who spoke to Moses. God revealed his truth to the Christians and the Jews, but you chose not to follow what was revealed."

Abraham closed his eyes for a few moments.

"This boy?" said Salah, pointing at Luc. "He chooses not to become a Muslim. Faith cannot be imposed by force. But he is in error. There is but one true religion."

"Ah, Salah!" said Abraham. "I though you were a tolerant man."

"Tolerance does not require agreement," said Salah. "I respect the boy's other virtues. Just as I respect your intelligence and your honesty, Abraham."

"So the boy is your slave, but you are educating him?" asked Abraham.

CHAPTER TWENTY-FIVE

Salah nodded. "How could I not? He was utterly igno-
rant, but he is curious and smart. I am, above all, a teacher.
He is already more than he was."

"Many free men would pay their entire fortunes to sit at
Salah's knee as you do," said Abraham to Luc.

"Yes, but they are free. I am not, and that is everything,"
said Luc.

"Isn't learning freedom?" asked Salah.

Luc rolled his bottom lip between his teeth and said
nothing.

Salah narrowed his eyes. "Against stupidity, even Allah
is helpless, don't you agree, Abraham?"

Abraham held out his palms. "You just said this boy is
smart."

"That doesn't mean he is not stupid."

"Ah, Salah, you speak in riddles. I came today to pay my
respects. I heard you were unwell, but I see you are yourself."

"Who else could I be?"

"No one," said Abraham, and he rose. "I shall not remain in Tunis."

"You will resettle once again, Abraham?"

"The wandering Jew," said Abraham, striking his heart
with two fingers. "I will go to Jerusalem."

"Jerusalem?" asked Salah.

"It has always been Jerusalem."

Tapping his cap, Abraham Zacuto turned and left.

When Luc rose to leave, Salah held up his hand and spoke in his deepest voice.

"If an egg falls on a rock, too bad for the egg. If a rock falls on an egg, too bad for the egg. As Abraham said, life is not fair, Luc. Look around. And remember, tenacity is admirable. Obstinacy is foolish. You are not a fool. Now, sit here next to me. We have work to do."

Luc looked down at his hands, which were clenched into fists. He spread his fingers and looked at Salah. Salah waited for a few moments, studying the boy before he spoke.

"You have just met a brilliant man, Luc. His life has been hard and unfair, but his learning has changed the world. Can you appreciate that?"

Luc nodded and sat down.

CHAPTER TWENTY-SIX

Christmas

IT RAINED FOR three days; the unusual cold was biting. Pons and Beatrice sat by the hearth drinking hot cider. Pons had collected bark, twigs, and stones, and he and Beatrice created a small stable with a manger on the wooden chest. They had just finished setting up the nativity scene when the door opened, and Mattie slogged in. She left her mud-stained wooden shoes by the door and snapped her soaked woolen cloak before draping it on a peg near the hearth.

"Awful weather to start our Christmas. Here, child, lentils and wheat sprouts for Saint Barbara's Day," she said, handing a little cloth sack to Beatrice. "Lovely stable," said Mattie bending to look at the assembled scene.

Beatrice and Pons joined her at the chest. "I can't wait to see this year's carvings," said Beatrice.

Mattie went to a shelf and, from behind a large basket, she pulled a wrapped bundle that she handed to Beatrice who carefully unwrapped four new figures. She kissed Mattie and set them around the manger. Pons put his hands on his knees and bent down to study the additions.

"Villagers," crowed Mattie. "Villagers to worship the Christ child."

Pons chuckled. "Am I really so ugly and crooked?"

"What do you mean?" asked Mattie, lifting the little figure of a fisherman. He was bareheaded and had a coil of tiny baited hooks draped over his shoulder. "This is a handsome, strong fisherman. What do you think, Beatrice?"

"Very handsome," she said, smiling at Pons.

"Well, you carved our Beatrice just right," said Pons. "A beauty. And the boy. I am glad to see him."

Beatrice picked up the statue of Luc. "It *is* Luc," she said, rubbing her thumb on the smooth left side of the head. "Wearing the shirt I made."

"Boy never took it off," said Mattie, picking up the statue of herself and setting it next to the one of the girl.

"See," said Beatrice, putting Luc's statue next to the one of Pons. "Luc belongs here."

"I made him for you," said Mattie, patting Beatrice's hand.

"It wouldn't feel right without him," said Beatrice.

"But you forgot someone, Mattie," said Pons.

Beatrice laughed. "Someone furry and brown."

Mattie went to the same shelf and pulled out a half-finished carving of a dog. "You mean Cadeau? I'll have him finished by tomorrow."

Mattie and Beatrice hung evergreen branches over the windows, and the cottage smelled of pine, wet wool, and wet dog.

"I met Oubert with his new bride in the village," said Mattie as she stood back to admire the Christmas decorations. "She's in the family way."

"He wasted no time," said Pons.

"Such a wan thing; this is no weather to be out, not in her state," said Mattie, shaking her head. "He could have servants to help her, but he wouldn't spend a coin to save his own neck, let alone a second wife."

Beatrice put her arm around the old woman.

"Oubert asked me to carve the holy family for him," said Mattie, pulling Beatrice close.

"I hope you set a high price," said Beatrice.

"Very high. And I refused to bargain, so there we are. Oubert will be paying for this year's Christmas feast. What do you think? A fat duck and chestnuts?"

"Mmm," said Beatrice.

"Blanche sent you olive wood. Hervé stopped by when you were in the village," said Pons.

"He asked about the dog," added Beatrice.

Cadeau was curled near the hearth. Beatrice knelt to pat him, and he rolled onto his back so she could rub his belly.

"You belong to Luc," said Beatrice.

"He is a fine dog," said Mattie. "Too fine for us. But then, so are you, Beatrice. Another Christmas with Pons and me? It's past time we think of your future."

"I am happy here, Mattie."

"I fear there is a change coming. Did you hear all the crows this morning?" asked Mattie.

"It's the rain they were complaining about," said Pons, cracking open the front door to check the rain drumming on the stone threshold.

"And Cadeau? You heard him howling last night," said Mattie, reaching in front of Pons to pull the door closed.

"He's howled before," said Beatrice, still rubbing the dog's fur.

Mattie frowned. "And things have happened before. They're signs. Mark my words. Something is about to happen."

"Dinner, I hope," replied Pons.

Just then there was a loud knock at the door. Cadeau jumped up and began barking. Pons looked at Mattie and crossed himself. Opening the door, he found Alain and the young soldier Henri.

Pons took a step back.

"We've come for the girl," said Alain, pushing the door

open and marching in with Henri, both drenched and dripping, their boots squelching and their cloaks clinging.

"No!" cried Beatrice.

"You whoreson!" said Pons. "How could you!"

"Hold your tongue, old man. I have done you all a great service. I bring good news."

"What news could be good that takes the girl?" asked Pons.

"Her father had a younger brother," said Alain, shaking water from his sopping cloak. Taking off his soaked hat, he hung it over Mattie's cape.

"I don't remember any uncles," said Beatrice.

"I remember him," said Mattie, moving Alain's wet hat to another peg. "He was just a boy when his father, Beatrice's grandfather, sent him off to be a page. That was before the pestilence struck. That plague took Beatrice's grandparents."

"It was a bad time. Lot of people died in my village. More than a dozen or so years ago," said Alain, nodding.

Mattie said, "Anyway, Beatrice never heard a word from him."

Water puddled under both soldiers. Henri just stood, drenched, hat in hand, eyes to the ground. Alain blew on his chubby hands and rubbed them together.

"Course not. He had nothing to offer the girl. But now Sir Étienne's brother—"

Beatrice cut Alain off. "Sir Étienne?"

"That's what I'm trying to tell you. The young count has restored your father's knighthood and his manor."

"What?" asked Beatrice. "But why?"

"Your uncle is this count's dear friend; they were pages together as boys. So the count investigated your father's case. He talked to everyone in his father's household. It's true Sir Étienne had debts and that he gambled. But he never stole. It was one of the stablemen. A lot of the servants knew, but the old count hadn't waited long enough to hear the true story."

"That would be just like the old count," said Mattie. "Well, amen to this. Sir Étienne's name has been cleared." Beatrice closed her eyes, and Mattie put her arm around the girl. "You see, I always said you were a lady."

Beatrice sighed, then she looked at Alain. "But why are you here to take me?"

"Let me finish what I have been trying to say. After my last visit, I told your uncle that I had seen you, and he was overjoyed."

"Overjoyed? Why?" asked Mattie.

"He has no other family. Like you said, the plague killed his parents. And then after his brother was killed, he thought the girl was lost."

"And so now he wants you to take me away?" asked Beatrice. "Why?"

"To *visit* him. I'm here to escort you. The count has invited you to spend Christmas in his castle with your uncle.

Your uncle sent this gift," said Alain, offering Beatrice a bundle wrapped in heavy sacking.

"Invited?" asked Beatrice. "Not ordered?"

"Right," said Alain. When Beatrice did not take the gift, Alain unwrapped it. He held out a thick fur wrap.

Mattie put her hand to her mouth and caught her breath.

"It's beautiful, and I appreciate it," said Beatrice, tentatively reaching out to touch the fur. "But I shall not go with you. This is my home, and this is where I plan to spend Christmas. I'll never leave Mattie and Pons."

Beatrice sat down, and Pons lowered himself onto the bench next to her. She put her head on his shoulder.

"What about Beatrice's mother?" asked Mattie. She was standing with her arms folded in front of her.

"Ah," said Alain. "Sad news there. She remains in the convent, and that's where she'll stay. She's gone," he said, knocking his head. "She remembers nothing. If you met her today, she wouldn't recognize you tomorrow. She has no idea who she is, or ever was. But the nuns are taking fine care of her."

Beatrice buried her face in Pons's shoulder. Mattie stood behind her and stroked her hair.

"You know we love you, right, Beatrice? But maybe this is the answer to my prayers," said Mattie.

"Not *my* prayers," sobbed Beatrice.

"You don't belong here in this simple life. Maybe you should go north. To visit. Maybe this is your chance to be the lady that you are," said Mattie.

"What's there for me there that I don't have here? Fancy clothes and fine meals? Parents who abandon their children? I don't want to be a lady. I like this life just fine. We have everything. And I love you and Pons. You'd never leave me. And I don't want to leave you," said Beatrice, turning to look at Mattie.

"How about a husband, a fine nobleman?" said Mattie, taking the girl's chin in her hand.

"Someone like the count, who murders the innocent and throws away his own son?" asked Beatrice bitterly. "Does this uncle whom I don't remember think I'll come running because he's sent me a fur cape?"

Alain took a step toward Beatrice, but stopped. "I have delivered my message. The cloak is yours," he said, laying it on the table. "I shall inform the count of your refusal."

Pons was rubbing his stiff fingers and shaking his head. "Beatrice, think about what you're doing. Turning down the count?"

"No harm will come to Pons and Mattie if I refuse?" asked Beatrice, looking at Alain, her eyes filling.

Alain answered with a shrug, "What do I know? I do what I am told. Nothing more. Nothing less."

"I wish that were true," said Pons. "You should have never said a word about Beatrice."

"You're fools, all of you," said Alain.

"Is the count like his father?" asked Beatrice, wiping her eyes.

CHAPTER TWENTY-SIX

"All the servants say he is a better man," said Alain, reaching for his hat.

"Has there ever been anyone worse than the old Muguet?" asked Mattie.

Alain extended his arm to Beatrice. "Return with me. Your uncle is most agreeable. He and the count hoped to share Christmas with you. Just for a visit."

"No," said Beatrice, standing. "This is where I shall be on Christmas. Tell my uncle and the count that I am too ill to travel."

Alain shook his head. "I won't do that."

"Beatrice, you cannot ask Alain to lie," said Pons.

Beatrice grabbed one of Mattie's knives and slashed the cushion of her thumb. She winced and said to Alain, "Then tell the count I've had a small accident. I cannot accept his invitation just now. Perhaps in the spring, for Easter."

"Lord, I hope there is no infection," said Mattie, rushing for a cloth to wrap the girl's bleeding hand.

"Now no one needs to lie, and I can stay. What about Luc? Did you tell the count he has a brother?" Beatrice asked Alain.

"No, because I don't believe there is any truth to that story, my lady."

"'My lady'?" asked Beatrice. "Now that I am a lady, does my request that you tell the count about Luc carry more weight?"

Alain took a deep breath. "If you insist, I shall convey

the story to his lordship. But think about what you are asking."

"There may be nothing but trouble here, Beatrice," said Pons.

"It's Luc's best chance. I must take it," said Beatrice.

1502

CHAPTER TWENTY-SEVEN

Geography

THROUGHOUT THAT AFRICAN winter, Luc spent less and less time helping Bes and more and more time studying under Salah. Bes was quick to remind the master and the boy that he needed no assistance. Still, sometimes Luc would catch the little man watching his lessons. Luc and Bes had come to a wary truce; the little man had begun to recognize that his master would not easily part with this special slave.

Though he had adapted and even thrived in this new life, Luc longed for home; in December he wondered whether he would ever be back for a Christmas. In the chilly months of December and then in January, the sky was often thick and even rainy, but any rain that fell disappeared into the dry earth. Throughout the winter, Luc's thoughts would often turn to home. He wondered who was taking care of Cadeau. Was he still at the cottage? With Beatrice?

He was daydreaming, remembering the windy afternoon when he had promised Beatrice a yellow silk dress, when he became aware that Salah was drumming his fingers on his knee, watching him. It was late February, and the old man was seated on pillows on the floor of his room with a shawl wrapped about his shoulders. Before him was a low table covered with books and scrolls. Behind were more stacks of books and a large clay ball. Salah shook his head and pointed to a cushion at his right knee. Luc knelt facing the old man as Salah reached for a tusk of ivory and a white coin.

"Do you know what these are?"

Luc took the tusk and turned it, sliding his thumb along the perfect surface.

"This is the tooth of an elephant," said the boy.

Salah nodded. "The elephant is a noble beast, but it is his tusk that men covet. You have seen carvings of ivory?"

"Yes. I have dusted yours. But ivory is not known in my country."

"Not widely known. It is very valuable, so it is known only to those of wealth."

"Not to a fisherman."

"No. Probably not, although there are whales with teeth of ivory."

"We fished for anchovies, not whales," answered Luc.

"Now, we fish for something larger than whales," said

Salah. "What's this?" asked the old man, offering the boy the white disk.

"It looks like a coin," said Luc, taking it and turning it over. "But it isn't made of gold or silver. It's just a disk of salt."

"No, it is a *coin* made of salt. South of the desert, below the great Sahara, salt is traded as gold. Weighed out equally, measure for measure, and sometimes even struck into coins like this."

"In Bizerte's souks, this coin would buy very little," said Luc, handing it back to Salah.

"Salt always has value, but far less here, where it is more abundant than gold. Things that are rare are more valuable."

"Not always," answered Luc, pointing to his ear. "A boy with one ear is nearly worthless."

"Your singular ear is no exception to that rule. Had you two ears, you might have been worked to death in a salt mine or ended up as a eunuch in a rich man's harem."

"Had I two ears, I would have fetched a better price. I would be more valuable."

"Yes, I see your argument, but it is not responsive."

"I do not understand."

"Because you were cheap, *I* purchased you. That was of more value to *you*."

Luc bowed his head.

"Perhaps you are luckier than you think, Luc."

"What do you mean?"

"Throw a lucky man into the sea, and he will come up with a fish in his mouth."

"I miss your lesson here," said Luc.

"Only because you choose not to listen. There is luck, and there is what you make of it. Who we are is not in our control, but what we make of ourselves is. Allah has given me the right of ownership of you, Luc, but I never forget that he could have given *you* the ownership of *me*."

Luc grinned. "I am grateful that I was not given to Bes."

"You have much to be grateful for. One hand is not enough to clap with. A single ear?" Salah shrugged. "It is why you are here. Be thankful. I am thankful that my bargain turned out to be a scholar and more. Of course, the nut does not reveal the tree it contains."

Luc looked down at his knees and his hands. He spread his fingers, and then he surveyed Salah's room, with its books and instruments. He turned his head and saw that the old man was watching him. Salah smiled.

"I understand," said Luc.

"Geography is today's subject," said the old man. "Nine hundred years ago, there was a rare Christian scholar in Seville named Isidore."

"Rare?" asked Luc, sitting back and drawing his knees to his chest, leaning forward to listen.

"Yes, a Christian scholar has always been rare. The Egyptians, the Greeks, and even some of the Romans were great scholars, but their learning would have been lost without my people. Isidore, unlike most of his primitive race—"

"Primitive like me, you mean?"

"Oh yes, Luc. And like you, Isidore was unusual. He was a Christian who appreciated and studied the ancients, a remarkable scholar. Isidore described the world as having four parts, three of them known: Asia, Europe, and Africa. And a fourth part, beyond the ocean, unknown."

"Beyond the Mediterranean?"

"Beyond the *Atlantic*. Lately, the greed of some Christian explorers has impelled them to venture boldly into the unknown in their quest for gold. Some believe that on the other side of the Atlantic is the rich land of Asia. I suspect these Europeans have miscalculated the size of the world. Fetch my scissors."

Luc jumped to his feet and retrieved the steel tool—a single piece of metal, forged into a loop with opposing blades that closed when the loop was squeezed. Luc had never seen scissors until he came to live with Salah, but then, he had rarely seen paper, and he had never held a book.

Salah rolled the clay ball toward him. "Now we shall build the world."

Luc raised his eyebrows. "Surely that is not the job of an old man and his slave?"

"Most assuredly that is the very task at hand."

The old man tossed Luc the scroll that he was holding in his lap.

"On this, you will find a map. An unusual map, printed

on gores across the width of the paper. Cut each gore carefully along its outside lines."

When Luc had twelve strips carefully cut from the sheet, the old man handed him a crock of wheat paste.

"Paste each piece carefully on that clay ball. The edges should just meet: I will hand them to you in correct order."

Luc pried open the crock's stopper; the paste smelled sour and was cold to his touch. He worked carefully, pasting the strips to the ball and scraping the excess glue with his nail. Once Luc had fitted the final strip, the surface was completely and perfectly papered.

"There, we have the world. Wonderful! Look at it, Luc!" said the old man, his eyes sparkling.

Luc hoisted the papered globe high above his head and smiled broadly. Then he brought the globe down to eye level and turned it, studied it.

"And the fourth part, Luc?" asked the old man, looking up from his cushion on the floor.

"Is a blank," said the boy.

"Precisely," said Salah, clapping his hands. "Precisely! Here I have collected maps and books—all the works I can find of explorers and travelers, of merchants and scholars," he said, turning his shoulders and waving at the stacks of manuscripts and folios. "I have the learning of the ancients, of Ptolemy and of Pliny. I have histories from the great Temujin, known as Genghis Khan, who ruled an empire bigger than a year's journey."

Salah signaled for Luc to sit, and the boy put the globe on the floor in front of the old man and sat across from him. Salah grabbed a small blue leather book and hugged it for a moment against his chest.

"Here is the account of Ibn Battuta, a Berber from Tangier who spent thirty years exploring Africa. He traveled the length of the rivers Nile and Niger, to Mombassa, and then he journeyed across the sea and over the deserts of Arabia, on to India and through the land of the Tartars to China."

He put the blue book on the low table and rooted around the manuscripts.

"I have logs from Arab seamen describing and mapping the Indian Ocean. And now, I have the writings of Christians who have begun to travel beyond their muddy villages. Here is a book of the journey east by a Venetian merchant family."

Salah handed a book to Luc.

"Learn to read well, Luc. You will know the world."

The old man pointed to a heavy folio bound between wooden boards, with a leather spine and heavy brass clasps. "There I have the works of a Frankish map maker, Henricus Martellus. That treasure was sold to me by the very man who found you."

"I wasn't lost," answered Luc hoarsely.

"Dawn does not come twice to wake a man," said the old man. "Luc, you learn so easily, and yet you do not change."

Luc shook his head. "When I think of my old life, when I remember it, I ache to be home. I try not to think of it, but I can't help it."

The old man pointed to his books and papers. "This is where you are. And there is so much here."

From the minarets of the city, the cries of the muezzins floated through the window. Salah turned to the boy. "Are you too childish, too stubborn to appreciate all you have gained? Shall I be disappointed?"

Salah stroked his beard. Luc struggled, searching for words, searching for calm. He felt his temper searing through his tight throat. He gazed at the old man and knew that he had disappointed him. And yet Luc was angry. Salah had given him so much; that was indisputable. But when Luc looked down at the bands around his ankles, he could not escape the reality of his life: he was another man's property. Yet the man was a good man, and maybe that counted for something.

"See to your work in the kitchen. I expect important guests today," said Salah, struggling to rise from the pillows.

Since the morning months ago, when Luc stitched the camel bite, Salah was increasingly weak and had trouble with his legs. Luc assisted him to his feet. Before he left, the boy put his right hand over his heart and bowed.

"I am better for all that you have taught me."

Salah lay his right hand on his own heart and nodded. "I am not nearly finished teaching you, Luc. Now leave. It is time for my prayers."

In the kitchen, Luc found Bes browning strips of veal with cinnamon and pepper in a large iron pan over the fire.

Handing Luc a long fork, the little man sniffed and said, "So the scholar is again the lowly slave?"

Luc said nothing. He was thinking about the geography lesson and how he had disappointed Salah. He was in no mood for Bes's banter.

Bes danced from one foot to the other; he had three pots on the fire, including a perforated kettle filled with ground wheat that he was steaming over a pot of broth for couscous. He tasted each dish and added salt or a spice.

"Brown the meat," he chittered to Luc. "Clean the birdcages, sweep the floor. Then beat the pillows."

Luc said nothing but closed his eyes and bowed. When the meat was done, he left with his broom.

When Luc finished his chores, Bes asked, "Do you know who our guests are?"

Luc said nothing.

"Tariq and his only son, Mohammed."

Luc sighed and shrugged. The names were meaningless to him.

Bes shook his head and hissed, "The old man and you spend all your days poring over books. You draw pictures of birds and leaves, and copy numbers and play with puzzles, but you don't know who Tariq is?"

Luc answered, "No." He closed his eyes and wished for quiet.

"Albino lizard," said Bes, and he spit into the fire. The gob sizzled, and he watched it before continuing.

"Tariq is the wealthiest merchant in the world. He has more camels than there are stars in the sky. When his caravan marches across the desert, the line is so long that you can see neither the beginning nor the end. And in his harem, there are countless women, all beautiful."

Bes put his hands on his hips and said, "Such a pretty lad. Perhaps I can persuade Tariq to buy you as a toy for the harem." He smiled crookedly. "The boat captain wanted to cut your neck, but me? I would cut you elsewhere." Bes raised his voice to a very high pitch. "You could be the fairest eunuch in the land, with your sun-yellow hair and your blue-sky eyes."

Luc said nothing.

Bes chewed the nail of his pinkie and tilted his head. "Or maybe I will sell you to Tariq's son. Mohammed has a stable of slaves whom he rents out by the day. They break stones and dig ditches. Sometimes his slaves are harnessed to pull heavy wagons like oxen. The worst work for whoever will pay the most. Mohammed cares nothing if the slave dies, so long as he is paid for the full day."

Bes floured a board and rolled dough to create pies of pigeon and fig. He grilled eggplant slices slathered in garlicky olive oil. He baked almond cakes with honey and currants. The little man had never taken more care, and Luc, meanwhile, busied himself in the courtyard, where a low table was set for Salah and his honored company. The late-February afternoon sun was hot, but the shaded courtyard was cool; the fountain water tinkled and pealed, and the birds chirped and trilled. Dust puffed from the pillows that Luc beat; he fetched extra cushions. He scrubbed the floor tiles until the iridescence of the blue and green glazes caught the light. He collected every lantern in the house, filled each one with oil, and trimmed every wick. Bes produced a saffron-and-aqua cloth to cover the table. With the candles and lamps, the pots of night-blooming jasmine, and the bright pillows, the courtyard was enchanting, and all was ready.

Luc found Salah asleep, and he gently woke the old man as the call for evening prayer sounded from the minarets of Bizerte. With Luc's help, the old man changed into a freshly laundered white caftan. Luc filled a basin with water, and Salah washed his face and his arms to his elbows. After he washed his feet, he knelt on his prayer rug with Luc's help.

"Leave me now," murmured Salah. "There is dirt under your nails. The Prophet said that cleanliness is half the faith. Surely you can accept that much of my religion."

Luc went out to the courtyard and scrubbed his hands and his face. Ever since the morning when Salah was ill, months earlier, Luc had helped him walk to a nearby bath-house, a *hammam*, where both the man and his slave were scoured and steamed. A bath had been a rare event in Luc's old life, but in this world, bathing was weekly. Not just for the wealthy, but for everyone. *Hammams* peppered the city; they were centers of the community. And Salah's faith called for him to wash before each of the five daily prayers, as well. Salah repeatedly reminded Luc that Allah loved those who accepted him and those who were clean.

Salah often talked of his faith, and although Luc listened, he held on to the faith of his birth. He knew that he was no longer the simple boy who herded pigs or fished, but he was not from this place; his home and his heart were across the sea.

CHAPTER TWENTY-EIGHT

Honored Guests

TARIQ AND HIS SON sailed in, trailed by servants bearing gifts for Salah. One led a new lamb, another clutched three plump hens. One man carried a caged gray parrot with a gray beak, lemon eyes, and red tail feathers; the handsome bird laughed like a girl and whistled like a man. More servants followed with baskets of pale pistachio nuts, rosy pomegranates, and yellow bananas, and they presented bright copper trays with pyramids of orange turmeric and umber cinnamon. A child servant carried a ball of straw in a silver bowl.

Bes pointed to the bowl and said to Luc, "Snow."

Luc frowned.

"Inside the straw is a ball of snow. Cold snow from the mountains," said Bes, with a smirk.

In his studies with Salah, Luc had read about snow, but he had never seen it. Salah handed the bowl to Luc and winked as Luc wiggled his little finger under the straw to touch the snow.

Tariq and his son were gigantic, almost as tall as Salah, and enormously fat. Each was draped in a brightly striped silk robe and stuffed into a vest embroidered with threads of gold and silver. Their turbans were pinned with feathered jewels, and as they passed, Luc smelled the heavy scent of precious oils.

Salah was seated, and Luc helped him stand to greet his guests.

"Salaam," said Salah with a low bow. "A rare pleasure. You honor me with your presence. There was no need for these wondrous gifts."

"You honor us, Hakim," said Tariq, bowing as low. "In all the lands where I have traveled, there is no one as learned or as wise as you."

His son, Mohammed, bowed to the old man and proffered a crimson leather folio.

Tariq held up his hand. "Later. *That* gift must be saved for the end of the evening."

Mohammed blushed and handed the book to a servant.

"Now, let our humble meal begin," said Salah. With a snap of his fingers, he directed everyone to sit.

Luc passed a basin of lemon water, and each man washed his hands. Bes appeared from the kitchen with a burnished copper bowl of couscous, which he placed in the center of the table, removing the lid with a bow. Each man dipped his right hand into the aromatic grain and began to eat. Luc followed Bes to the kitchen, and together they returned with the feast. Each dish was fragrant and perfect, and the men ate and talked. Luc and Bes sat just beyond the table with the merchant's servants and waited for Salah and his guests to finish.

"We have just returned from our journeys, wise one," said Mohammed proudly. "We took musk from India to the king of Timbuktu. And now to you, as well."

Mohammed pulled a tiny crystal flask of dark purple grains from the pouch on his belt. Using his thumb and his forefinger, he jimmied out the wooden stopper; for a moment, the air filled with a delightful, earthy smell. He replaced the stopper and handed the bottle to Salah, who turned to hand it to Luc.

"My hands are not trustworthy for something so precious."

"We took musk and many other goods," continued Tariq. "Baskets of Christian wheat and salted fish. Wool cloth from the merchants of Genoa, barrels of wine from Sicily, vats of oily anchovies from Marseille, rice from here. All this we carried by camel caravan through the desert. An endless journey, sleeping through torrid days, traveling by night with burning torches. Finally we reached the salt mines of the Tuareg and their miserable villages of salt bricks and camel skins."

"Dreadful places with bitter water and biting flies," added Mohammed.

Tariq continued. "The slaves in the salt mines last maybe a month. The lucky ones die within their first week."

Bes elbowed Luc in the ribs. "That should have been your fate."

"We traded the Tuareg for great slabs of salt and continued through the desert. The Sahara mocks anyone who pretends to know his way. The wind will take a hill from one spot and throw it to another. Our lives depended on the skill of our blind guide, who plotted our way though the desert with his soul and his heart, and, most importantly, with his nose," said Tariq, tapping the side of his own long nose. "At last, we reached Timbuktu near the River Niger."

"Where we saw crocodiles as big as fishing boats," added Mohammed. "Man-eaters."

"Timbuktu is an impressive city, a Muslim place with an old and massive mosque," continued Tariq. "There is a fine university with many black scholars, and the city is ruled by a learned king. We visited his palace. He is as dark as his ebony throne; a dignified, wise king. But before us, he had an audience with a savage tribe from the south."

Mohammed interrupted, "Cannibals! The king presented them with a slave girl, and they ate her."

Bes clapped his hands. "I hear the palm of the hand is the best cut."

Salah shook his head and put a finger to his lips, and Tariq rolled his eyes and continued.

"I thank Allah that we returned safely and with much

profit. Timbuktu is truly a city of gold. They have so much gold that they will trade it for equal weights of salt. One visit will make a man rich enough for his lifetime."

"That is good, for I never wish to make that journey again," added his son. "The mosquitoes alone nearly bled me to death."

Tariq frowned at Mohammed and turned to his host.

"Salah, even in Timbuktu, your fame is great. We dined with a scholar who asked if we knew of you. I was proud to reply that I counted you among my dearest friends."

"I am honored to be so counted," said Salah.

Then Tariq signaled to Mohammed for the crimson folio. "This I acquired in Genoa. It is a printing of a letter from a Genoan admiral who sailed for the infernal King Ferdinand. May all Ferdinand's ships end their voyages on the bottom of the sea."

Mohammed handed the folio to Salah.

"This is the account of the admiral who crossed the Atlantic and reached the islands off the coast of China," said Mohammed.

Salah raised an eyebrow and smiled. "China? I have heard of this man although I thought he claimed to have reached India by crossing the Atlantic. Either the world is smaller than I thought, or Asia is greater. Perhaps both. In any event, it is a wondrous gift. A great treasure. Luc, take this to my room along with the musk."

As Luc rose, Bes came forward. "Master, I was thinking that you should make a gift to your guests."

Salah frowned.

Bes persisted. "Luc would be an extraordinary addition to their harem."

Bes bowed to Tariq. "*Sayyid*, you must see his golden hair. It rivals the gold you brought from Timbuktu."

Tariq squinted at Luc, who had turned to leave but stopped.

"That slave? Come here," demanded Tariq.

Luc looked at his master, wide-eyed, his heart thumping, his hands suddenly cold. Salah glared at Bes and turned to Tariq.

"I would not dream of it. Bes failed to tell you that the boy is unfortunate. If he removed his turban, you would see that he was born with but one ear."

"One ear?" Mohammed frowned. "Hideous! Why do you keep such a freak?"

"Allah has a reason for all his creations. Who am I to question? I care not if my servants are deformed. It is how they perform that matters," answered Salah.

Tariq shrugged. "Well, the short one has a big mouth."

"Yes," said Salah. "A man's ruin lies in his tongue. I doubt you would want him, but Bes is yours for the asking."

CHAPTER TWENTY-NINE

March Visitors

JANUARY TURNED UNSEASONABLY warm, with bright days and cool nights, but the wind blustered, and the sea was rough. Pons fished occasionally, although since Luc had been taken, he rarely went out in his boat. He fished from the shore, wading in to his knees and casting his net with a twirl. He brought home barely enough fish for himself, Mattie, and Beatrice. Through the dark winter days, he and Beatrice wove baskets and made ropes and mended nets. Mattie was carving a set of chessmen for Saint Olive's new young priest. When Father Émile had visited the cottage in the course of acquainting himself with his new parish, he had been amazed and delighted by her fish. He asked if he might commission her to carve a chess set for him. He described the thirty-two pieces she would have to shape, and Mattie agreed to undertake the work.

"Your talent is a wonder, Mattie. Surely it is a gift from the Lord."

Mattie looked at the young priest with one eye closed and a big smile. "A gift, eh? Well then, I suppose I must make your chess set for free."

Father Émile flashed the silver coin in his palm. "I expected to pay you, Mattie."

She shook her head. "A fortune, that is. But I'd rather have your prayers."

"Especially if you'll pray to the Lord to return Luc to us," said Beatrice.

Mattie sighed and shook her head. "I was thinking of asking for more fish," she muttered under her breath.

Each day, her knife peeled away curls of linden wood until a rook or a bishop or a knight emerged. The rooks looked very much like the Church of Saint Olive, and the bishops resembled Father Émile. He came once during the first week to see her work, twice the second week, and by the third week, the priest in his black cassock was stopping by every afternoon. Each day his smile grew wider.

"The king has the face of a certain fisherman, does he not?" asked the priest one afternoon.

Pons smiled. "I'll wager the queen won't look like that fisherman's sister."

"Don't you take that bet, Father," said Mattie, as she unwrapped an unfinished figure. It was a beautiful queen, and she looked like Beatrice.

"More like a princess," said Pons, and Beatrice rolled her eyes.

Each of Mattie's pawns resembled a different inhabitant of the village of Mouette, and Father Émile delighted in identifying his new parishioners.

One day in early March, the four of them were sitting at the table sharing bread and cheese that Father Émile had brought. Father Émile was teaching Pons and Beatrice about the game of chess. Mattie had no interest in learning.

"Why would I waste good light playing when I could be carving?" she asked.

Before Émile could answer, there was a knock on the door. Cadeau barked. His bark was echoed from outside. All four rose, and Pons opened the door and found two young horsemen. Cadeau was nose to nose with a dog who was almost his twin; but unlike Luc's dog Cadeau, who was brown everywhere except his muzzle, this dog had two white paws. The horsemen were both tall; one had very dark hair, and the other had light brown curls. The man with the curled hair tipped his feathered hat to Pons. He wore a maroon cape and wide charcoal britches with tall leather boots.

"Old man, good day. I am looking for my niece, the lady Beatrice. Are you Pons?"

Pons nodded.

"I am Bertrand, and this is my neighbor, Louis, who had business to attend to nearby."

Pons straightened his shirt and patted his hair down. He bowed. "Sirs, please come in. We have only very humble fare, but you are welcome to share it. Your niece is inside."

Bertrand pointed to Cadeau as the two dogs sniffed each other, tails wagging. "Is that your dog?" he asked.

Pons replied with a puzzled look and pointed to the visitors's dog. "Yours, sir?" he asked.

"No, he belongs to Louis," said Bertrand. "A remarkable likeness. Where is yours from?"

"A long story, sir," answered Pons. "Come inside, please."

The two young men stamped their boots on the stone threshold to knock off any dirt.

"Where is my niece?" asked Bertrand, straining to look beyond Pons, into the cottage.

Beatrice stepped forward.

Bertrand drew in a breath. "Alain did not do you justice when he called you beautiful. For truly, you are astonishing."

He took her hand and kissed it. Beatrice lowered her head and blushed. "Forgive me. I was a boy when you lost your father. Let me make it up to you. I have our family's manor, and you must again call it home." He shook his head. "I do not remember your mother well. I always heard she was pretty, but nothing like you."

He looked at the girl with dark brown hair that tumbled to her waist in shiny curls. She had clear blue eyes, high cheek bones, and full lips. Her skin was creamy except for the pink of her blushing cheeks. Bertrand just stared at her.

The other young man said nothing. He was taller than Bertrand, leaner, with fine dark hair and light eyes. He wore a worn beige doublet and heavy black hose. He had a simple cap, but his boots were high and fine.

Bertrand kissed Mattie's hand. "Dear Mattie, thank you. You must come with my niece, because I was told she will not leave you. You'll have a place of honor in my household."

Mattie bit her lip and took her hand back.

"And Pons?" Bertrand said, bowing deeply to the old man. "You, too, will be most welcome. I cannot repay you for your loyalty and service, but I shall take care of you. You took Beatrice because of nothing more than the goodness of your hearts."

Father Émile said, "Goodness is its own reward."

"Too few recognize that, Father. In any case, I should like Pons and Mattie to come with Beatrice. I have no other family, and neither does my niece. I must confess that I had forgotten she existed until Alain reminded me."

Beatrice spoke. "Thank you. But we must talk about this. Mattie and Pons have a life here in the village. And I don't know if I wish to live close to the Muguets."

"The Muguets?" asked Bertrand. "Don't give *that* family a thought."

"How could I not? I still have nightmares about my father's death."

"Well—" said Bertrand.

But Beatrice continued before he had a chance to say more. "And then there is Luc," she said. "Do you know if Alain told the count about Luc?"

"Ah, yes," said Bertrand, nodding. "The story about the boy. Perhaps we should take Pons up on his offer of refreshment, eh, Louis?"

Bertrand removed his cape and hung it from a peg. He and Louis sat at the table, and Pons joined them along with Beatrice and the priest. Mattie poured wine and sliced more cheese and bread. Bertrand kept looking at Beatrice and shaking his head. Louis removed his hat and held it in his lap. He looked around the cottage at the fish.

"Who carved all this?" he asked, with a wave of his hand. "I've never seen anything like it. Ever."

"Mattie," answered Beatrice.

"Wait," said the priest. "May I show them, Mattie?"

Mattie shrugged, and the priest pushed a wooden box filled with Mattie's chess pieces across the table toward the two visitors.

Louis picked up four or five of the figures, examining each carefully. When he got to the queen, he looked at Beatrice and shook his head. Then he turned to Mattie. "This is your work?"

She nodded.

"You have amazing skill," said Louis. He looked up again at the suspended fish, his mouth half open.

"I'm speechless," said Bertrand. "Speechless."

Mattie said, "Thank you, my lords."

"Oh no," said Bertrand quickly, shaking his head. "I am family, and Louis?" he said, pointing to his companion. "He's just a farmer. You needn't pay him any respect at all."

"Mattie, if you decide to come north with Bertrand, I will pay you to carve for me," said Louis, ignoring Bertrand and still looking at the fish. "I have never seen anything like this."

"You can charge him a lot, Mattie," added Bertrand. "Louis is a *very rich* farmer."

Louis sipped his wine and wiped his mouth on the shoulder of his doublet.

Beatrice watched him.

"May we talk about Luc?" she asked. Bertrand nodded, and Beatrice continued.

"Luc was raised in the hills above this village in an olive grove that was given to his family by the last Count de Muguet."

"That much of the story was confirmed," said Bertrand. "The property was indeed the Muguets', and the old count transferred it to a servant. A groom or some such."

"The count had a second son," continued Beatrice, going to the door and letting in both dogs. She knelt and patted the new dog. Cadeau whined.

"Yes, he was named Francis," said Bertrand. "He died shortly after birth. He is buried in the family's tomb. Except for the current count, all the old count's children are deceased. Two daughters died of plague, thirteen years ago. The same plague that took my parents. The count's daughters are buried in the Muguet tomb with his son, Francis."

"But the count's second son did not die. That infant in the tomb must be the son of the servants who were given the olive grove," said Beatrice, standing and smoothing her gray dress. "Count de Muguet killed their son and forced them to raise Luc, the count's younger son."

"That's absurd. Why would he do such a thing?" asked Bertrand.

"Because the count's son was deformed," said Beatrice.

"Deformed?" asked Bertrand.

"He was born with just one ear."

"Surely someone would be able to confirm that," said Louis.

"Father Thierry could," said Beatrice.

"He is dead," said Louis.

Beatrice watched the two men, especially Louis.

"Is that your dog, Louis?" asked Beatrice.

"Yes."

"Where did you get him?"

"From my father."

"Our dog is remarkably similar, don't you think?" she asked.

"Yes. Surprisingly similar," answered Louis.

"Our dog belongs to Luc. Sir Guy gave him to Luc."

CHAPTER TWENTY-NINE

"That is interesting. Sir Guy, eh?" asked Louis.

"Alain said the puppy was a gift to Sir Guy from the count," said Beatrice.

Louis cocked his head and frowned at the girl.

"From *your father*, my lord," she said to him. "You have the same eyes as your brother, Luc."

CHAPTER THIRTY

Louis

WHEN BEATRICE CONFRONTED the young count, he didn't respond. He said nothing more to anyone. He simply stood up and left the cottage. Bertrand and his friend Louis—who Beatrice had rightly guessed was the new Count de Muguet—had ridden four days, over the mountains and to the sea, to meet her: the beautiful but stubborn Beatrice who had refused her uncle's Christmas invitation. She was far more beautiful than either had expected. Bertrand was amused when the young woman quickly deduced his friend's identity, but he was surprised by the count's silence, and worried when Louis insisted on an abrupt departure.

When they had planned the trip, Louis was simply curious to meet his friend's long-lost niece. Now his thoughts were spinning from the strange, almost magical cottage with the carved fish and the beautiful girl. His father had killed the young woman's father. Wrongly. And the boy named Luc? Louis had hardly listened when the gossipy Alain told him that outrageous tale. Now he was mystified about Luc, and he was intrigued by the boy's dog. Could anyone unravel this tangled history? Since his father's death, Louis had no family. He'd lost his only sisters to the plague; his little brother, Francis, had died after a birth that had taken their mother as well.

Could it be that I have a living brother?

He was afraid to hope.

"My niece didn't offend you, did she, Louis?" asked Bertrand as they mounted their horses.

The young count shook his head but said nothing.

"My niece is exquisite, isn't she?" asked Bertrand as they trotted away from the fishing village. "I had no idea she would be so lovely."

Louis did not respond.

"You're a talkative companion, my friend. Do you promise that Beatrice did not offend you with that absurd talk of a brother?" asked Bertrand.

Louis nodded, but he held up his hand, signaling Bertrand to be quiet.

They rode in silence. For four days, Louis said almost nothing as they traveled, stopping only to eat and sleep, homeward over the mountains and into the valley where both Beatrice and Luc had been born. The branches of the oaks, elms, and beeches had puffed out green buds, and the willows were sending out yellow shoots. Louis's dog trotted happily along, detouring to chase rabbits and squirrels.

When they reached the outer wall of Louis's castle, Bertrand tipped his hat. "You've barely spoken for four days, my friend. What is it?"

"Forgive me," said the young count.

Bertrand smiled. "No need to apologize. Thank you for accompanying me on this journey. I hope to persuade Beatrice to join me in my home," Bertrand said, turning his horse to ride home. "Do you approve?" he called back.

"Yes. That would be good for both of you."

Louis nudged his horse forward, then he pulled back on the reins.

"Bertrand?" he called, turning his horse back around.

"Yes, my lord?" answered Bertrand, stopping and turning in his saddle.

Louis closed his eyes. "Louis, just Louis."

Bertrand grinned, but Louis did not smile. "How many people do you think my father killed?" he asked.

Bertrand looked away from Louis. "With his own sword?" asked Bertrand softly.

"A weighty question," Louis snorted. "You do not have to answer. Farewell, Bertrand."

Louis pulled his horse around again, and trotted into the courtyard. A groom ran to take the horse. Another servant rushed from the château with a mug of wine.

"Fetch Alain. Have him meet me in the large hall," ordered Louis, dismounting and taking a swallow before wiping his mouth on his shoulder.

"Yes, my lord," said the servant.

Louis strode inside, with his dog growling playfully and nipping at his boot heels.

"Good to be home, isn't it?" said Louis, reaching down to scratch behind his dog's ears.

The hall was a large room with tall glass windows and a gilded coffered ceiling. A huge wool-and-silk tapestry hung on one wall showing a life-size hunting scene. Iron torches with thick wax candles guttered on each side of a massive stone fireplace. In front of the hearth were two high-backed wooden armchairs and a polished bench. Louis dropped into a chair and stretched his boots across the bench. His dog lay at his feet. A servant appeared and added logs to the fire.

Another servant bowed and asked, "Are you hungry, my lord?"

"No. Where is Alain?" asked Louis, sipping from the mug.

"Here I am, my lord," said Alain, who had just entered the room. He bowed to Louis. "I trust my directions led you to the fisherman's cottage?"

"Sit," said Louis, sitting up and pointing to the bench.

"Tell me everything you know about the boy called Luc. Anything you've heard."

Alain dropped onto the bench, his large belly settling on his thighs, stretching the cloth of his tunic.

"For his last six years, I was Sir Guy's trusted aide. We visited the boy's house two times every year."

"Was Sir Guy collecting rents for my father?"

Alain cleared his throat. "Not really, my lord. That was the only place where he was involved with your father's rents. That little village of Mouette where Pons lives."

"You collected rents at the olive grove. That wasn't in the same village."

"No, sir. It was odd. The olive grove where the boy lived was in the next village, on a hill, right above Mouette. There were three farms where we collected rents in the hill village. Then we would go down to the fishing village and gather salted fish from your father's tenants there. But we never collected rent at the olive grove. I never thought the rents in either village were anything more than an excuse for Sir Guy to visit the olive grove."

"Why did you think that?" asked Louis, settling back in his chair. His dog sat up and rested his head in his master's lap. Louis stroked his muzzle.

"Well, sir, your father had men whose job it was to collect rents. He didn't waste knights for that. Not someone as important as Sir Guy. And then, of course, when we went to the grove, like I said, we didn't collect rent. We brought gifts."

Alain cleared his throat a few times. His stomach growled, and he patted it and smiled sheepishly.

"Gifts?" asked Louis, sipping from his mug.

"Yes, my lord. Generous gifts. Hams, woolen cloth, casks of wine. That sort of thing. I began to suspect that Luc might be the bastard of Sir Guy."

Louis sat up straight and asked, "Why did you think that?"

"Aside from the gifts and Sir Guy's interest in this family?"

Louis nodded.

"Well, my lord, Sir Guy always talked to the children in the family. The olive grower had three sons, but the oldest, Luc, was different from the other two."

"How?"

"In every way. Sir Guy always spent extra time talking to Luc; he was very partial to that child. He gave the boy that valuable puppy from your father."

Louis nodded and sat back in the chair.

"Luc looked nothing like the younger sons. He had light hair, and he was more delicate. Pascal, the olive grower, and his younger sons are stocky, with heads of dark curls, and dark eyes. Luc had very light eyes."

"Like mine?" asked Louis softly, looking away from Alain and into the fire.

"My lord?"

"Never mind," said Louis, resting his chin in his hand.

"And of course, Luc had only one ear."

"Yes," said Louis, turning to Alain. "Strange."

"That is certain, my lord," said Alain, nodding. "Peculiar to look at—startling, actually—but the boy heard well enough. I got used to it, and there was nothing strange about him otherwise. A handsome, well-spoken lad, but he and the father never got along."

"How do you mean?"

"The father, Pascal, drinks heavily. Never once offered Sir Guy and me a drink, either." Alain looked at Louis's mug hopefully and cleared his throat a few times. "Sorry, my lord, my throat's very dry."

Louis nodded. "Go on, Alain. About the father?"

"Yes, my lord. The father is a mean, unfriendly sort. Over the years I knew him, he got worse. Sir Guy worried that Pascal mistreated the boy. I think he spoke to Pascal about it. But not in front of me. Still, I was shocked to find Luc apprenticed to the old fisherman."

"Yes, why?"

"Well, the olive farm is substantial. A good stone house, too. It seemed odd for the eldest son to leave his father's household and go to that humble cottage. Of course, that happened after Sir Guy's death. I never saw Pascal again after that. I still went to the hill farms and to Mouette, but there were no more gifts, so I didn't visit the olive grove.

Even now I still collect the rents like before, because no one knows why it was set up that way. Probably should use a rent collector, my lord. It makes more sense."

Louis nodded. "I shall look into it."

"Anyway, I like the old man, Pons, so I can see how Luc might prefer him to that father. And then there's that beautiful girl. I mean the lady Beatrice."

"Sir Guy never told you anything about Luc?"

"Never, my lord. Just the opposite. I was ordered never to mention the boy. Not our visits and, especially, not the boy. Or his lack of an ear. Like I said, there was no order to continue the gifts. Probably because it was all so secret. But I kept my word to Sir Guy. I never said anything about Luc. Except, of course, to you, my lord."

"Thank you, Alain. You may go. Stop in the kitchen, and get some food and drink if you like."

Alain grinned, bowed, and left.

Louis called for his steward. He was a middle-aged man of middling height with wispy brown hair. He was dressed in the dark-blue livery of the Muguet family, but unlike the other servants, his tunic was trimmed with silver braid, and he wore a wide leather belt from which dangled a large iron ring with keys of all sizes. He was a quiet man who stepped lightly and spoke softly, but the keys clanked and jangled, so that his presence was always announced before he appeared.

"How long have you worked in this household?" Louis asked, pointing to the bench.

The steward sat on the edge of the bench with his knees locked together and his hands folded tightly in his lap. "Twenty-three years, my lord," said the steward proudly. "I've served as steward for six years, sir."

"Do you remember the last infant my mother bore, before she died?"

"I remember that there was a son who died within days, but I never saw the baby."

"Did you hear anything unusual about the infant?"

"No, my lord."

"Who would have been present for the birth? The midwife?"

The steward started to say something then stopped. He swallowed and picked at a piece of lint on his sleeve.

"What is it?" asked Louis. "What about the midwife?"

"Well, my lord, the midwife died shortly after the birth of the child."

"Died?"

The steward nodded.

"How?" asked Louis.

The steward grimaced.

"Was her death sudden?"

The steward hesitated. "I believe so, my lord."

Louis nodded. "Was the baby baptized?"

The steward pulled at his ear. "I think so. Named, wasn't he?"

"Yes—Francis."

"My father was steward then. He would know more, if he were alive."

"The priest, Father Thierry, is no longer living, either. Who else might have helped with the birth or with the infant?" asked Louis.

The steward put a finger to his lips and thought. "Well, Father Thierry had an assistant, but he's been gone at least fifteen years. Left around the time your mother died, I think. And the wet nurse moved away, about the same time. I can't recall her name, but maybe I can find that out."

"Check with everyone who was here. Let me know if there is anyone who might know about the baby."

"Anything in particular my lord?" asked the steward, keys banging as he stood up.

"Everything," answered Louis.

CHAPTER THIRTY-ONE

Promises

THE GRAY-AND-RED parrot sat on Luc's shoulder, where it had perched ever since it had been given to Salah by Tariq five weeks earlier. Luc had constructed a hanging roost in a corner of Salah's room and another in the kitchen, high enough to be safe from Cat. But usually, the bird sat on the boy's shoulder.

Luc had begun teaching the bird greetings and small talk in French.

Salah sighed. "I should punish you, Luc, for teaching the bird anything but Arabic."

Luc tipped his head. "But then the bird could talk to Bes."

Salah frowned. "Ah, Luc. He who seeks a flawless friend remains friendless."

"Master, you have said that the rain wets the leopard's skin, but it will not wash out the spots."

"I also said, if there were no fault, there would be no pardon. Bes has tried to be civil with you for months, but you remain unfriendly."

"But—"

"No, Luc. I know Bes was cruel to you."

"Very."

Luc was dusting the books on Salah's desk. He turned his face to the bird on his shoulder, and the parrot nuzzled the boy.

Salah steepled his hands. "Bes felt threatened."

"By me? A powerless slave?"

Salah put up a hand. "Your relentless self-pity blinds you."

"Blinds me to what?"

"To what you have. I no longer blame Bes. It is you who are wrong."

"He still has my ear."

"Your ear?" Salah pushed himself back from the desk, and the chair legs squealed on the tile floor.

"My wooden ear," said Luc.

"Have you asked for it back?"

"No."

"Because you rarely speak to him?"

"He knows I want it back. It's mine."

Salah shook his head. "He waits for you to ask, and you

wait for him to give? Allah has no mercy for those who have no mercy for their fellow man."

Luc frowned and brought the bird to the perch, where it sat whistling and singing. Salah was rubbing his hands together, blowing into them.

"Shall I light a fire, master?" asked Luc.

Although it was a mild day in April, and the room was comfortable, Salah nodded. As Luc knelt to light the charcoal in the iron brazier, Salah handed the boy a brown nugget.

"Drop this into the fire, Luc."

"What is it, master?" asked Luc, examining the opaque lump in his hand.

"Myrrh. The tears of a thorn tree."

"Tears?"

"It is the sap of an Arabian tree. The myrrh soothes, and the charcoal warms. I am very cold today."

Bes entered the room, and the parrot began to squawk. The little man stood on his toes and spoke gently to the bird, but when he extended his finger, the parrot chomped down and drew blood. Bes yelped, and put his bleeding finger into his mouth.

Luc said nothing.

"Damn both you and that infernal creature," the little man snarled at Luc. Before he could say any more, there was a crash, and Salah slumped to the floor.

Luc and Bes rushed to help the old man, who had struck

his head on a corner of his table; blood pulsed from a gash on his forehead. Luc pressed a cloth against the cut to stanch the flow. Bes positioned a pillow under Salah's head and tried to make him comfortable on the floor.

"Press this against his wound," ordered Luc, handing the cloth to Bes. Luc tucked a blanket around the old man and rushed to fill the silver pitcher. He washed Salah's bloody face. Salah's eyes fluttered, and he looked at the boy fearfully for a moment. Then he closed his eyes again. Luc checked the wound. Bes watched.

Luc said, "It's not a deep cut."

"But there was so much blood," said Bes, wrinkling his nose.

"The bleeding has already stopped. I'll clean the cut and wrap his head. The wound doesn't need to be stitched."

"The master has never been the same since that day you treated Ibi's cheek," said Bes softly.

Salah opened his eyes and blinked a few times. Luc bent close.

"Can you speak, master?" asked Luc.

Salah tried, but he only uttered garbled sounds.

"Raise your right hand," said Luc.

The old man closed his eyes, and lifted his right hand just barely above his lap.

"The left hand?" asked Luc gently.

The old man closed his eyes again, and nothing happened.

Luc took Salah's left hand in his own.

"Can you squeeze my finger?" he asked.

Nothing happened. Salah closed his eyes.

Bes whispered in Luc's ear. "It's much worse this time, right?"

Luc chewed his lip. "I don't know."

Bes began to sob. "Salah is my life. What am I to do?"

The old man stirred and looked at Bes. He tried to talk, but still nothing came out as a word.

"Hush," said Luc to both Bes and Salah. "You need to rest, Salah. We'll stay right here with you."

"Good night," piped the bird in a baby voice from his perch. "Pretty bird."

Bes shook his head. "Damn bird."

Luc half smiled at the little man. "At least he hasn't broken into song."

Bes took a deep breath and smiled back. The old man was watching Bes and Luc, and he smiled crookedly—only the right side of his mouth turned up.

Luc squinted at Salah, and Salah closed his eyes.

"He might sleep now," said Luc. "Stay with him, Bes. Call me if he stirs. I'll brew him some willow-bark tea. Then I can take over the watch." Luc offered the bird his finger, and the creature hopped on and toddled up his arm to his shoulder.

"I'll be back soon," Luc told Bes.

So they took turns sitting with the old man as he slept

fitfully through the morning. At the call for the midday prayer, Salah awoke and sipped the tea that Luc held to his lips. He was bewildered; he raised his right hand to his head and touched the bandage. His left arm dangled, and the left side of his face drooped. Luc reached for Salah's right hand, and the old man's fingers tightened over the boy's hand.

"Are you feeling any better, master?"

The old man locked eyes with Luc. "Worse thith time," he whispered.

Luc nodded. "Yes."

Salah let go of Luc's hand and tapped his bandage.

Luc said, "You hit your head. The cut is clean and shallow. It should heal quickly."

The old man whispered, "Promith."

"Promise what?" asked Luc.

The old man blinked. "Stay till I die."

"I am your slave," said Luc. "You don't need my promise."

"No. Promith."

"I promise, Salah. For the rest of your life, I shall be right here. Even if I could, I would not leave you," said Luc, and he covered his heart with his right hand.

Salah nodded. "When I die, you'll be free."

The old man closed his eyes. Luc said nothing, but he felt the rush of heat to his cheeks and the quickened beat of his heart. He took a deep breath and looked at Salah, but the old man was already asleep.

CHAPTER THIRTY-TWO

Reading

SPRING WAS ENDING, and heat thickened the air. Salah improved, but he did not recover. His speech had returned, but his left arm and the left side of his face were paralyzed; he could shuffle only a few steps with a cane. One morning in late May, with Bes's help, Luc settled Salah in the courtyard, where they piled pillows in an alcove that faced the bubbling fountain. The caged birds sang, and the garden was filled with bright roses. Luc was reading aloud a story about Sinbad the Sailor from a glorious manuscript that Salah had acquired in Egypt many years before. It was richly illustrated with depictions of sea voyages, monsters, and treasures. Though he stumbled often, Luc was growing to love reading these tales of adventure.

"Well done, Luc," said Salah when the boy reached the tale's end. "It's lovely to listen to Sinbad while sitting here on a silk cushion, but if I were a young man, I would travel. I would venture beyond the ends of the known world. When I am gone, Luc, cross the Atlantic. I would give anything to be a part of that adventure."

Luc closed the book. "I may, Salah. But first I will return and see Pons and his sister and Beatrice."

"Is she beautiful, this Beatrice?"

"Very," said Luc, blushing.

"The whisper of a pretty girl is heard farther away than the lion's roar."

"Was there never a pretty woman for you, Salah?" asked Luc.

Salah closed his eyes. "I was always too deep in my studies. I never bothered to know anyone very well."

"Except Bes."

The old man smiled at Luc. "Yes. And now you."

Luc was silent for a while.

Salah tugged at his beard. "After you have visited the fisherman and his wife—"

"His sister," corrected Luc.

"The fisherman and his sister and the beautiful Beatrice—after you have visited them, Luc, what will you do?"

"I shall visit my mother and my brothers."

"And your father?"

"I don't know if he is my father. But yes. Even him."

"Can it be, my boy, that you have learned to forgive?"

"I don't know, master."

A lopsided smile spread on Salah's face.

"The wisest man is the one who can forgive," said Salah.

Luc smiled. "Do you know whom I really miss?"

Salah asked, "Is there yet another girl?"

Luc shook his head. "I miss my dog."

"Such an odd race, with your pet dogs. How you cling to your primitive ways, Luc! Stubborn you remain."

"But not obstinate?"

"You have a fine mind, Luc. Much too fine to just fish and repair nets."

Luc said, "I think I would have been a good fisherman."

"I have no doubt of that," said the old man. "After I am gone, I know you will go home, but not to fish."

"No, not to fish. I don't know what I'll do. But I still have much to learn from you. I don't expect to go home soon."

"Death rides a fast horse."

"In your case, I hope he has fallen from the horse."

"At least for a little while longer, yes, my boy?"

"Yes, master."

Salah nodded. "It is in the hands of Allah. Will you consider a proposition from me?"

Luc raised his eyebrows. "A proposition?"

"Yes, there is something I want you to do after I am gone."

CHAPTER THIRTY-TWO

"Of course."

"Take Bes."

"Bes?"

"Yes." The old man nodded. "He will be lost without me."

Luc arched his brows and bit his lip.

"You have come to understand him. He is loyal and skilled, but he has no sense of the world. He would not last long on his own, despite his quick tongue."

"Because of his quick tongue," said Luc.

"Yes," said Salah. "The safety of a man is in the sweetness of his tongue. Bes's tongue is sharp; it will bring him harm. Will you take him with you?"

"What do I have to offer Bes?"

"More than you know, Luc. More than you ever dreamed."

CHAPTER THIRTY-THREE

May's Move

LUC HAD BEEN gone for more than a year—twice the time he had lived with Pons and Mattie. The heart-shaped leaves of the linden were green and open, and the sky was the cloudless pale blue of a matchless May morning. Beatrice sat on the bench with her back to the now empty cottage, staring at the sea. She held a letter in one hand and with the other, she picked at berries in a basket on her lap. She wondered what Luc would do if he returned. Father Émile had promised to tell the boy where they had moved. But if he came back, would Luc move north with them? She knew he loved fishing and the sea.

Mattie tucked her hair into her hat and sat down on the bench. She was wearing her better dress, slate wool with a wide band of brown wool along the hem of the skirt. Underneath, she wore a plain linen smock that was gathered at her neck with a drawstring. She fixed a new ribbon around the crown of the wide-brimmed straw hat that she had made for Beatrice.

"I'll miss these sounds," said Beatrice.

"Noisy gulls?" asked Mattie.

Beatrice nodded and said, "I love the smell of this wind."

"And the fish? Pshaw," said Mattie, pinching her nose. "Wait until you smell the pine trees and the fields of lavender and rosemary."

"This is a good thing, Mattie, isn't it? Moving north?"

"Yes, Beatrice," answered Mattie, but her voice was husky, and she wiped away a tear.

In April, Bertrand had sent a messenger to Beatrice repeating his offer to come live with him. Beatrice had finally sent a note back accepting her uncle's invitation because she realized that Pons was struggling now to put food on their table. She had also included a letter to the count about Luc. Yesterday, Bertrand had arrived with a servant, horses, a mule driver in the Muguet blue, and four mules to move his niece and Mattie and Pons north. He also carried a reply from Louis to Beatrice.

Mattie elbowed Beatrice. "Those berries were your favorites when you were a little girl."

Beatrice looked at the basket filled with deep-red strawberries, none bigger than a pea, a gift from Bertrand's garden.

She put two strawberries in her mouth and tried to remember.

Mattie and Beatrice watched as Bertrand and his servant loaded the four pack mules. Two mules were carrying nothing but Mattie's fish carvings for the young count.

"Why does he want my fish?" Mattie had asked Bertrand. "He's offered me a fortune for them."

"He's talked about your cottage and the fish ever since our visit. When he heard you were moving, he started to prepare a room for them in the castle."

"Well, I am glad then," said Mattie. "I may carve something else for my new home."

Bertrand was dressed in a willow-green jacket that fell mid-thigh, with a ruffled linen tunic and fawn-colored hose. He wore short boots and a brown felt hat that sported two green rooster tail feathers.

Mattie motioned with her chin and whispered to Beatrice, "He is a bit of dandy, isn't he?"

The girl smiled and nodded.

Mattie rolled her eyes and tossed a few strawberries into her mouth. She motioned at Pons with her chin. "My brother has never been on a horse, but he says it can't be worse than the boat in a gale."

"Bertrand promised these mares are gentle, slow walkers," said Beatrice, folding the letter from Louis.

"Well, what did the young count say?" asked Mattie, peeking at the letter. "Aside from wanting my fish? What does the count say about Luc?"

"My letter didn't persuade him that Luc is his brother."

"So he won't help?" asked Mattie. She reached down and picked a couple of buttercups that she spotted by her foot. Mattie tucked the flowers into a ribbon on the crown of Beatrice's hat.

"Actually, he will," said Beatrice, opening the letter again. "He's decided to search for Luc anyway; he's hired agents."

"Why, if he thinks the boy's not his brother?" asked Mattie.

Beatrice pointed to a line in the letter. "He says injustices were done by his father."

"Injustices? That's a pretty word for it," said Mattie, looking over the girl's shoulder at the meaningless marks on the page.

Beatrice took a deep breath. "He's Luc's only chance."

"True, but if the boy *is* found, he'll have you to thank. Luc's been gone a long time, and not a day goes by you don't think about him," said Mattie.

"I've felt so helpless, Mattie. And now I'm a little scared. What lies ahead? For us?"

"I don't know, Beatrice. You and your uncle are saving us all."

"You saved me first."

Mattie put her arm around the girl. "But it is Pons and me who need saving now. We wouldn't be able to pay the rent for much longer. Pons is too old for the sea. And done with it.

My brother never got over losing Luc. He blames himself for not being strong enough to save the boy."

"If Pons had been stronger, they'd have taken him too."

Mattie nodded. "Maybe. In any case, your uncle's invitation is our salvation. For all his fancy clothes, Bertrand seems a good man."

"I think so," said Beatrice. "Generous."

She watched Bertrand as Pons and the mule driver loaded the last of the mules. She liked the way her uncle talked to Mattie and Pons.

"Your father was a generous man, Beatrice. But gambling was his ruin. Bertrand has his brother's good side without the bad."

Beatrice laughed, "I think he would rather spend his money on feathers than gambling."

Mattie elbowed Beatrice and nodded. "He'll find you a husband, and then I'll take care of your children. If I'm not too old."

Beatrice and Mattie rose as Bertrand patted Pons on the back and walked over to them.

"Ready to mount up?" he asked. "We have at least four long days ahead of us."

"Here's your hat," said Mattie, handing it to Beatrice. "You tie it tight."

Beatrice kissed Mattie on the forehead and sighed, "Mattie insists on treating me like a lady."

"As she should," said Bertrand.

Mattie covered her mouth and held a finger up. Then she turned and went into the cottage. Beatrice tied the hat and followed her, and they looked around for the last time. With the beams stripped of fish, the cottage was empty and still. The dirt floor was dry, and there was a bitter tang in the air; the walls nearest the hearth were smoke-smudged and dark. Beatrice climbed the loft ladder for a last look through the little window where she had watched the moon for more than eight years. She backed down and looked over to the corner of the room where Luc used to sleep. Mattie took her arm, and they stepped outside and hugged each other.

"I've been happy here, Mattie. I dread going back to the north. I have some ugly memories."

"I know, Beatrice. But that was a long time ago."

Bertrand watched the women and turned away. He linked his fingers and cupped his hands and helped Pons mount his horse. Up in the saddle, Pons looked toward the sea, where sunlight quivered on the water.

"I've lived here all my life. Thought I'd live here forever," said Pons.

Bertrand patted the old man's leg and said, "I hope you'll love the mountains, Pons."

"What about Luc? Has the count really begun to look for him?" asked Pons.

"At great expense."

Beatrice overheard her uncle's answer as she and Mattie mounted their mares.

"Why *is* the count searching for Luc?" asked Beatrice later as she rode away from Mouette alongside her uncle. "Since he doesn't believe Luc is his brother."

"I don't really know. Maybe it's your mermaid spell," answered Bertrand, smiling at his niece.

Beatrice shook her head, and Bertrand continued, "Louis has no doubt that his real brother is buried in the family tomb, but he's hired agents in Genoa who have African contacts. Still, Beatrice, how do you find one boy across a wide sea?"

"He'll be found for the very reason that his father disposed of him."

"I don't understand," said Bertrand.

"He is the boy with one ear. That makes him unforgettable."

Beatrice twisted strands of her mount's mane around her fingers. When she last rode a horse, Beatrice had been a little girl on a small pony. Now, she relaxed into the saddle of the black mare and rolled with its comfortable gait. Bertrand complimented her riding. As they rode farther from the sea and higher into the hills, the land was greener and the air was cooler. The lemon, orange, and mulberry trees of the coast gave way to chestnuts and walnuts, oaks and pines. Beatrice was wearing her gray dress with her linen undersmock. She was cold, and she rubbed her arms.

"You're chilled?" asked Bertrand, and he reached into a saddlebag and produced a lavender wool cape. She swung the cape over her shoulders.

"Thank you, Uncle. I don't think I ever thanked you for the beautiful cape you sent last Christmas."

He said nothing, but he smiled broadly, and they rode without speaking until the sun was at its highest, and Bertrand pointed to a pair of shade trees near a moving stream. "We'll rest here. The horses need water, and I need bread."

Beatrice was warm as she dismounted, but when she tried to return the cape to her uncle, he refused.

"Keep it, Beatrice. I like to see you in a color. You must have some new clothes for your new life."

Beatrice said nothing as she folded the cape, tucked it under her arm, and sat down. She untied her hat and shook her hair free. Pons and Mattie were walking together, stretching and stopping to rub at shoulders and calves. Beatrice watched them and worried that she had taken them from their home, from her home. Had she made a terrible mistake accepting her uncle's offer? Did she really have another choice? She smoothed her dress and straightened her sleeves. Then she looked at Bertrand and found he was looking at her as he chewed his bread. His servant had spread a cloth and produced cheese and sausage and bread from one of the mule packs.

"How shall I fill my days in your house?" Beatrice asked.

"*Our* house."

"Until you have a wife."

"I'm in no hurry. You shall have a husband well before I marry. *If* I marry. You are very beautiful. And we are an old family. Thanks to Louis, our name has been cleared."

"But I have lived as a peasant since my father's death. Mattie brags that I can read and write, but I read no better than a child. I don't know how to be a lady, and I have no property."

"Perhaps I can persuade Louis to help me provide you with a suitable dowry."

"Why would he do that?" asked Beatrice, breaking off some bread to feed Cadeau.

Bertrand shrugged.

"More atonement?" she asked. After Beatrice fed him some bread and some of the cheese, Cadeau lay down next to her and fell asleep so soundly he began to snore. She stroked his head.

Bertrand patted the dog a couple of times and said, "You can't fault Louis for that, Beatrice. Because of him, our family has the manor back, but we are anything but rich. Besides, his wealth is enormous. He's making amends for the deeds of his father."

Mattie and Pons joined Beatrice and Bertrand, and after everyone had eaten and drunk and rested, they continued their journey. Toward sunset, Beatrice dropped back and plodded along with Mattie and Pons. Mattie reminisced about their journey almost nine years earlier, when she and Beatrice struggled on foot over the hills and the mountains to the sea. It was a hard journey but Mattie had been determined to return home, and little Beatrice had never whined.

"You were just a seed of a girl," said Mattie.

"Nothing more than a sardine," added Pons. "I couldn't believe my eyes when the two of you straggled into the yard. You and that skinny little girl."

"But that little girl could already read," said Mattie, shaking her head.

"They breed them smart up north," said Pons. "Luc was a quick one, too."

"He couldn't read," said Mattie.

"He could read the fish and the sky as well as anyone. That boy had eyes like no one else. Saw things way before most men. Born to fish," said Pons.

The journey home was slower than Bertrand had expected. Each day before sunset, Bertrand's servant found a farm or a monastery where they could lodge for the night.

On the fourth day, they passed through an empty village. The thatch was gone from the roofs, and the walls of most of the houses were crumbling or fallen. The fields were returning to forest. Bertrand pointed to the remains of a chapel.

"This village lost everyone in the terrible black death a century and a half ago."

Beatrice said. "I've heard stories. And that was the same sickness that took my grandmother and grandfather when I was two."

"My parents." Bertrand nodded. "The plague still comes back now and then." He glanced at his niece and added, "You and I are all that's left of the family now."

Family? wondered Beatrice. Mattie and Pons had been her family for more than half her life. Here was this stranger who was her only blood relative, talking about family. "You weren't there when the count killed my father, were you?" she asked him.

"No, Beatrice."

She nodded but said nothing more.

Pons was increasingly stiff from riding, and on the fifth morning he asked to walk a bit. Beatrice joined him. For a while Bertrand rode ahead, but he, too, dismounted and walked. Only Mattie refused to dismount.

"I vowed I'd never do this walk again, and I am not going to break that vow."

On the sixth day, as the afternoon sky blushed, they crested a green hillside dotted with sheep. Spread below was Bertrand's honey-colored stone manor amid an orchard of white pear blossoms. The old mares broke into a trot as they neared the stable. Beatrice was quiet, seeing paths and trees she had not thought of for years. She pulled her mount to a stop as memories of her childhood and her parents flooded back. She closed her eyes, fighting tears. Mattie trotted up, bouncing precariously on her plump mare, and reached for the girl.

"It's lovely. We were happy here before. We will be happy again."

Pons had lagged behind. When his horse caught up on the hilltop, he turned to his sister.

"Is that the place?" he asked.

Mattie nodded.

As the sun set, Pons watched the distant hills go from gold to blue. He scanned the valley and turned to Bertrand, a wide smile spreading on his old face.

"Thank you."

Bertrand smiled, and taking the reins in one hand, he gestured across the horizon, from left to right, with an outstretched palm. "Home."

CHAPTER THIRTY-FOUR

Inland

WHEN BEATRICE WAS a child, she and Mattie had shared a small, sunny room in the manor. Now, Bertrand led Beatrice to a different chamber, a large room with a tall chest, a high wooden bed, and a glazed window that overlooked a green meadow with a ragged brook.

Mattie and Pons were settled into a cottage near the kitchen garden. Mattie was delighted to find a stack of fruitwood, a new set of tools, and a bench outside where she could work on fine days. Bertrand had propped a fishing pole against the cottage door.

"Bertrand says there's a stream with trout as big as my arm," said Pons, picking up the pole; his voice cracked.

"He's a good man," said Mattie.

Pons nodded.

"Generous and easy," said Mattie.

Tired from the long journey, Mattie, Pons, Beatrice, and even Cadeau slept soundly that night. The next morning, Beatrice was strolling in the kitchen garden with Bertrand when Mattie and Pons, carrying the fishing pole, joined them. Bertrand was showing his niece the herbs, stumbling to identify the plants. Beatrice supplied the correct names for him.

"Our Beatrice knows her herbs. She is a wonder in the garden," said Mattie.

Bertrand nodded. "I am beginning to gather that, Mattie. Are you and Pons well settled?"

Mattie answered, "Gloriously. But it's strange to be back."

Pons just stood twirling the fishing pole and nodding.

Bertrand said, "The count invited all of us to come to the castle to hang Mattie's carvings."

"Surely not today?" said Mattie. "I'm weary, and I can't see my brother climbing back up on a horse without more rest."

"Of course. Louis can wait a few days more, though to tell you the truth, he has been most impatient to hang the carvings."

Beatrice said nothing.

A few more days passed, and one evening Bertrand and Beatrice shared a simple late supper with Pons and Mattie in the manor house kitchen. With its two sleeping chambers, and its hall with four glazed windows, the house was far grander than the fishing cottage. There were also several tenant cottages and a massive stone barn. But the large kitchen was the heart of the manor, and the place where meals for the servants and the master were eaten. The kitchen shelves were filled with crocks and baskets; sausages and hams hung from hooks on the rafters along with braids of garlic and bunches of drying herbs. Most evenings, everyone gathered by the kitchen hearth, with Bertrand in the only high-backed chair.

Beatrice dragged her hand along the polished table edge; she looked up at Mattie, who watched from across the table. When Beatrice began picking at a hangnail, Mattie covered the girl's hand with her own.

"I won't go. I can't return to the place my father was murdered," said Beatrice. "I still have nightmares about that morning. I'll never go back there."

"I understand," said Mattie.

Beatrice snapped her fingers under the table, and Cadeau lumbered over and put his head in her lap. She patted him. Bertrand cleared his throat but let the matter drop without a word.

The next morning, Bertrand, Pons, and Mattie set off. The manor house was a half morning's ride from the ancient Muguet castle. Long before they arrived, Bertrand pointed in the distance to the tall feudal towers that had been begun four centuries earlier by the first Count de Muguet when he returned from the first crusade. The party rode on, through an arched gateway into the infamous courtyard that Mattie, like Beatrice, dreaded seeing again. Everything had been altered, and Mattie was relieved to find a garden covering the courtyard and large new windows added to the château. The wide door was open. Out bounded the brown-and-white dog and his tall owner, Louis, Count de Muguet.

"Welcome," he said.

Three grooms in dark-blue tunics rushed to take the horses.

"Where is Beatrice?" asked the count.

"She's tired from the journey," said Bertrand.

"Still?" asked the count. "Perhaps next time." He turned to Mattie and Pons. "Welcome to my home. I haven't opened the bundles of your carvings, Mattie. I've waited for you. You must see the room I have prepared. Come."

As Mattie stepped inside the great hall, she stopped. She looked up and around, and she shook her head. The château was still a part of a vast ancient fortress, but light from the new glazed windows played across recently tiled black, rose, and cream floors. Mattie stepped into a pool of shimmering sunlight. She touched the bright new tapestries that hid the cold stone walls. She smelled beeswax and flowers. The place was the same but different, as different as this son was from his father. Louis beckoned, and they hurried along the hall to a staircase that spiraled up a round turret. Iron wall torches lit the way.

Louis climbed only three steps before he turned. "Forgive me, I should have asked if you were thirsty, but I wanted you to see the room. Shall we take refreshment first?"

"No, my lord," said Mattie with a chuckle. "Let me see where my fish will swim."

Louis rushed up the tower stairs taking two steps at a time and, at the top, he stopped at a small doorway. Pons and Mattie were breathless from the climb.

Bertrand brought up the rear. "Well, my friend, I don't think I have seen you this excited since we were boys. Open the door."

Louis turned to Mattie. "Please Mattie, I'm not good with words, but your fish are a treasure. I started to prepare this room as soon as I heard you would be moving. I prayed you would let me buy your carvings." Louis sighed and shook his head and sighed again. "That they are now mine, that perhaps one day I will have children who—well, I . . ." And he opened the door.

No one said a word. The round room was small, but its walls were pierced with large windows. The windows had leaded panes of turquoise, sapphire, cobalt, sky, and pale-blue glass. The floor was sand-colored tile, and the blue-painted ceiling was hatched with pegged wooden beams. Sunlight dappled the stone walls and the floor with all the blues from the windows, and the room glimmered.

"Pegs to hang the fish," said Louis, pointing to the ceiling. "Is there something else I should do?"

Pons was wide-eyed and speechless, but Mattie watched the count and began to laugh.

"This room won't do at all, my lord," said Mattie, stifling her laughter and wiping her eyes with her sleeve.

The count went pale. Bertrand's jaw dropped, and he removed his jaunty cap.

"You can't be serious, Mattie," said Bertrand, stroking his hat feathers.

"I can't be serious?" asked Mattie. She laughed again, harder. "I'm not even a bit serious. This is the most wondrous place I have seen in my long life. It's like standing on the floor of the sea. All you need is a mermaid."

"A mermaid? Can you carve one?" asked the count.

Mattie jammed her tongue in her cheek and looked up at the ceiling. "For now, let's get the fish swimming."

With Mattie's direction, three servants began to hang her carved fish, using blue silk thread. Pons squeezed himself against a wall, but Louis and Bertrand kept getting in the way, and Mattie banished everyone except the servants. The count and Bertrand took Pons to see the castle and the grounds.

When the three men returned, Louis dashed up the stairs and pounded at the tower door.

Mattie answered, "Not yet, sir. I'll send one of my helpers to fetch you."

"How much longer?" asked Louis.

"Soon, my lord, soon," said Mattie.

"But—"

"Before the sun sets; trust me."

Pons and Bertrand waited at the bottom of the tower stairs and followed the count into the great hall, where he dropped into his favorite chair. The spring day was warm, so there was no fire burning. Instead, the hearth was spread with sweet greens and flower petals.

Wine and fruit were set out on a table. Pons had never been in a place like the château, had never met a nobleman, other than Sir Guy, but as the day wore on, he liked the young count more and more. Louis had asked the old man about fishing in the sea, and he had taken Pons to see where he fished for trout. The old man was fascinated by the eel pond, and the count had delighted in showing him the gardens and parkland around the castle. Now Pons sat in the hall, cutting an early peach, listening and nodding his head, as the two younger men tried to engage him in their conversation.

"My father increased our holdings significantly, but the castle has been in our family beyond memory, just as the manor always belonged to Bertrand and Beatrice's family," said the young count, smiling at Pons.

"It's been a long while since anyone added to my family's holdings. And Étienne gambled away all that was left," said Bertrand, sitting down in the other chair by the fireplace.

"My father made it easy for a man to lose," answered Louis. He stood and began to pace about the hall.

Bertrand twirled his feathered hat in his hands and watched his impatient friend. Louis sighed and dropped again into his chair across from Bertrand.

Bertrand stretched over and patted Louis's shoulder. "You are a good man."

Count de Muguet held his goblet with both hands and sipped his wine. He looked over at the windows in the hall. "The light is beginning to fade. I hoped to see the room in daylight today. I like the way the sun hits the windows."

A smiling servant appeared in the hall and announced that the room was finished; Louis bolted up to the tower room, where Mattie stood outside the closed door. She curtsied and opened the door.

Louis clapped his hands, and everyone—Mattie, Pons, Bertrand, and the servants—began to clap and cheer. The room was a wonder.

CHAPTER THIRTY-FIVE

The Captain Visits

SALAH WAS FAILING. His mind remained sharp, but, even with help, he was no longer able to walk. Each morning, Bes and Luc propped Salah in his room on a carpeted platform with bolsters and pillows. As word of his decline spread, there were fewer visitors and patients, but neither Salah nor Luc was sorry, as the old man's diminishing energy was spent teaching the boy. One sunny morning in early July, Luc was showing Salah new tricks he had taught the parrot.

"How would you like to live with Bes?" he asked the bird, which was perched on his finger.

The bird spread its clipped wings and flittered to the carpet next to Salah. It rolled onto its back with its feet in the air and was still.

"You would rather be dead?" asked Luc, bending down to the bird.

The parrot hopped back onto Luc's finger and nodded enthusiastically.

"Show Salah where you want to go."

Clasping the boy's finger with its feet, the bird rotated in a full circle; when it was again upright on Luc's finger, it puffed out its chest and sang out in Arabic, "Around the world!"

Salah clapped his right hand to his thigh. "Wonderful," he whispered.

The parrot fluttered up to Luc's shoulder and nuzzled the boy's cheek with its gray beak.

"Such a smart creature," said Salah. "Bes is envious. He cannot make friends with that parrot. But you have a way."

"I have a secret," said Luc, dumping the contents of a sack into his palm, displaying a handful of shelled nuts and dried bits of fruit.

"I should have known," said the old man.

Bes appeared at the doorway with a visitor. Luc was startled to recognize the captain of the dhow, the slaver who had stolen him from his old life. He blinked and breathed deeply.

The captain bowed to Salah, and then he pointed to Luc.

"The blond boy has grown a cubit. I should have bargained harder."

Salah answered, "He was underfed and filthy."

"That is how I found him. In a broken-down boat with a worthless old man."

"There is always an answer, but it is not always correct," said Salah.

The captain took a step back. "May we speak in private, Hakim?"

"Leave us, Luc," said Salah with a wave of his hand.

With the parrot on his shoulder, Luc backed out of the room and found Bes in the kitchen.

"Did you invite that slaver here?" asked Luc angrily. "Are you still trying to have me sold?"

"No," said Bes. "I had nothing to do with his visit. He came to the door and asked to see the master. But he came about you."

"And why do you think that?" rasped Luc.

"Because he asked me if the slave with one ear was still here. He asked many questions, all about you."

"Like what?"

"He wanted to know if Salah was happy with you."

"And your answer?"

"I said you were slothful and as stupid as a walnut."

"For once you have done me a favor."

"I have done many favors for you, locust."

Bes poured goat's milk into a shallow bowl and set it down for Cat. Luc collapsed to the floor, wrapping his arms about his knees and putting his head down. The parrot sat on his shoulder and started to hum.

CHAPTER THIRTY-FIVE

Bes spit on the floor. "Quiet, stupid bird."

"Shhh," said Luc to the parrot. Then he looked at the little man. "Am I in danger, Bes?"

"What kind of danger?"

"The old man promised me my freedom. He wouldn't sell me, would he?"

"I don't think he'll sell you, but what do I know?"

"More than you say," said Luc, turning the metal band on his ankle.

Bes winked at the boy. "I'll see what I can learn."

"I may need your help."

"You have always needed my help. But the old man needs you. I need him. You need me. We are a circle."

"A strange circle."

"Old man, short man, freak."

Luc frowned.

"I'll go to the market later. Maybe I'll find that giant Berber with the kola teeth."

"Hassan. He was kinder than the captain."

"Everyone is kinder than the captain."

"Everyone but you," said Luc.

"Ha! I like that," said Bes, rubbing his hands together. "I have always wanted to be known for something other than my height. Stay with the old man. I will see what I can learn." He handed Luc a dish of honey in a pool of olive oil and a fist-sized round of warm, salted bread for Salah.

As soon as Luc heard the captain leave, he returned to

Salah's room, where he found the old man sleeping. Luc sat by the window, with the bird on his shoulder, and thought about home. He watched the old man's fitful breathing. Looking about the room, he saw the beautiful mosaic tiles he had scrubbed, the intricate woolen rugs he had cleaned and beaten. He saw the high table where he had lanced abscesses and splinted legs, where he had stitched Ibi's cheek. He looked at Salah's piles of books, many of which he could now read. He saw the globe that he and Salah had created. Luc considered his months in this house. He was now in his second year of bondage. Except it wasn't really bondage. As Salah had promised, Luc had been given a gift. He had known nothing of the world—nothing of geography or science or math or medicine. He hadn't been able to read, and he had never heard a poem. He hadn't even known that he wanted to know things. In his old life he had mastered olives, pigs, and fish; he had always been keen to do tasks well. Now he realized that he wanted more than skills: he wanted understanding. He wanted knowledge. That was the old man's gift to him.

When Luc heard Bes return, he rushed to the kitchen, where he found the little man sweeping the ashes from the fireplace.

"What did you learn?"

Bes hesitated.

"You learned something; I can see it in your face," said Luc, snatching the broom.

"What do you see, stupid Christian? Do you think you can read my Egyptian face?" asked Bes, turning his back to Luc.

"You found out something that you don't want to tell me."

Bes wrinkled his nose, and turned to face Luc. "I am not sure that I learned anything."

"Tell me, so I can judge."

"You?"

"Please, Bes?" asked Luc, laying the broom against the wall.

"Give me the bird," said Bes, pointing to the parrot on Luc's shoulder.

"The bird belongs to Salah."

Bes held out his finger and was bitten again.

"Ouch! Feathered fiend!"

Then Bes leaned close the parrot; he opened his mouth wide and snapped his jaws in the air. "One bite and your head will roll. Then I'll feed what's left of you to Cat."

"Horrid dwarf," said Luc, pulling the parrot close to his chest.

"Damn you, Luc. Why should I tell you anything?"

"Because you said you would."

Bes shook his head. "I learned nothing of use. I planted many questions."

"Bes, have you any kindness?

"Kindness? What's that? Nothing I have experienced from you."

Bes took up the broom again and began to sweep. Sooty dust swirled, and he coughed as he whisked the ashes into a pan. When he finished, he wiped his smudged face on a cloth and turned to Luc.

"Let us see what sprouts from my questions. Trust me."

"I trust Salah," said Luc.

"That is enough," said Bes.

"Salah would say trust in Allah," said Luc.

"Yes, he would. He would say trust in Allah, but tie your camel. But then, you are an infidel."

"So are you, Bes."

"What would you do if you were free, Luc?"

"I would go home."

"You would leave the old man?"

"I am not free. What does it matter?"

CHAPTER THIRTY-SIX

Tariq's Revelation

SALAH WAS DYING. He slept fitfully; he was awake in snatches. When he spoke, he whispered. Luc and Bes dribbled sugared water into his mouth and cooled the old man with a palm fan that had been rubbed with jasmine oil. On the last afternoon in July, Tariq, the rich merchant, came to call.

"Salah is asleep, *sayyid*. He cannot be disturbed," said Bes.

"I am here to see the boy," said Tariq.

"What boy?" asked Bes.

"The blond slave."

Bes shrugged.

"Luc," said Tariq. "Fetch him."

"He is no longer here," said Bes.

"Is that so?" Tariq bellowed, "If you see him, tell Luc that I have news of his family."

Luc appeared in the doorway, and Tariq dismissed Bes.

"I knew you were lying," said the wealthy merchant.

The little man narrowed his eyes, and clenched his fists. Luc bowed to Tariq.

"Leave us, little man," said the merchant. "I need to talk to Luc of private matters."

"You and the slave? I must consult the master," said Bes, shaking his head.

Luc put a hand up to stop Bes. "Tariq and I will go to the courtyard. I will hear his news."

"Be off, little man, before I take a whip to you," snarled Tariq.

Bes glared at Tariq, but he hurried to the kitchen.

Luc led his visitor to an alcove, where the fat merchant eased himself onto a cushion and signaled to the boy to sit across from him.

"How is Salah?" asked Tariq.

"He is gravely ill."

"He has been, for the most part, a good master?"

"In all parts. He has been more than a master."

"I have never known Salah to be dishonest."

"Nor have I."

"Until now," said Tariq, pulling a perfumed kerchief from his sleeve and mopping his glistening face.

Luc spread his hands in front of him. "I do not understand."

"Two months ago, maybe three, inquiries began in Tunis and then in this small city of Bizerte."

"Inquiries?"

Tariq nodded. "A Genoan was looking for a boy who had been taken from a fishing boat."

Luc nodded. "Many boys have been stolen."

"He was looking for a particular boy."

"Yes?"

"A boy with one ear."

Luc squeezed his eyes shut.

"Yes, there is only one," said Tariq softly. "Salah is a venerated wise man, a powerful man. He knows all there is to know, and that frightens many. Even for money, no one would approach you without his permission."

Only the splashing water of the fountain sounded cool; the air was so hot and still that the songbirds were silent; the shade of the alcove where Luc and Tariq sat offered little comfort. The fat man was breathing heavily. He pulled a rolled woven disk from his belt, unfurled it, and fanned himself.

"What would anyone want with me?" asked Luc.

"A handsome reward has been offered for your return."

"A reward?"

"Yes. And your passage back home."

"But who offered the reward?" asked the boy.

"Your family, I should think," answered Tariq, with a shrug.

"My family has no wealth, and my father would never—"

Luc stopped because he remembered the doubts that the heavy soldier, Alain, had planted. Who was his father?

Tariq mopped his face. "I do not know who offered the reward, but that is of little concern. It is a substantial sum."

"How much?" asked Luc, very puzzled.

"It doesn't matter. Salah has never cared about money. Besides, he is a very wealthy man."

"I don't understand. Did Salah know this?" asked Luc.

"Oh, yes. A few weeks ago, the slaver tried to buy you back."

"He wanted to buy me back for what?"

"To collect the reward. But the old man refused, and he made the slaver vow not to tell you. I heard that Salah paid the slaver for his silence."

"How do you know this?"

"I trade with Genoan merchants. Your story is well known; the agents were told you were dead."

"Dead?" Luc rose and looked away. Then he turned and sat down. Tariq watched the boy and fanned himself.

"But who is looking for me?" asked Luc.

Tariq said, "Someone rich enough to offer a princely reward. Money for a boy of great wealth. Not a fisherman."

"And Salah kept this from me? He told them I was dead?"

"Yes."

"Why would you bring me this news? You are Salah's friend. And the reward would mean nothing to you."

Tariq nodded. "I respect your master. But I am an honest man. The Genoans trust me. I have long traded with them, and I value my name and my virtue. I could not lie when they asked me if you were truly dead."

"So now they know I'm alive?"

"Yes. They will come here soon."

Luc frowned. "Salah is mortally ill. I will not leave him. I gave my word."

"Your master did not tell you of the search. He tried to scuttle the search."

"I promised him."

"His betrayal would cancel your obligation."

"He is very near death, and he needs me. I will stay with him until the end."

"You are a credit to your people."

"My people? I wonder who they are."

Tariq answered, "Important people, I would think. The reward is substantial."

"That is a mystery. I am from a simple peasant family. Perhaps it is a mistake."

"You think there is another boy with one ear?"

"No."

"As I said, you are a credit to your people."

"If I am a credit to anyone, it is to Salah."

"Stay in this land, Luc. I like you. I have made inquiries

about you. You are skilled in surgery, knowledgeable about geography. You know the astrolabe. You speak Arabic like an Arab. Salah has told me that you are very, very smart. And now I know you are loyal. After he is gone, and you are free, I will find you an excellent position in my business or with the Christian traders. You will be a wealthy man in no time."

"Thank you. After Salah dies, I will go home. But I may return to accept your offer."

"If you accept the true faith, I will give you one of my daughters in marriage. I have six daughters, all beautiful."

"I am humbled by your confidence in me."

"And if you remain a Christian, well, there is still a place for you in my business. But no daughter," laughed Tariq.

Tariq lumbered to a stand, tucked the fan into his belt, and mopped his face with the soggy kerchief. He placed his right hand over his heart, then touched his fingers to his forehead and nodded to Luc. "Go in peace, my boy. I look forward to our next meeting."

"Thank you."

Bes appeared all too quickly and led the merchant out. Luc shook his head.

"How long have you known?" asked Luc when Bes returned.

"Not long," answered Bes, sitting down in the alcove across from Luc. Cat appeared and sat beside the little man.

"How long?" repeated Luc.

"Only since the visit of the slaver. Hassan told me."

CHAPTER THIRTY-SIX

"You said you learned nothing."

"I promised not to tell."

Bes waved his own fan as he settled back into the cushions and crossed his legs. Now and then he fanned Cat, who preened and leaned into the little breeze that Bes created.

"You should have told me," said Luc, folding up his sleeves.

"I promised Salah I would not tell you."

"I promised Salah I would stay."

"Salah did not tell you, either."

"I know. He thought I would leave. But I won't."

"Not even now, when you know he deceived you and the Genoans?" Bes raised his chin and fanned his neck.

"Salah is the kindest, wisest person I have ever known. I will stay. He is dying. If he failed me once, I forgive him," said Luc, standing up.

Bes stood. As Luc began to walk away, he tugged on the boy's shirt. "Will you forgive me, Luc?"

Luc turned. "Forgive you?"

"Yes."

"Why should I forgive *you*?" asked Luc, with a half smile.

"You don't know who I am. Do you, Luc?"

The little man did a jig.

"You are Bes," said Luc, sticking out his tongue and doing a poor imitation of Bes's little dance.

"Do you know who Bes is?"

"He's a dwarf who tortures me."

"Bes is an Egyptian god," said the little man, taking a deep bow.

"Is he, now? Well, I'll try to remember that. But I'm a Christian, so I won't be praying to you. Tell me something, Bes."

"I will tell you anything. No more secrets."

"Good." Luc pointed at Cat. "Tell me why there are only cats in Arab houses, never dogs."

"Arabs have dogs."

"But never in the house."

Bes frowned. "Because a dog will chase away any angels."

Luc laughed, "In my country, dogs chase away strangers."

"A stranger might be an angel in disguise," said Bes.

"Or just a stranger," said Luc.

CHAPTER THIRTY-SEVEN

Rumors

THROUGHOUT THE EARLY summer, Louis appeared often at Bertrand's manor. Sometimes he and Bertrand rode or hunted together. Sometimes he stayed for dinner. Again and again, he invited Bertrand and Beatrice to join him for a meal or to visit his home. Bertrand always accepted; Beatrice always refused. Louis sent gifts to the household: peaches from his orchard, cheese from his sheep, and lavender-scented cakes of soap. When he sent a bolt of deep-blue silk, Beatrice suggested that Bertrand return it.

"I will not," said Bertrand. "I'll use some for a tunic for myself. But there is enough for a new dress for you, too."

"I don't want his gifts. I want him to believe me. To believe Luc is his brother." Bertrand glanced at his niece. He said nothing for a moment. They were strolling in a new garden that had been Beatrice's idea. Pons and Bertrand's gardener were dividing bulbs. Bertrand stopped and turned toward her.

"No one could fault you for your loyalty and persistence, but the boy has been missing for what? Two years?"

"Not that long," said Beatrice, patting Cadeau, who followed her everywhere.

"Long enough. Louis has continued the search because he knows you want to find the boy. But you're not fair to Louis."

"If he believed me, he would be searching for Luc for *himself*, not for me."

"Louis is my best friend. Everything I have I owe to him. Everything you have, too."

"I lost everything because of his father."

"His father was evil. But Louis is a good man. A very good man. When Étienne was declared a criminal, you and I both suffered. But we were innocent."

"*Father* was innocent, too."

"That's not my point. Don't you remember how unfair and how terrible it was to be tainted by the supposed crimes of someone else?"

As they walked on without talking, Beatrice kicked a pebble. Cadeau rushed forward and pounced on the pebble. But when the dog found it was just a stone, he dropped it and turned to Beatrice, wagging his tail and waiting for a new game.

Bertrand smiled. "He's a great dog."

Beatrice nodded.

"You know, there were three puppies in the litter when Louis's dog and Cadeau were born," said Bertrand.

"Three? Who has the other dog?" she asked.

"Louis's father killed it."

Beatrice stopped and frowned at her uncle.

He nodded and continued, "Louis was home for Christmas when the litter was born. I was visiting. I'll never forget it. The third puppy was a lovely female, perfect in every way, except she had a pink nose. *She* was the puppy Louis wanted. But the old count took one look at that nose, and he wrung the little creature's neck."

"How horrible!" gasped Beatrice. "What's wrong with a pink nose?"

"Nothing. But it should have been black. The old count hated anything imperfect. Like his tiny thumbs? He would have cut them off if he could have attached normal ones."

Beatrice covered her mouth. She said nothing, but she thought of Luc.

Bertrand shook his head and stopped. "Louis knows all too well the pain his father caused. Can you imagine what his childhood was like?"

"You were pages together, right?" asked Beatrice, thinking about Louis for the first time.

"Since we were seven. Louis was lucky that he spent at least part of his youth in a distant castle as a page to a good man. And away from his father. You won't find a better person than Louis anywhere. Besides, Beatrice, if you believe Luc is his brother, then the old count was Luc's father too. Can you forgive one son and not the other?"

Beatrice sighed.

Bertrand took her hands and stood back, looking at her.

"You are as loyal as you are beautiful. Almost perfect," he said.

"Almost?" asked Mattie, who had caught up to Bertrand and Beatrice in the garden.

"Yes. She is a rather stubborn creature," he said, still holding her hands.

Beatrice pulled back her hands and walked a few steps away to talk to the gardener about where to transplant some bluebells. Then she turned and linked her arm in Bertrand's, and they walked on.

"You are a very good man, Uncle, and a good friend."

"It is time we start looking for a suitor for you, Beatrice," said Bertrand.

"Amen to that," added Mattie, walking a few steps behind.

"Are you both trying to get rid of me?" Beatrice asked.

"No, anything but," said Bertrand. "But maybe then you will give up this hopeless search for Luc. First, let's get rid of that old gray dress. We'll have a beautiful new dress made for you."

"Of blue silk?" laughed Beatrice.

Bertrand nodded, and the three ambled back to the house, where they found Louis waiting in the hall, looking somber. He was sitting on the edge of a bench with his dog at his feet. The dog wagged its tail and began to play with Cadeau.

"Hello, Beatrice, Bertrand. Hello, Mattie," said Louis, standing.

"Hello, Louis. Is something wrong?" asked Bertrand.

"Beatrice. I have news." His face was pale, and his lips were pursed.

"News? News of Luc?" asked Beatrice, stopping.

"Yes, there was a rumor of a slave with one ear in a port near the city of Tunis."

Beatrice clapped her hands.

"Where is Tunis?" asked Mattie.

"In Africa. But wait," cautioned Louis. "Despite a large reward, no one has come up with the boy."

"But they will. They must," said Beatrice.

"No, Beatrice. My agents have heard that that boy is dead."

"No, no, no," said Beatrice, covering her mouth with a hand and shaking her head. Then she looked up. "But that's just a rumor, isn't it? They don't know that for certain?"

"I believe it is a report. I do not know that it is confirmed."

"So we don't know that he is *not* alive. And now we know better where to look," said Beatrice.

Louis shook his head. "My agents say it is time to give up."

Beatrice began to cry. Mattie took the girl into her arms and held her tightly. When she could speak again, Beatrice wiped her eyes and turned to Louis.

"Would you quit now if you were searching for a brother? Because of a rumor?" she asked.

Bertrand frowned at his niece. "Beatrice, be reasonable. Louis has committed a fortune to this hunt. You must accept that the boy is not alive."

Beatrice pulled away from Mattie and stepped back from everyone. Her face was streaked and red, and she glared at Louis.

"The count did not answer my question."

Louis pressed his knuckles to his lips and looked hard at Beatrice. "Luc isn't my brother. I have looked for him because it was right. I am sorry that the news is not better, but Luc is lost, forever."

"If you believed he was your brother, would you abandon him?" demanded Beatrice.

Louis sighed, "He is not my brother."

"You are wrong, my lord," snapped Beatrice.

"Beatrice, hold your tongue," said Bertrand.

Louis continued, "My baby brother, Francis, is buried in the family tomb in our chapel. I don't know who Luc was, but he wasn't my brother. I agree that he had some connection to my father's household. Perhaps he was Sir Guy's bastard."

CHAPTER THIRTY-SEVEN

"You never questioned Blanche, did you?"

"Blanche?"

"The woman who raised Luc."

"Alain questioned her husband."

"Pascal had everything to lose by admitting the truth."

"Alain assured the man that he would lose nothing."

"Alain gave him your word?"

"Yes."

Beatrice smiled. "*Your* word? The word of Count de Muguet?"

"My word, yes."

"Those people would never trust your word. They know nothing of you, and they knew the worst of your father. Would they confess that they had lost the count's son? How terrified they must be to hear your dreaded name, Muguet!"

"Beatrice, you go too far!" said Bertrand, stepping between Beatrice and Louis.

"I know. But I also know what it is to be abandoned, my lord," said Beatrice, turning away from everyone.

"Can't you call me by my Christian name?" asked Louis quietly.

"Yes," said Beatrice, but she did not.

"Do you know why I have searched for the boy?" asked Louis, standing right behind her.

Beatrice turned and looked at Louis. "You said you searched because it was right."

"Yes. And to secure your forgiveness."

"Mine?"

"Is it too much to hope that you will forgive me?"

"Forgive you for what?"

"Forgive me for being a Muguet. For what my father did to your father. And for what that did to you."

Beatrice said nothing. She hid her tear-streaked face in her hands.

"I am so sorry, Louis," said Bertrand, putting an arm around Beatrice's shoulders. "She's very emotional about the boy. About everything. Forgive her. Forgive me."

Louis looked at Beatrice for a moment, blinking very slowly.

"I'm sorry," said Louis, holding up his hand and looking down. "Good-bye."

He turned and left.

CHAPTER THIRTY-EIGHT

Freedom

SALAH SIPPED FROM a cup that Bes held to his lips. He brushed away the little man and whispered for Luc. Salah was a husk, winnowed to bone and skin. Luc was astonished to find Cat sitting in the old man's lap, purring. Salah stroked the cat with his good hand. Luc shielded the parrot on his shoulder as he leaned in to hear Salah.

"I must tell you about ransom."

"I know, Salah. Tariq told me."

"Forgive me?"

The old man coughed.

Luc nodded and covered Salah's hand with his. "I owe you everything."

The parrot hopped from Luc's shoulder to his head. Cat

didn't move, but he followed the bird with his eyes. The boy rose and put the bird on its perch as Salah turned to Bes.

"Box."

Bes went to a shelf and, standing on his toes, stretched for a thick leather book and tipped it out. The old man nodded, and Bes opened the book: inside, the pages had been carved out so that the middle of the book was hollow. Bes removed a fitted leather box that held a leather pouch and a folded sheet of paper.

"Cup your hands, Luc," whispered Salah.

Bes poured the sack's contents into Luc's palms: five huge pearls, a handful of large diamonds and rubies, and more than two dozen heavy gold coins.

"This is yours, Luc," said Bes. "The master has given the same to me. Here is the paper setting you free."

Salah closed his eyes. His breathing was ragged, and he dozed. Luc poured the treasure back into the sack and tied it inside a larger pouch that hung from his belt. Then he sat on the floor across from Bes and next to Salah.

He rubbed his eyes and took a deep breath. "This is more than I thought to earn in a lifetime. In several lifetimes."

"And Tariq has offered to make you far richer," said Bes. "I heard him."

"Yes. I thought I had lost everything, but now?" Luc took Salah's hand and covered it with his other hand. "This is enough for anything." Luc shook his head. "Maybe it's enough even for Beatrice."

"Beatrice? Is that a place?" asked Bes.

"No, Beatrice is the most beautiful girl in the world."

"And she lives where you came from?"

"Yes."

"Is her father as rich as Tariq?"

Luc laughed.

"Richer?" asked Bes, wide-eyed.

"She has no fortune."

"Stupid man. Will you marry her?" asked Bes.

Luc shrugged. "I never thought I was good enough."

"Now that you are rich, you are?"

"Perhaps."

"Is that what you want?"

"I don't know, Bes. She may have married someone else. What do I want?" Luc looked around at Salah's room; then he turned to Bes and said, "I used to want my old life back. But not now. I no longer know what I want. I don't even know who I am. After Salah is gone, I must go back and find out."

"Take me. I will serve you."

"You are as rich as I am. Why would you serve me?"

"I will lose all that Salah gave me, and then I will be on the street."

"You do not have to lose it," said Luc.

"I will, though."

"I thought you were a god."

"I am Bes," said the little man. He held a pearl between

his thumb and his forefinger. He rolled it in the sunlight, catching the nacreous sheen. "Pearls are wondrous, Luc. Had you ever seen one before?"

"Not before I came to this house."

"They are formed when an oyster swallows a moonlit dewdrop. Pearls are scarce, but one this large and perfect is as rare as a man with one ear," said the little man with a half smile. "Take my treasure, Luc. And me."

"Bes—"

Bes put his finger to his lips and handed Luc the pearl.

Then Bes held out his fist to Luc. He turned and opened his hand, and offered Luc the wooden ear. Luc took the ear and looked at Bes.

Neither noticed that Salah had awakened and was listening, watching.

"Luc," he whispered.

"Yes, master," said Luc, leaning in.

"Forgive."

The old man closed his eyes and coughed softly. Then his breathing sputtered, slowed, and stopped, until the only sound was the purr of Cat. The old man died with Bes and Luc each holding one of his hands.

CHAPTER THIRTY-NINE

Beatrice and Louis

IT WAS AUGUST, and the fields were a patchwork of color: gold wheat, green barley, and purple lavender. Beatrice joined her uncle and his servants to bring wine, cheese, bread, and onions to a wheat-field where the harvesters were binding armfuls of straw into toast-smelling bundles. She wore a new blue silk dress with a rose linen underdress that was trimmed with crimson ribbon along her collarbone and wrists. Her hair was braided, weaving in twists of the same red ribbon, and the braid was pinned up in back so that her long neck was bare. The sun was hot, and, for once, Beatrice wished she had worn a hat.

"Louis never visits anymore," said Beatrice, taking Bertrand's arm as they strolled back toward the manor.

"No," said Bertrand. "He refuses my invitations. When I attempt to visit him at the castle, he's always away or too occupied to see me."

"It's my fault, isn't it, Uncle?"

"That business about Luc was very painful."

Beatrice knelt in front of Cadeau, who was walking at her side. She laid her head on the dog's neck and stroked his head.

"I've been very selfish. I never considered Louis in all this. Or you, Uncle. Louis is your dearest friend."

"Yes, he is."

Bertrand patted his niece's shoulder. He was dressed in a tunic of the same blue silk, and he wore a wide-brimmed straw hat with a golden feather.

"And you were right, he has nothing of his father in him," she said, looking up at her uncle.

"Just the burden of his father's bad deeds."

Beatrice stood up and asked, "Shall I write to him? To tell him how sorry I am? How unfair I was?"

"That would be very good, I think," he said, offering her his arm. "That new dress suits you. You look especially beautiful today, Niece. Now let's see your pretty garden. I love all the yellows and blues."

Beatrice cocked her head and glanced at him. "The colors, eh, Uncle?"

Before they reached the garden gate, Beatrice heard hurried steps on the pebbled path, and Cadeau barked. When she and Bertrand turned, they found Louis, walking quickly to catch up with them.

"Hello, my friend," said Bertrand, clapping Louis on the back. "We were just talking about you. I've missed you."

Louis nodded, but said nothing. He fell in next to Bertrand.

"*We* have," said Beatrice softly.

"We're going to see my niece's garden. Will you join us?" asked Bertrand.

Louis nodded. He was dressed in a muslin tunic and ragged hose. His straight dark hair was damp, and he brushed it back from his forehead. He looked more like a field-worker than the lord of a great castle.

"Beatrice has created a perfect little garden with such pleasing colors," said Bertrand, opening the gate.

Louis walked ahead and looked about the garden.

"Interesting," he said.

"Interesting?" said Bertrand. "What sort of praise is that? You don't find this to be a lovely garden?"

Louis smiled. Beatrice was quiet. He explored the garden, examining the plants. He stopped at a black-barked sapling with yellow-green leaves.

"A mirabelle?" he asked.

"Yes," answered Beatrice.

"Well?" asked Bertrand. "Don't you find it pretty, my friend?"

Louis turned to Bertrand. "Oh yes, this garden is pretty, Bertrand. And the colors are pleasing. But—"

"*But!* But what, Louis?" asked Bertrand, disappointed.

"It's pretty enough, but, really, this garden is all about fragrance. From the honeysuckle on the gate to the lavender growing alongside rosemary hedges." Louis walked about, pointing. "Between the stepping stones, Beatrice has planted at least two kinds of thyme, and that's verbena over there and sweet woodruff here under the tree. My every step crushes leaves and adds more scent. Those rose beds are edged with sweet alyssum. It's lovely to see, but it *smells* marvelous."

Bertrand took a step back and rubbed his forehead. He marched about the garden, leaning over, leaning down, sniffing, snuffling.

"Fragrance?" Bertrand muttered, and turned to Louis. "Fragrance?"

Louis nodded. Bertrand turned to Beatrice. She nodded. Bertrand grinned and shook his head. "So *I* was too wooden-headed to understand this garden? But not Louis. Oh no. *He* got it right away."

Beatrice watched Louis. He was leaning down to smell a flower when she finally spoke.

"Louis?"

"*Louis?*" Louis looked up and smiled. "Not *my lord?*"

"I was going to write to you," she said.

"Write to me? Whatever for?" he asked.

"I wanted to apologize—"

"You've been avoiding us, Louis," said Bertrand. "We haven't seen you for weeks."

"You thought I was angry?"

"Yes," said Bertrand. "We both did."

"No," he said, with a sidelong glance at Beatrice. "Just busy."

He walked a little farther into the garden.

"And afraid," he added.

"Afraid?" asked Bertrand.

Louis leaned over to snap off a verbena sprig; he crushed the leaves between his fingers and held them to his nose.

"All spring and summer I've listened as Beatrice insisted that Luc was my brother. To have a living brother? At first I was enthralled. But then, as I thought about it, I didn't want to believe her. Think, Beatrice. This would be my father's most monstrous crime, against his own son, against my brother, and against the innocent child of a servant. I might even learn that Father was responsible for the death of my mother."

Beatrice said nothing, but she remembered what Blanche had said—that there had been rumor, that Louis's father had indeed committed this heinous act.

A noticeable wind had picked up, and Beatrice felt her skirt fill, and loose strands of her hair whip her face. Cadeau whined. Louis stepped toward her just as a blaze of lightning turned everything white. They all looked up at the sky.

"Don't worry. It's just heat lightning," said Bertrand.

The sky was banded with a luminous violet, and the tree leaves showed their silver undersides. The air was hot, but this wind was cold.

Suddenly, the heavens thundered.

"Run!" shouted Beatrice.

Cadeau broke into a gallop, and Beatrice gathered her skirts and took off with Louis sprinting at her side. They reached the house just as the sky opened. She laughed and coughed and caught her breath. Louis had just reached out to brush a loose curl from her eyes when Bertrand stomped into the house. He was soaked.

"Ruined," he said, wringing the hem of his tunic. "This silk is ruined. And my shoes?" he asked, lifting one foot to display the sodden leather. "Hopeless." He looked up. "And you two, dry as can be? Well, I'm glad for Beatrice's new dress, anyway. You must excuse me, but I need to change."

Bertrand sloshed off. Beatrice stepped into the hall, and Louis followed. The room went white with another burst of lightning, and this time the thunder followed immediately. Rain sheeted along the windowpanes. Louis walked to the window to watch. Without turning, he spoke.

"Beatrice, I never stopped the search for Luc," he said.

"Thank you," she said.

"And I sent my steward to speak with Blanche."

Beatrice took a step toward Louis.

He continued. "He's a gentle man. I hope Blanche will be comfortable enough to talk openly with him."

"Louis, whatever you learn—"

He turned and faced her, "About Luc?"

"And about your father—"

Louis sighed and nodded.

"You aren't to blame for his deeds."

He pressed his knuckles against his mouth, stepped toward her and said, "I don't want to give you a false hope, but there has been another report from Africa. I do not know if Luc has been found alive, but expect I shall know more soon."

Beatrice took a deep breath that puffed out her cheeks. "I have always hoped . . . thank you.

Louis smiled at her. "Will you ever come to the castle? To see the room with Mattie's fish?"

Beatrice looked at Louis and smiled. He put his hands together as though he was praying.

"Please," he said.

Beatrice nodded.

CHAPTER FORTY

Returning

A WEEK LATER, a servant brought a note from Louis inviting Beatrice and Bertrand, Mattie and Pons to the castle. It was a gentle horse ride on a bright September morning. Throughout the countryside, reapers were swinging their sickles and leveling the last flaxen fields of wheat. The leaves on ripening grapevines striped the hillsides with yellow. Cadeau bounded along, circling widely around Beatrice's horse.

"I'm starting to enjoy riding," said Pons proudly, patting his mount on its withers as the castle towers came into view.

"I'm not," said Mattie. "But it's better than walking." She looked up at the sky and pointed to a high-soaring bird.

Beatrice looked up as the bird dipped and cried. She turned to Mattie.

"Can that be a gull?"

Mattie nodded.

"Here?" asked Beatrice.

"I never saw one so far from the sea," said the old woman. "It's the boy, I think."

"Luc?" asked Beatrice, watching the bird disappear over the hills.

Mattie nodded. "His spirit. He's come to see that we are all well."

Tears filled Beatrice's eyes.

"He's with us. And he knows we are safe. It's a good sign, Beatrice," said Mattie.

"But he's gone?" asked Beatrice, her cheeks wet.

Mattie nodded.

They continued in silence. Riding through the castle walls, despite her tears, Beatrice noticed the transformation. Flowers and shade trees filled the dreaded courtyard, and water splashed and flowed over the tiers of a grand new fountain in the center. Louis and his dog stood in the doorway. The dogs jumped at each other and were off at a run, chasing each other around the garden.

"Welcome," said Louis, smiling. He wore a silk tunic of the same blue but a darker hue than the new dress that Beatrice wore. When he noticed her tears, he said, "What a fool I am. It's too hard for you to return here, Beatrice."

She shook her head and wiped her eyes. "No. It was something else."

Louis exhaled. He was holding a perfect white lily, and he handed it to her.

"Come," said Louis, taking her other hand and helping Beatrice from her horse. "I can't wait for you to see the tower room."

Bertrand hung back and climbed the stairs with Mattie and Pons. He turned to Mattie and said, "You know, the count is in love with Beatrice."

"You think that's news to me?" asked Mattie.

"It's news to me," said Pons.

"Of course it is, Brother. If it doesn't swim, you don't understand it."

"How does she feel?" asked Bertrand.

"Good sir, she is *your* niece. You ask her yourself."

"But the tears?"

"The tears were about Luc. She knows he is gone."

Bertrand nodded.

The steward stood at the entrance to the room; he smiled at Beatrice but said nothing. She and Louis waited for the others to reach the top of the stairs.

Then Louis turned to Beatrice and said, "Beatrice, this room . . . well, I—"

"Open the door, my lord," said Mattie, her hands on her hips.

With that, Louis made a slight bow to Beatrice and nodded to his steward who unlatched the wooden door.

Beatrice stepped in. Colored sunlight flooded the room,

and Beatrice walked into the center, held out her arms, and twirled around and around. The blues of the windowpanes flickered on her hands and arms and turned the white lily aqua. Two small windows were ajar, and the suspended fish swayed above her.

"Now you really *are* a mermaid," said Mattie, loosening Beatrice's hair so that it cascaded around her blue dress.

Beatrice laughed and spun around.

Pons scratched his chin. "It's a wonder."

Bertrand patted Louis on the back and said, "Well?"

Louis held up his hand. They heard a peculiar vibrating sound.

"I have a surprise," said Louis. "For Beatrice. For all of you."

A bald little man playing a peculiar drumlike instrument danced through the doorway and into the room. He was dressed in a shirt of saffron silk with short ginger pants and bright green leggings. He capered about the room, pirouetting around each person. Then he stopped playing his drum, turned toward the door, and clapped his hands. The steward entered carrying a large cloth sack that he deposited in front of the little man. The little man rummaged in the sack, muttering to himself; he withdrew a small string-tied packet that he tried to hand to Pons, but the old man stepped back, and the little man yammered at him in a foreign tongue.

"It's all right, Pons," said Louis. "He has a gift for you."

Pons took the package and turned it over and over.

"Open it, Brother," said Mattie impatiently.

Pons nodded and began to unwrap the square package. Inside was a hinged leather box. He slid the catch with his thumb, opened the box, and removed an ivory bowl with a glass cover.

"What is this?" Pons asked, displaying the ivory bowl.

"It's called a compass," said Louis. "See the little needle? See how it dances? It will always pivot and point to the north."

Pons shook his head. "Magic?"

"No, not magic. But extraordinary," said Louis with a half smile.

Pons nodded and turned the bowl, watching the needle spin. "Never in my life!" he said.

Meanwhile, the little man dragged his sack to Mattie and pulled out a flat bundle that he handed to her. She took the package and opened it. Inside she found a beautiful crimson cape. The lamb's wool was soft and tightly woven, and she smiled broadly at Louis as the little man danced across the room to Beatrice. He bowed deeply and presented her with the biggest parcel, a thick long roll tied with ribbons of orange, green, and yellow. First she untied the ribbons, then Beatrice unrolled the sackcloth wrapping, dropping it on the floor. She shook out a bright yellow silk dress and held it up against her chest.

"But how?" Beatrice asked Louis. "How did you know?"

Louis smiled and turned to the doorway.

In stepped a tall blond gentleman wearing a buttercup-yellow silk tunic. A handsome gray-and-red bird sat on his shoulder. The gentleman put his arm around Louis's shoulders. The two stood linked, one with dark hair, one with gold, both with the same extraordinary blue eyes, the same remarkable smile. Together they bowed to Beatrice: the count and his brother, the boy with one ear.

ACKNOWLEDGMENTS

My thanks to: The encyclopedic Janet Pascal for her knowledge and vigilance.

My divine literary agent, Jill Kneerim, for her patience, wisdom, and humor.

My masterly editor Joy Peskin for her relentlessness and her vision.

Thanks also to my early readers: AL, AR, BK, CF, EP, GA, GL, JG, LH, MJ, MS, MT, PM, and VB, as well as to Maddy, KP, Anna & Richmond, JS, and Anonymous for inspiration and education.

And especially, with love, I want to thank CBL, WHGB, NBL, GEB, FBL, and SFS.